DRAGONKYN

DRAGONKYN

by

Nathan Smith Jones

iread
books

This is a work of fiction. The characters, organizations, names, incidents, places, and dialogue are either products of the author's imagination or are used fictitiously, and are not to be construed as real. The views expressed within this work are the sole responsibility of the author and do not necessarily reflect the position of iRead Books, LLC., or any other entity.

ISBN 13: 978-0-9996600-0-3

Published and Distributed by iread books

Originally published and Distributed by Sweetwater Books, an imprint of Cedar Fort, Inc. 2373 W. 700 S., Springville, UT 84663

LIBRARY OF CONGRESS CATALOGING-IN-PUBLICATION DATA

Names: Jones, Nathan Smith, author.
Title: Dragonkyn / Nathan Smith Jones.
Description: Provo, Utah: iread Books
Inc., [2016] | Summary: Teenage Marc discovers he carries ancient dragon DNA.
Identifiers: LCCN 2016048878 (print) | LCCN 2016049631 (ebook) | ISBN
9780999660003 (perfect bound : alk. paper) | ISBN 9780999660010 (epub, pdf, mobi)
Subjects: LCSH: Young adult fiction. | CYAC: Dragons--Fiction. | LCGFT: Action and adventure fiction. | Fantasy fiction. | Bildungsromans.
Classification: LCC PZ7.J72414 Dr 2016 (print) | LCC PZ7.J72414 (ebook) | DDC [Fic]--dc23
LC record available at https://lccn.loc.gov/2016048878

Cover design by Priscilla Chaves
Cover design © 2017 Nathan Smith Jones
Edited and typeset by Erica Myers and Jessica Romrell

Printed in the United States of America

10 9 8 7 6 5 4 3 2 1

Printed on acid-free paper

For my children

CONTENTS

Contents

ONE

The Chase and Grilled Cheese

Marc was too busy running from Deputy Brandwhite to notice how different things were that night, the subtle changes in the air that whisper the unimaginable things that lie in one's future. He ran with get-me-outta-here urgency, feet pounding the earth like fists on a punching bag.

Marc's navy blue t-shirt didn't exactly camouflage him as he ran, but he figured it didn't matter. He was almost to the grassy field near the freeway where he'd lost the deputy before. Reaching the dry waist-high grass, he slowed. *Idiot*, he thought.

Deputy Brandwhite was a young, overzealous cop who always wore his full-brim deputy hat like he was a Canadian Mountie. Marc was proud of the fact that after a year and four attempts, Brandwhite, who loved chasing some of the poor kids in town, still hadn't caught him. The deputy claimed Marc was responsible for some of the vandalism to the school, which wasn't true. Many kids thought he targeted Marc because he was embarrassed at not having found the kid who really did it, and blaming one of the poor kids was easier than a formal investigation. It had all become such a big hassle, a dumb game. But Marc still ran, more out of being easily intimidated than any fear of being in trouble. Marc couldn't help but smile, knowing it wasn't that hard to outrun the guy.

Turning back, he thought he'd lost the cop, until his panicked eyes were caught in the headlights of Brandwhite's cruiser.

Trying to swallow as his ravenous lungs sucked air, he felt the headlight beams behind him bouncing strangely.

Looking back, his eyes widened again, and he continued fast. *He jumped the curb! He drove into the field!*

"Ahhgh!" Marc shouted half with alarm, half with effort as he pumped his arms and legs. He zigzagged, struggling to get deeper into the grassy field. The police cruiser's grill was eating up grass and shrub, hungry to run down a dark-haired, almost-fifteen-year-old kid. Brandwhite had never done that before, but four attempts tend to try one's ego.

Marc could have sworn he heard cackling laughter. Anyone'd be nuts to take a car into that grassy field, but hey, Brandwhite didn't mind. He wasn't the one paying the car's maintenance.

It was Marc's zigzagging that saved him. He did it just enough that he was able to get into the tallest grass, hiding from view.

That's when the cruiser stopped, its engine breathing fire from the chase. Brandwhite lugged his lanky body, beady eyes, and plain face from his car and continued the chase on foot.

When Marc got to the thickest and tallest of the grasses in the field, some as tall as he was, he stopped near his favorite spot, a large, forgotten drainage pipe beneath I-70—a freeway that twisted and turned like the Colorado River it mirrored.

He listened, cursing his angry, loud exhales that might give away his position.

Marc's feet started getting numb from crouching there in the grass, so, hearing nothing but the lonely squawk of a bird, he stood and exhaled loudly. Eyes wide in panic, he dropped himself to a crouching position again—swallowing the last of the exhale—when he saw Deputy Brandwhite's back to him thirty feet away, closer to his hideout than he'd ever been before.

"I'm gonna find you some day, boy!" the deputy called out. Luckily, Brandwhite didn't know Marc's name, and none of the kids at school would tell him. For this reason, it always felt like just a big, dumb game instead of any actual trouble. "I know you did it!" the deputy said with a mischievous chuckle.

Tiptoeing, wincing when a step made a sound, Marc slowly stepped backward, his green-hazel eyes never leaving

Brandwhite's direction. He made his way to the drainage pipe itself, hidden by the thickest and wettest of the grass.

When Marc reached the drainage pipe, he looked back with a wry smile and ducked into the darkness to freedom, slipping away from Brandwhite yet again.

He was so busy escaping Brandwhite's dork patrol that he hadn't noticed there had been something strange that night, something in the air, accompanied by the faint smell of flint and steel. When he got home, covered in dirt and grass, he was able to jump into the shower before his mom saw what he looked like.

He had never told his mom about Deputy Brandwhite's late-night pursuits; he didn't want her to worry. She worried enough as it was about not having health insurance, made even worse by the fact that he had two thin, inexplicable lumps on top of his already-too-large-for-his-age shoulder blades. Was it some kind of tumor? She tried looking it up online, but found nothing, and since they never caused him pain, she assured him she'd have a doctor look at it in a couple months when a former boss promised her the back-pay she was due. Marc wondered if all moms were implanted with some kind of addiction-to-worrying device in their brains when their child was born, which took over *most* of their brain when their kid turned twelve.

His dreams that night were odd, as if affected by the strangeness in the air itself.

He was running again, his feet stuck in some kind of dark sand, but this time it wasn't from Brandwhite. It was some kind of creature, lumbering after him in what looked like a dark forest. A snake's eyes suddenly peered at him, overtaking all of the dream after the creature chased him. The thin irises seemed human almost, filled with such fear and terror that it frightened him, and he moved in his sleep.

The dream itself seemed forged from fire, encircling and weaving its way all throughout it—flames framing the scary snake eyes. Then, in another part of the dream, he was somehow even speaking this fire, which he thought was, well, weird.

Marc woke up with a start, but pushed away any feelings about the significance of the dreams, other than how strange they were. His head was already filled with all of the complaints about his life that already cluttered his mind as much as his clothes and *Rockies* baseball paraphernalia cluttered his bedroom.

Jenny Mondragon (pronounced *Mahn*-druggin) never worried about how clean his room was, but she did worry about his schooling, which is why she made Marc write something, anything, as another 'summer assignment.' She would often assign him some kind of homework once during the summer when she felt he wasn't doing enough reading or writing, or when she felt she wasn't monitoring it enough.

He wrote the following:

Searching for something
Outside the home.
Gotta do something
To feel less alone.
Searching for something
Outside the home.
You can't find it here, so
You gotta go roam.
Searching for something
Outside the home.
Heart's been feeling
Cold as a stone.

When she saw that he had written something, she gathered her keys from the countertop with a frown.

"I'm just worried about you, is all."

"Aren't you gonna read it?" Marc asked.

"I have to go. I'm already late! I'll read it when I get home from work, I promise," she said.

"Barely read anything I write," he mumbled to himself, crumpling up the poem.

"You just don't seem yourself lately."

"Maybe there's a clue in what I wrote. Crazy thought."

"Are you depressed?" she asked.

"No, mom, not depressed. Just, I don't know," Marc said.

"'I don't know.' It's all I ever hear from you. If you don't know, then who does?" Jenny said as early-morning light crept through the blinds.

"Now you're worrying about me not knowing exactly how I feel?" Marc asked, but all his mom did was exhale an exasperated why-do-you-have-to-be-such-a-smart-aleck-when-I'm-seriously-worried-right-now sigh as she went out the door, leaving Marc once again feeling like he was to blame for everything.

It wasn't that Marc was whiny; Marc hated whiners. It was partly because he always thought that something interesting would happen to him before now, but nothing had. This odd premonition was something he always felt deep down. He almost told his mom about this, because they were sort of close, but he didn't want to express something hard to explain and come across as whiny in the process, so he always kept it to himself. Sure, Marc was restless, but who wouldn't be? Marc figured anyone would want to bust out of the tiny run-down house they rented in the small town of Rifle, Colorado, where dusty yellow boulders on the mountains sat like blunt thorns the earth had finally worked out of its skin.

Jenny and Marc, her only child, genuinely liked each other's company—well, except for what came to be known as the 'ice cream deception.' To save money and protect her son's teeth from decay, Jenny told her toddler that the ice cream truck that often came through their neighborhood was a dance truck. They would stop everything and have an impromptu, mother-son dance party whenever they would hear its tinny jingle, but when Marc turned eight, he discovered that the truck sold ice cream. That and Santa Claus were the two great childhood disillusions Marc had had to get over.

All of his summer boredom was about to disappear fast, however, and it all began with a grilled cheese sandwich.

Yeah. A sandwich. Crazy.

Alone and barefoot, he crossed the peeling-linoleum kitchen floor and opened the side door of the house for the cooler morning air, even though there were three fans in the house going full blast, droning on like tiny, monotone robots. Marc took the crisp air into his lungs with closed eyes, the scent of fresh hay from a distant farm soothing him. He didn't even mind the hint of cow manure that came with it.

That's when he chuckled to himself, thinking of the time he told a kid online from back east that cow manure to him smelled like home. The kid said he was crazy and Marc just laughed. He moved from the door and sat at the kitchen table, idly picking at the chair's cracked, plastic seat cover. The print was yellow and faded, *but at least it matched the floor*, his mom always said with a laugh.

Marc stared at the picture on the fridge that he drew when he was six that his mom refused to throw away or place in a box, and he felt bad about their fight. His vision blurred, and a lone tear fell to his jeans, a tiny dark spot the size of a dime appearing near the pocket. He cursed to himself, wiped his eyes, got up, grabbed his baseball bat from his room and went outside.

He lived on the wrong side of town with the smaller, older, one-level homes that people usually rented. Across the street, scattered toys of molded plastic punctuated front lawns with happy colors. Marc swung a few hits on the decrepit wooden fence of the old abandoned house next door. It had the same layout and color as his own house, but it had fallen into disrepair, abandoned by owner and tenant alike. The house seemed the unkempt, evil twin of Marc's house.

After smacking the old fence a few times, knocking a few imagined baseballs out of the imagined ballpark, he went back into his house feeling better. Entering the side door, Marc decided to make himself a grilled cheese sandwich.

He clattered the pan onto the electric stove and waited for it to get hot. Leaning against the stove with one hand, he let his thoughts run; he wondered if the customers at the diner were treating his mother as well as she treated them. He wondered why the word *abbreviated* was such a long word.

His hand felt really warm all of a sudden, and he looked down.

When he saw that he had turned on the wrong burner, a guttural scream involuntarily filled the house. His hand had been directly on the big, red-glowing stove top the entire time.

Snatching his hand away, his first thought was that his body must be in shock. He clutched the wrist of his burned hand and turned away, afraid to touch or look at it, anticipating all the throbbing, stinging agony about to come flooding in.

Just calm down. Get through this, he told himself.

The pain was—

The . . .

The . . .

. . . pain?

As his breathing slowed, Marc stared at his hand. Instead of a melted mass of flesh and bone, he stared incredulously at a perfect hand without so much as a smudge.

There never had been any pain, none at all.

Marc couldn't be sure how many minutes he spent staring at his hand. He went to the stove, keeping his hand up, never letting it leave his sight, like a stranger he couldn't trust. Slowly putting his other hand close to the big, red, glowing circle, he sensed the heat, getting warmer and warmer, but when he touched it, nothing. It didn't hurt. Sure, it felt warm, intensely warm, but shouldn't a hot burner feel more than *intensely warm*?

He experimented further, pressing his upper arm to the hot burner, then his other arm, then his bare feet, and finally his face.

Nothing. Just a warmth that said, yes, you should be feeling more than this, but you don't.

He decided to test it again, digging through a few drawers in the living room coffee table until he found a lighter his Uncle

Bill had left a while back. He stared, disbelieving, at the small flame as it curved around his fingers, bathing them like yellow running water from a faucet turned upside down.

He stood there, amazed. Not a burn, not a bit of pain, nothing, only a deep warmth. It didn't bother him at all.

"I'm impervious to all harm!"

TWO

Mom Almost Faints

He had to tell his mom. He had so many questions: *How could this be? Why was this happening? What could it mean? Why am I shaking? Isn't this a good thing?* He took a quick shower and dressed, his hair dripping water on his pant leg and socks as he put his shoes on. Jumping onto his rust-lined bike, he pedaled to the diner where his mom worked as a waitress.

The skeptical part of him, the side that listened to the self doubt his brain seemed so good at generating, sounded the alarm.

There's a logical explanation for all this, and you know it, his skeptical side said in his mind, and the voice sounded a lot like his dad before he left.

How? he answered.

I dunno, but you're sure gonna feel stupid when someone points out what's really going on. You're a moron.

The buzz of insects was loud in the summer air. As Marc pedaled past a vacant lot, his faded yellow t-shirt lightly flapping as he did, he suddenly couldn't imagine why he had let himself sit in his house, weeping about his outcast state. Sure, he was poor, and couldn't get a job, despite how often he explained he was almost fifteen; but none of that mattered now. Thoughts of being some kind of pain-free superhero filled his mind as the sound of the pedals, crankset, and chain of his bike worked together in rhythmic time.

But the nagging thoughts wouldn't leave him alone.

You're an idiot, the voice said that sounded like his father's.

What else could it be? Marc asked his skeptical, self-doubting side.

Remember when you were seven, and you thought your hand had special heat-generating powers because the chocolate peanuts melted in your hand? This has to be something similar.

Shut up. You were right there, too! No matter how hard I tried, I couldn't get burned!

Maybe the stove top is broken, genius. Ever think of that? You're so stupid. You can't do anything right.

Marc pedaled faster as cars rumbled past, trying to outrun his father's words that always tore at his self-esteem. He jumped a curb, passing a portly, balding man sitting on his front porch with eyes that wondered what the hurry was all about.

As Marc pedaled, he realized that he had wanted to bust out of his life not because it was some jail he was trapped in, not really. He was sick and tired of it all; his scrawny body incapable of building any muscle, this dumb little town, the way a lot of people would look down at him and his mom at church because she was a single mom and they were poorer than most, the would-be suitors—*more like losers,* he always thought—that came by the house wanting to date his mom, and the annoying pity-looks the older check-out person always gave them at the market whenever his mom handed over the food stamps or used her EBT card.

The chain on his bike rattled as the tires hit the driveway into the parking lot of the Big Creek Diner. The name no doubt referred to the nearby river. The diner itself was a white, squat, stand-alone building, about the size of a mini-mart. It wasn't much to look at, but it always stayed busy. Marc was convinced that the reason was because the food was good, his mom served it with a smile, and it was probably the best place to meet someone in town. The AC of the diner turned his sweat cool when he entered, as the sound of clashing silverware met him at the door. His mom turned from a table when she saw him, and her eyes immediately widened with concern.

"Marc, what's wrong?" she asked.

"I gotta tell you something. Real quick."

"Honey, I can't—" she started, but he took her hand anyway and led her to the space by the kitchen door, across from the bathrooms. On the way there, he grabbed a clean fork from a recently-bussed table.

"Mom, you're not gonna believe this," he said.

"Are you okay?" she asked.

"Yes, Mom, I'm okay, I'm okay." Out of breath, he stalled on purpose to build up to the big announcement.

"Ready?" he asked with pride.

She nodded.

"You're not going to believe it, but I'm impervious to all harm!" With that, he stabbed himself in the forearm with the fork.

Marc had no idea why his mom's face went pale and the other waitress screamed until he saw the dark, red blood gurgling from his own arm. That's when he heard himself scream too.

Later, in the back office of the diner, his arm now a steady throb wrapped in gauze, Marc tried to explain.

"But what were you thinking?" Jenny asked again, gathering the bandage packaging.

"Mom, please—"

"Honey," she said, putting the packaging in the small, black trashcan by the door.

"I need something hot. Get me something hot, and it'll prove—"

"Marc, I know you're probably stressed about—"

"Get me something hot, Mom. Please! It'll explain everything."

"Is this about a girl? Is that the reason for this craziness?" she asked.

"Mom, I can't get burned. Okay? I said it. Now you know."

"Well, no one wants to get hurt in a relationship, honey. I know exactly how you feel, but you're so young. There's no rush for you to get a girlfriend, and it's definitely not something to hurt yourself over."

Marc stared at her. "Mom. What are you talking about?"

"What?" she asked.

"Mom, you're not making any sense," he said, and at this his mom looked at him with level eyes and a raised eyebrow.

"The boy who comes to my work and stabs himself with a fork for no reason tells me *I'm* not making any sense?"

"Let's just go into the kitchen and I'll show you," Marc pleaded. "Really quick. You'll see!"

"Honey, I just want to know what you were thinking. I know some kids around here cut themselves—" his mom said, and they both spoke over each other.

"Oh, come on, Mom—"

"I'm just saying, so, maybe fork mutilation is—" she said.

"Do you really think—"

"—the new thing kids are doing, but I want you to know that I love you anyway," she said with a sigh. "I mean, you rarely if ever come to my work, and when you do, you announce something and stab yourself with a fork? What would *you* think if you were me?"

Marc still had Uncle Bill's lighter in his pocket, and was about to take it out when her boss called her over to talk to her. He didn't want her to get into trouble with the guy so he told her he'd talk to her later, shoveling a lame excuse.

"Thanks for the band-aid, mom!" he said, loud enough for her boss to hear.

Marc wondered if his friend Luke was home and headed there.

Marc's best friend Luke was hilarious, loyal and true, the type of friend anyone would want to have. Luke was on a trip with his family and said they'd be back right about then. Marc had rarely taken a trip, except a few trips camping when he was young before his dad left. Luke's family was far from rich, but it seemed they were compared to Marc and his mom. *Talking to Luke would be so much easier with a phone*, Marc thought darkly as he pedaled, jealous of those kids at school who had their own phones.

THREE

Swindling People with New Powers

By the time Marc reached Luke's house, the sun sat lower in the sky, casting shadows as long and deep as giant talons. Standing on the left pedal as he neared the house, Marc stepped off his bike as if stepping off an escalator, letting it land in the grass of Luke's semi-green front lawn. Luke's family wasn't home yet, and Marc sighed a swearword born from the frustration of holding in a secret like a full bladder.

"Who the fuss are you?"

It took a second before Marc realized who was speaking. He turned to see a nosy, freckle faced boy in a dingy tank top.

"Huh?" asked Marc, still out of breath.

"Who are you?"

"Did you really say 'fuss'?" asked Marc.

"Yes."

"Is that supposed to be a swear word?"

"Duh," said the young boy, as if everyone knew.

Marc blinked. "Uh, okay," he said. "Do you know where the Rendats are?" he added, gesturing to Luke's home, but the freckle-faced kid just stared at him.

"Hello?" Marc asked again.

"Not sure."

"You've been a big help," Marc said dryly.

"Thanks," the boy said, not aware of the sarcasm.

Marc started when a big black labrador behind him dashed past in pursuit of an imagined threat.

"Don't mind him. That's Bear. He don't bite. So, what happened to your arm?"

"Nothing."

"You're older than me, aren't you?" said the boy, and it was at this point that Marc's nose sounded the alarm that the boy probably hadn't bathed in months.

"Uh, probably. How old are you?" Marc asked.

"Nine." The sun on the boy's hair made it look blonder than it was.

"Cool," said Marc, his eyes on his bike on the front lawn. "I'm only a few years older."

"I made almost twenty-five dollars selling lemonade yesterday. Wanna see?"

"Wow. Sure," said Marc.

The boy took a wad of dollar bills out of his pocket, stowaway quarters clinking onto the sidewalk as he did.

"That's cool," Marc said, when a fiendishly clever idea entered his mind. "Hey, uh. I'll bet you ten dollars I can burn myself with fire and I won't get hurt."

"Whuuuuuh?" the boy said with an exhale.

"Serious. Wanna bet?" asked Marc.

"How long are you gonna have your hand over the flame?" asked the boy.

"Oh, thirty seconds."

"Thirty seconds?"

"Yep," said Marc, his nose sounding the alarm again about the boy's stench. He stifled the impulse to gag or say anything about it.

"No, a minute!" said the boy with delight in his eyes.

"Okay, a minute," Marc agreed. "Is it a bet?"

"It's a bet!" said the boy.

Marc had his uncle's lighter in his pocket. He took it out and showed the boy, while Marc's nose argued that ten dollars wasn't worth standing in the nuclear blast of the boy's stench. With twenty seconds left in the minute, the boy finally spoke in hushed amazement. "How are you doing that?" he asked, hypnotized by what he saw.

"It's a magic trick. Now pay up."

The boy handed him the money without a hint of disappointment in his eyes, still fixed on Marc's hand. "But seriously. How'd you do that?"

"I told you. It's magic," said Marc as he pedaled away.

"Seriously! Tell me! I won't get mad!" the boy yelled after him. "Promise! I won't ask for the money back!"

Nearly a block away, Marc called back to him. "How do you know this lighter makes real fire?"

"Hey, wait! Do they sell those? How much for it?" the boy yelled after him, but Marc and his bike—and his nose—were thankfully already down the street.

Marc stopped at the Quick-Mart on the corner to spend his newfound fortune, pushing away the guilt tugging at him as he opened the glass door.

Great. The first thing I do when I realize I have special powers is to hustle some poor kid who probably spent the day slaving away making gallons of lemonade.

He got over it quickly. He was hungry and poor.

Four

A New Friend

Outside the Quick-Mart, sitting on his bike, eating his burrito, Marc watched a gray jay on the ground near the road pick at a torn piece of hotdog bun.

Marc then noticed an older boy, wearing a white hoodie, standing near the large ice locker.

They exchanged a glance. Marc gave him a courtesy smile with a half nod.

"I'm new in town," said the teen.

"Oh. Uh, great," said Marc, pretending to care.

"Been around for a little while. Visiting family," said the boy, looking away toward the town's water tower and the trees beneath it.

Another uncomfortable pause. "Anyone I know?" asked Marc, trying to be polite.

"The Trammels on Birch street. Know 'em?" The boy's eyes were narrow and striking, his fingers loosely holding an intricately colored longboard.

"Nope," Marc said. Another pause. "I'm Marc."

"I'm Steve. Steve Yabloka." When he said this, they both looked up when a small, black Nissan on the street facing the store screeched its braking tires, blaring its horn at a slower car.

"Good meeting you. Nice longboard."

"Thanks. You should get one."

"I wish I had the money," said Marc, his mouth full with the last bite of his burrito.

"Money isn't a problem," said Steve.

Marc stared at him, ran a hand through his hair, and lifted a quizzical eyebrow. "Must be nice," Marc said.

"It isn't a problem for you, either. I can get you one."

"You can?" asked Marc, suddenly more interested. He sipped his drink, trying to act casual.

"Sure. For free," Steve said, a gust of wind hurrying past his hair.

"Free?" Marc paused, unsure now. "Cool. So, uh, what's the catch?"

"Nothing. You just seem cool. I'll get you one."

"Really?"

"Sure," he said, the light breeze carrying sounds of distant traffic.

"Why would you buy me one? You don't even know me," Marc said, itching his arm.

"Well, I have to make friends somehow, right?"

A smile from Marc. "Do you have lots of new, uh, friends, then?"

"Oh, sure. I have several on my payroll," he said with a rueful smile.

Marc chuckled and itched his arm again, figuring it was a mosquito bite.

"What's your address? I'll bring it over."

"You're seriously going to buy me one of those?" Marc asked.

"Sure, why not?"

Marc looked at his arm and his eyes flew open in alarm. There were black smudges on his fingers and arm where twelve mosquitoes had died in what looked like a kamikaze mission trying to penetrate his skin. Questions firing in his mind made him stumble over his next words as he wiped his hand on his jeans.

"Uh, uh, cool. Um, I'm—I'm at 137 East Eden Drive." As Marc said this, he stepped to the side as a heavy construction worker strode past them towards the store. Marc met his suspicious gaze, but looked away first. *Geesh, calm down, Mondragon*, he told himself as the man lumbered into the store. *It's not like I'm doing anything wrong.*

"Great. Easy to remember." Steve's voice interrupted his thoughts. "So, what's your story?"

Marc kicked the same tiny rock into the curb over and over as he spoke, gesturing with the soda, its straw leaning sadly to the side. "My mom grew up here, and when my dad died we moved here where her parents are. But they, uh, they moved to Arizona a year ago. She works at the diner."

The boy seemed disinterested, his gaze off in the distance toward the water tower again. "That's cool," he finally said after a pause.

"What I'm saying is I know how you feel, being new and all," said Marc, holding his empty cup.

"Sucks about your dad."

"Thanks. I was young when he died, like five." Marc's cup lowered a bit.

Steve nodded. "Yeah, that sucks."

An awkwardness settled in until Marc saw Luke's family's white Chevy pull onto their street. "Well, there's my friend's family. Better go."

"See ya," Steve said as Marc pedaled away toward Luke's house. When Marc glanced back at Steve, he could've sworn he saw a corner of Steve's mouth tug into a light, self-satisfied grin.

FIVE

MEANWHILE, IN NEW YORK CITY . . .

The homeless man had witnessed murder before, but never like this. He was just waking up, still groggy from the previous night's alcohol. As he awakened, the first city sounds of morning fading in, he lay still beneath the refuse at the back of the dead-end alley; a damp cardboard box, a few newspaper sections, and plastic sheeting.

At the side of the alley's opening was a fire escape ladder, casting the meanest of shadows against its building.

As the man considered his cold feet on a morning that would turn into a perfectly warm day, he heard a boy coughing. He looked through the five-inch gap in the debris that covered him, the only part of his vision not obstructed, and saw the boy at the alley's entrance, moving toward him. The boy looked thirteen, a bit older perhaps. He was dark-haired and shirtless, and his body contorted this way and that in pain, stumbling at times. The tall building cast the boy in shadow as he approached.

The homeless man stayed motionless with steady, shallow breathing. It was a game he liked to play, trying to make himself invisible, like a child pretending to sleep when mom checks on him. He was already invisible to most of society anyway.

Another figure, a blonde business man in his 30s, passed by in the sun-bathed street but stopped when he noticed the boy. *Nice suit*, the homeless man noted.

"Hello?" the businessman called to the boy. "You okay, kid?"

The boy just growled something. It was a bit menacing, but the boy's voice cracked, and the homeless man sensed anger, not vulnerability, below its surface

Business man approached the boy and offered him his gray suit jacket. Professional man waited a bit, and the homeless man continued watching the two dark silhouettes against the proscenium backdrop of the bright street behind them.

"Not the warmest day out here. Looks like you could use a co—" he began, but a burst of light exploded near the boy's face and the homeless man stopped breathing when he saw the business man's head completely engulfed in flames, screaming. The boy slashed and stabbed at the business man's torso and the it opened, though the homeless man couldn't see it well since the boy obstructed his view.

The screaming stopped, and the taller man fell, his hands not protesting, as his head and shoulders burned on. The boy took a wallet, keys, and phone from the business man's pants, put on the previously offered jacket, and stood.

The homeless man still hadn't breathed, so he exhaled slowly, trying to minimize any movement. His fearful eyes stayed on the boy's shadowed face. The boy looked all around, back in the direction of the homeless man, then turned, walking out of the alley with a confident gait.

"Okay. Got it," Detective O'Leary said, writing in a small wire-bound pad with a stubby pencil. His kids wrote things in the cloud. Him? He had his feet on the ground. Old school. Talking to the doctors in the sterile basement room at the county coroner's office was part of the job, but he never got used to the smell. "And eh, anything else on Extra Crispy?"

"Quite grisly," the young pathologist said, emotionless, focusing on the charred remains.

O'Leary put the pad and pencil back in his shirt and turned for the door. "So, I can get the full write up on that next week, right, Doc?" he asked as he walked impatiently toward the double doors. He counted down under his breath as he approached the exit. "Four, three, two . . ."

"Oh, Detective?"

Rolling his eyes, O'Leary muttered under his breath, "Every time," before doing the standard about-face. He could never leave the good doctor's presence on the first try. "Something more, Doc?"

"One last thing." Dr. Worthington was touching the side of his head with the back of his gloved hand, and O'Leary wondered if the doctor was dealing with a headache or worked too much. "In all my years as a medical examiner, I've never seen anything quite like it."

"Doc, you say that about three times a year," O'Leary teased.

"Well, yes, that's true, because I'm still relatively young, but this time, it's even more true. I've never heard of or read about this anywhere else. Right when I think I've seen it all . . ." The doctor paused, and O'Leary figured the doctor was quietly translating the big words into something he could understand.

"It's the accelerant on the body," the doctor said flatly.

So much for translating.

"Huh?" O'Leary was impatient with the doctor's dramatic pauses. "In English, please?"

"Well, it's simply not what you would find in any flamethrower. I dug a bit deeper, figuratively speaking, because of the particular hue on the skin that I'd never seen before. It's a plasma-type substance, but the strange part is that it carries DNA."

"What about the guy's DNA? It's all whacked or something?" O'Leary asked.

"No, no, not the victim's DNA, the *accelerant of the fire itself* has deoxyribonucleic acid *in* it. Strangest thing I've ever seen as an examiner." Dr. Worthington seemed to relish the drama and scientific mystery of it all, as if something that left him stumped was akin to a yearly bonus. "It's as if the flamethrower itself were alive."

"That's weird." O'Leary paused before saying the well-practiced, "Well, put it in the report, I'll tackle it later. Thanks again

Doc. Have a good night." He briskly left the room and ascended to the street where he sucked in some fresh air to purge the stench of the lab coating his lungs.

SIX

Impervious to Their Gorgeousness

Luke's room looked a lot like Marc's room, except that it was bigger and in a nicer house.

As the flame caressed Marc's hand, Luke sounded a lot like his nine-year-old neighbor. "Whoa." He froze, as if taking his eyes off Marc's hand would ruin the trick. "How are you . . ." he paused, fascinated, ". . . doing that, Donkle?" Luke dropped the potato chip bag into his lap. *Donkle* was short for *Donkleshorts*, an affectionate nickname Luke had given Marc on the first day of fourth grade when they'd met. All the kids had made fun of Marc all day for wearing the loud, three-sizes-too-big "poor-kid" shorts his mom bought him at the second-hand store. Luke was the only one who befriended him, making his shorts seem cool by giving them a nickname.

"Cool, huh?" asked Marc with mystified eyes, his hand still a stranger he was getting to know.

"Yeah. Totally."

A pause.

"But seriously," Luke said. "How are you doing that? Did you coat your hand with something?"

"No!" A neighbor bellowed right on cue from outside Luke's window. After a quick pause of worry, Luke and Marc burst into laughter, direct sunlight lighting up Luke's brown hair as he leaned forward.

"My thoughts exactly," said Marc, smiling. "Your new neighbor is crazy," he said. "And he's right! It's one-hundred-percent my hand. I have no idea how. I just realized it today."

"You just realized today that fire can't hurt you?"

"Luke, it's not just fire. *Nothing* hot can hurt me."

"Hot plates?" Luke asked.

"Nope."

"Hot grease?" Luke asked, and Marc shook his head. "Hot lava?" he tried.

"Probably not," said Marc.

"Not even hot *girls* can hurt you?" Luke giggled.

"No! I'm impervious to their gorgeousness!" Marc's and Luke's quiet laugh overtook their bodies for a few seconds.

A pause, filled with the sound of the loud, angry neighbor negotiating a flowerbed with his dog. Marc spoke first.

"Have you met that new kid named Steve?" he asked, and Luke, whose mouth searched out the last of the salt-and-vinegar potato-chip dust out of the bag, said "Nuh-uh" with a small, muffled echo.

"Yeah. He's new, but I dunno. Something's off about that kid," Marc said under his breath. After smiling at Luke and the potato chip bag for a moment, Marc asked, "So, what now?"

"What do you mean, *what now*?" Luke asked, crumpling the potato chip bag and grabbing the bottle of water from his desk. "Marc, this is a superpower! This is an honest-to-God superpower! Holy jafoozle-rabbits! What do we do with it?"

"I don't know. I—" Marc began.

"This never happened to one of my friends before!"

"You think it's happened to any of *my* friends *or* me?" Marc said.

"Where do you think this came from?" asked Luke.

"I don't know, it's like—" Marc started, but then he interrupted himself. "Wait!" he said. "My dreams!"

"Your dreams! Yes! Wait—your dreams?"

"I remember my dreams!" said Marc, his eyes focused on replaying the memory, those same feelings of dread enveloping him as he did.

"And that's cool *why* exactly?"

From the kitchen, Luke's mom called out to him and his sister for them to come eat, which was always the signal that friends had to go home.

"Okay, Mom!" yelled Luke, but Marc continued.

"I never remember my dreams, but now I can remember that I've had the same dream over and over the last couple weeks!" Marc exclaimed, then mumbled under his breath, "Have I ever remembered them before? Have they ever felt this real or repeated this many times?"

"Donk! Are you gonna tell me what the dream is, or am I gonna have to cut you deep?" Luke said, making his voice sound as super thug as possible.

"Oh, sorry. Okay. So, here's the dream. I'm flying. I'm flying high, then I'm flying low, going all over the place I guess, then I'm flying low above a small small town, like, really old. I'm hearing people shrieking and crying—"

"Crying?" Luke interrupted. "Crying like 'I'm sad' crying?"

"Uh, yeah, but it's also out of fear I think? Maybe—anyway, but here's the thing. There was fire everywhere, and..." he paused.

"And," Luke prodded.

"And I was *causing* it," Marc said.

"You were causing it? Like you're flying around, like some pyromaniac superhero or something?"

"How *was* I causing it?" Marc asked under his breath, lost in thought.

"Hello?" Luke asked.

"Sorry," said Marc. "Uh, no, it's not like I'm lighting fires with a lighter or something. It's like I'm dumping bursts of fire all over a small town that looks like it's from a long time ago."

"Weird," said Luke. He looked up. "Bro! What if you have some kind of like a magic DVD player, and it gives you the powers of the movie you're watching! Like you're watching *Firestarter* or something, and now you can't get burned!"

So random, Marc thought. "Uh, yeah," Marc said with a smile. "Maybe."

"Just a thought that popped in my head. Oh! What if you're, like, part dragon or something?" said Luke, stifling laughter.

"Funny," said Marc. *Like that's possible.*

"Okay, okay," Luke said, thinking. "Wait. Can anything else hurt you?"

"Yeah. Forks."

"Forks?" Luke asked, and Marc lifted his arm to show the bandage. "When I saw that nothing could burn me, I thought that nothing could hurt me, so I . . . tested it—"

"With a fork?" Luke said, filling in the blank.

"Yep."

Luke lost it. His laughter echoed in his small room and he fell on a heap of dirty clothes, then rolled on the carpet. "You stabbed yourself with a fork?"

"Yeah. At my mom's work."

"While she was serving *food*?" Luke asked as his laugh turned into a cackle, punctuating it with slapping the floor.

"Shut up! It isn't funny!" As Luke kept laughing, Marc had to give in and a chuckle escaped him. "Okay. Fine. It's a little funny," Marc mumbled, a smile tugging at his mouth.

"This is the best afternoon," Luke said, recovering. "That made my year."

Luke's mom yelled for him to come and eat for the second time, and the tone in her voice meant business.

"OK!" Luke called. Luke's mom once told them both that she thought they acted a few years younger than they actually were, and Marc always wondered if she meant it as an insult or a compliment. Luke then turned to Marc. "Marc, listen. Don't worry. We'll figure this out, okay?"

"Okay," said Marc. "Should I tell someone?"

"Are you serious? And wind up in some kind of a lab with doctors jabbing you with *more* forks? No way. Don't risk it."

"So, what do we do?" asked Marc.

"Meet me at the baseball field tomorrow to make our plans for world domination! What else?" said Luke.

"Okay, but don't tell anyone," said Marc.

"I won't."

"Promise?" said Marc.

"I swear on a stack of comic books," said Luke, his eyes as serious as if he had said 'Bibles.'

SEVEN

More Strange Powers: Did I Do That?

On the day before school started, Marc woke up with a sore throat. It burned. A lot. *Great,* he thought. *I can only feel burning* inside *me. Nice trade-off.*

The sore throat got so bad that before he was able to hang out with Luke to make his plans, his mom insisted that he go to the doctor's office.

With the lighter in his pocket, Marc wanted to tell his mom about his newfound powers as they sat in the library-quiet waiting room, but he didn't. There was a lot he had to figure out first, and the thought of being some lab rat and getting experimented on by government freaks because his mom got worried helped him keep his mouth shut. The epic fail in the diner only added to the fact that he needed to keep this hidden, at least until he knew more about what was going on.

Sitting in the antiseptic waiting room, Marc and his mom waited until a nurse finally called, mispronouncing their last name as always, and escorted them to their own personal walk-in closet of an examining room. Finally, a guy named Dr. Frenz, wearing a lab coat and a peninsula of light brown hair, finally checked Marc's vitals and swabbed the inside of his throat. After more waiting, he came in the examining room with a sigh and a tone of voice that said he'd rather be anywhere else.

"Uh, Marc, is it?" and Marc nodded. "Well, I'm guessing it's strep."

"You're not sure?" asked Jenny.

"Uh, the test came back inconclusive, which is odd, but..." the doctor paused, his eyes distracted. "Uh, sorry. Um, anyway, I'll tell you what. I'll write you a scrip for amoxicillin for now and I'll send the culture to the lab in Colorado Springs and if there's anything out of the ordinary, I'll give you a call. Does that work?"

"Does that amoxa-whatever-it's-called cost a lot?" asked Jenny.

"Uh, no, not a whole lot," said the doctor, whose eyes judged them as the less-than-wealthy clients they were.

Historic Downtown Rifle had a little something for everyone. It had theaters, a Civic Center, parks where the community could gather, and teenagers determined to raise harmless havoc. That evening, the downtown was more quiet than usual. Meeting at the baseball field ended up with Marc and Luke meeting downtown. When they got together to discuss their plans, it devolved into just hanging out. They found a crumpled dollar in an alley, spent it in the town's only arcade, and laughed about their lack of action in the action-packed summer they had planned. It was their last day of freedom, the day before school started.

"Do you think it'll be hard keeping this a secret? I mean, this is a pretty big thing to keep secret," said Marc as the sun slipped behind the mountains.

"Yeah, it's big, but not as big as some things," Luke said with a giggle and a smirk, his eyes darting to the ground. "Besides. Parents are so into their own lives, they're not going to stop to think about what we're going through, let alone whether or not my best friend has cool fireproof powers."

He and Luke approached the street. A light breeze mussed Marc's dark brown hair as he came to a stop on the sidewalk. Four or five cars waiting for a stoplight, all in a row, were to his right. Marc's breathing slowed and the hairs on the back of his neck stood on end. The last car was a red Dodge. Looking left to see if a car was coming was as second nature to Marc as breathing by now, thanks to his mom. To his left, he saw an older man with a large nose and what seemed to be his five-year-old granddaughter in pigtails and sizes-too-big overalls at his side.

That was when Marc saw the blue sedan.

It came screeching fast around the corner, the sheriff's patrol car screaming after it.

When its driver saw the line of cars in the way, the sidewalk became an option, and this was when time seemed to slow even more, though when Marc played it back in his mind later, it went too fast to even consider what actually happened.

At seventy miles an hour, the car jumped the curb only ten feet from the old man and his grandkid, coming straight for them.

All Marc could do was lift his arm in their direction.

As he did so, Marc's eyes widened in slow motion.

An almost-imperceptible shiver passed through him when he raised his hand.

Inexplicably, the blue sedan turned on its side, and by the time the old man yanked the girl back, the sedan's undercarriage faced them, rushing past, the back two wheels missing the girl by inches.

The sedan continued skidding on its side with a loud, cringe-inducing scraping sound, and fell upside down back into the street, past Marc and Luke, hitting the back of the red Dodge that waited for the light to change, shedding broken glass as it did.

The blue sedan and red truck burst with vocal obscenities for different reasons. The patrol car stopped behind both and barked stern orders to the upside-down man in the blue sedan.

Marc and Luke stood there with disbelieving eyes, still as a photo.

They blinked, and as an ambulance sounded in the distance and concerned citizens came rushing toward them, they got out of there.

Riding their bikes around, they talked about it, and the more Luke went on about it, Marc looked down at his hand, as if the difference between his hand and any other was visible.

"But Donk, seriously! What *was* that? Do you have more powers?"

"I don't kn—"

"I mean, was that you? Or did the car hit something that made it flip on its side?"

"I'm not sure," said Marc, a bit dazed.

"Come on! Yes you are!"

"No I'm not! I'm honestly not sure. It might have been me, but it all happened so fast," Marc said, turning his bike around the corner to Luke's house.

"It was you, bro, because cars don't move like that," Luke said. "What do you call it again, when you can move things with your mind?" asked Luke.

"I don't know," said Marc. "I think it starts with a 'K' or something."

"Naw, doesn't it start with a 'T'? I thought it started with a 'T'," said Luke.

"Oh, Christmas nuts!" said Marc.

"No, it's not Christmas nuts," Luke said with no irony.

"No, no!" Marc said. "I messed up. Aaugh! I'm late getting home. What time is it?"

"Uh, past nine," said Luke.

"I'm in so much trouble for being out so late."

Suppressing a laugh, Luke asked, "Do you want my mom to write you a note?"

Marc's eyes kept moving, trying to think of a solution. "My mom's birthday is the day after tomorrow. If I bring her a cake and surprise her, I think she'll soften up."

"A two-day-early birthday cake? You sure?"

"I think so," said Marc.

"That's a stretch."

"Worth a try," Marc said, and then added, "Can I borrow ten bucks?"

"Serious?" The way Luke said it, Marc heard the unspoken, *again*?

"C'mon. It's either that or I don't see you for a month 'cause I'm grounded."

"Fine," Luke said, begrudgingly.

Later, as Marc rode his bike slowly home, holding the cake in one hand, he watched the dark sky above him. After turning the bike to avoid a puddle, he looked up at the bright stars, amazed at the many mysteries this world held, and knew he was now a part of one of them. The many darkened houses that surrounded him were filled with people who had no clue about all he was going through, that all of this was real, and when he felt tempted to disbelieve it despite all he had experienced recently, a poster that his seventh-grade English teacher had on her wall came to his mind, a line from *Hamlet*, "There are more things in heaven and earth, Horatio, than are dreamt of in your philosophy."

When Marc entered his home, he could smell the dinner his mom had eaten by herself.

"Where have you been? It's the first day of school tomorrow!" Jenny Mondragon's voice was raised, but she was never good at yelling, even when she wanted to.

"What do you mean?" said Marc, feigning ignorance.

"Don't give me that, Marc. You know very well."

"Mom, you said I could stay out late with Luke."

"When did I say that?" Jenny asked.

"I said I was going to get home after dark, like, today. Earlier. Didn't I say today?"

"No, and I never said ten p.m. I've been worried sick!" she said, her face twisted with emotion.

"Mom, I could have sworn I said today. Didn't I?"

"You're grounded."

"Grounded? Come on, Mom. Serious?"

"Yes!" she said firmly.

"Even though I brought you a birthday cake?" Marc asked with an innocent look.

"Yes! Even though you, you—wait. You what?" His mom's face went from unyielding to bewilderment in an instant.

"Wait right there, Mom. Hold up." Marc walked back to the front door and retrieved the box from the front porch. By the time he had it out of the box and presented it to her, she had tears in her eyes.

"Oh, honey, thank you!"

"I hope it cheers you up, Mom. You deserve a break. It, uh, took a while to find the right cake. Luckily, the one store was open after nine."

She paused, looking at him. "You're getting to be so tall. You may end up being taller than your father. Oh, listen to me go on and on."

"I like it. It's okay," Marc said, the pain in his throat throbbing. He rubbed his neck, wincing.

"Throat still bothering you?" she asked.

"Mom, stop worrying about me. Think of yourself for once," Marc said. She looked at him, and he knew deep down that she knew part of the reason for the cake was to soften her response to his tardiness, though she never called him on it.

"Well, are you going to light the candles, or what?" Marc asked, pleased to see his mom happy. She giggled and ran to the kitchen. After a moment, she returned. "Here are the candles. Let me see where those matches went," she said, heading back into the kitchen.

When Marc placed the candles onto the cake, the scratchiness in his throat became too much. He felt like he would gag. An odd sensation welled up inside him—something related to the impending coughing spasm, but separate at the same time. When he coughed, his eyes involuntarily squeezed shut and his throat burned.

When he opened his eyes, the candles were lit, the frosting lightly scorched and drooping, melted on one side, and his throat felt like he just threw up, times seven, a weird chemical taste in his mouth.

"You had matches?" his mom asked as she came around the corner.

"Uh—" Marc managed, wiping away watery eyes. "I had, uh, Uncle Bill's lighter," he said, coughing. "Just realized, uh, that I had it."

"Oh, great!" she said, putting the box of matches down on the ancient dining room table. Marc stared in disbelief. Did that really just happen? Did he really just cough out some fire from his own mouth? He decided to stifle the million questions that burned in his mind and wonder about them another time.

"Happy birthday, Mom," Marc said.

"Oh, honey, thank you," she said, blushing.

EIGHT

Stone Stajinski and Drakesel

More than a thousand miles away, a wealthy man searched for someone to carry out a deadly task.

"Hold it!" Stone Stajinski commanded, walking to the elevator like he owned the place. The man and woman in the elevator jerked arms out to hold the door for this stranger dressed in all-black tactical gear, eyeing the black steel of Stone's 9mm pistol in its holster. Stone, in his early forties, with hard, ambivalent eyes, stared at the metal doors as the elevator's other occupants eyed him warily through the uncomfortable silence. Stone's presence was pure strength: crew cut, black armband on one forearm.

The other, younger man in the elevator made the mistake of trying to lighten the mood. Perhaps he did it to prove he wasn't the least bit intimidated by the man in black. "Let me guess. You're from accounting," he said with a chuckle. Stone stood motionless, as if the man hadn't said a word.

"I'm just joking. But wow. Your outfit looks pretty intense for this office building. Where are you from, and more importantly, should we be worried?" the young man dared ask, turning with a smile to the only other passenger in the elevator, a pretty young lady in a business suit who, by the forced apathy in her eye, seemed more fearful of Stone than impressed with the young man's fearless banter.

Stone maintained his rigidity, and when his hard, indifferent eyes bore into him, the young businessman wilted. Like a chided schoolboy, he looked everywhere except Stone's eyes, wishing he were anywhere else.

A tinny-sounding bell chimed, the elevator doors opened, and Stone stalked out, leaving the other two shifting nervously in their shoes.

When Stone entered the large, luxurious office, he sat without a word in a chair opposite the expansive desk, despite the warm greeting by James Leopold Drakesel. The scent of sterile affluence hung in the air.

"How are you?" Drakesel asked, but his question went unanswered. Drakesel was in his late fifties, with the distinguished graying hair and large, determined eyes that seemed to come standard on successful businessmen.

A well-dressed man with a bow tie sat in a slightly less-expensive chair in the corner, scrutinizing Stone. He looked to be in his early thirties, not a face anyone would remember. His demeanor was as straight-to-business as Stone's, but in a more academic way. Drakesel gestured to the man. "This is Jonathan, my right hand."

"Are you saying he's your butler?" Stone asked.

"Sure," is all Jonathan said. He delivered it with sarcasm, not the least bit intimidated by the big, bad tough guy. Jonathan's eyes never left Stone.

"Can I get you anything?" Drakesel asked.

Only Stone's eyes moved to meet his. "Yes. The reason I'm here."

"Oh, of course. You're to-the-point. I like that. Well, as I said on the phone, I know they're out there. I know it. My family, for more generations than you can imagine, have entrusted me to protect what they've built," Drakesel said.

Stone stared at him with cold, emotionless eyes, letting a long pause punctuate how ridiculous he thought the whole thing was before continuing. "Mr. Drakesel—"

"Uh, it's pronounced *Drake-suhl*," said James.

Stone only continued. "Have you stopped to consider that this could all be just some big myth, some old ghost story your family's been chasing?"

"Do you like money, Stone?"

"I don't need this job, Mr. Drakesel," he said, rising from his chair.

"I can find another just like you," said Drakesel, to which Stone exhaled a short chuckle and a tug of a confident smile that bore no teeth.

"No. You can't," said Stone.

Jonathan wore a light smile, a look that said, *is this Stone guy for real?*

Eyes met eyes, a manly contest of wills, until Drakesel sighed, sat down, and said, "It's real. Generations of my family haven't put this much energy into stopping something that doesn't exist."

Stone exhaled. "Yet you want me to track these people and kill them?"

"I wouldn't say that," Drakesel said.

"No?"

"Of course not. Not if you're somehow recording this, hoping to twist what I say into something incriminating," Drakesel said.

A look of begrudging respect shone in Stone's eyes. *This guy isn't dumb.*

"So, what's in it for you?" asked Stone. "What do you care about someone or something your family fought a long time ago, real or imagined?"

"Well, as I said, my family has an interest in protecting its wealth from threats past, present, and future." Drakesel said, pausing for effect, letting the words sink in. When the man in black said nothing, Drakesel hastily added, "Uh, m-my family's surname, in fact, actually comes from a middle-French word meaning 'dragonslayer.'"

"That's fascinating," Stone said dismissively. "But how can you be so sure that these kids even exist?"

"I'm sure," said Drakesel. "I won't explain to you how I know. I'm also sure that time is running out."

"Sounds dramatic," Stone said, unimpressed.

"If you don't want the job, don't take it," Drakesel said vehemently, then composed himself and continued, businesslike. "Sign the non-disclosure contract in front of you and go," he said, suddenly concerning himself with something on his tablet.

Without moving his head or neck, Stone eyed the contract on the desk, then looked back up to Drakesel. "Still here."

"Okay."

"Why don't you just hire me to get them behind bars? I'm sure they've broken some kind of law if you're afraid that they will come after your family's fortune."

Drakesel moved to the floor-to-ceiling window facing the East River and stared at the mute traffic below. "No. We must get them before their powers grow too strong."

"Powers. Right," Stone mumbled dismissively as he got up from the chair and turned, but then stopped with a resigned exhale and looked back at Drakesel. "Mr. Drakesel, if you're this determined, I suggest we start with any strange phenomena. Hospitals, research labs—anything someone out there might come across as the least bit off, even if it sounds crazy. The crazier the claim, the more we need to look into it."

"Yes. That's good. I'll start my men on database searches."

A long pause followed, and Stone's eyes turned from serious to threatening.

Drakesel looked up at him with a question in his eyes, as if wondering what he had done to provoke it, and finally Stone spoke. "If all of this turns out to be some sick rich guy who wants to kill kids for fun, or to retaliate against some rival's children, I will find you, Mr. Drakesel. And you won't go to jail. You'll cease to live." Stone said this firmly but matter-of-factly as he signed the non-disclosure form on the desk.

"Yes, I understand," Drakesel finally said, looking over at Jonathan, who shifted in his seat with expressionless, scrutinizing eyes that never left Stone. By the time Drakesel said this, however, Stone was already to the office door.

"Send me anything your men find, and my team will track down those leads," said Stone, throwing the words over his shoulder as he walked out.

"Good, yes," Drakesel called after him, hope rising in his voice. "We have your bank information to transfer the funds," he said. When Stone left, Jonathan approached Drakesel and spoke of their plan with business-like calm and hushed tones.

NINE

THE DRAGON IN THE DREAM

Marc saw dragons flying all around him, and what's more, he knew them. He knew them well, for he was one of them.

His large body landed on the peak of a stony mountain, his enormous, taloned wings settling as he surveyed the view.

Just below him were two other dragons, one of a color darker than night, and the other a deep red. Their thirst and lust for his fall off the precipice gleamed in their eyes like cat-eyed cigarette ends in the dark.

Adrenaline coursed through him; his heart pounded with the nervous, fearful energy of any creature preparing for a fight.

In the second part of the dream, however, all the danger fell away.

Marc sat in a massive white room, its edges faded and barely perceptible.

A large dragon, whose size, majesty, and very presence caught him in a spell of wonder, approached him.

"To this were you born," said the dragon. As it spoke in its deep baritone, Marc watched it, mesmerized. He didn't dare speak. More than twenty feet high, the dragon seemed to be made of solid, charcoal-grey granite. Its back was lined with deep copper, and its front splattered with grey and black scales, coursing down its snowy white bosom. When it spoke, its mouth looked crooked on the sides, pulled around wide jaws.

"I will guide you with these dreams, since the others are slow to find you," said the dragon, its lean muscles packaged in scales of iron.

Without warning, a single thought burned into Marc's consciousness, commanding every part of his attention:

I am part dragon.

Marc awoke in his bed with most of the covers on the floor. He opened his eyes and looked at the clock on his nightstand: 1:37 a.m.

Marc moved to pick up the blankets from the floor, trying to shake thoughts of bright eyes in dark places turning in his direction.

He thought of flying, of his new relationship with fire.

Part dragon? he thought.

The thought seemed so far from reality that he tried dismissing it. A nervous chuckle escaped him. Dragons were fantastical, mythical creatures. It wasn't like they were real. After all, this was just a dream, right?

The thought persisted.

If he were part dragon, he reasoned, it would make a lot of sense. Marc thought of the lighter's fire under his fingers, his weird cough scorching his mom's cake, and the other unexplained phenomena currently happening in his life. In the midst of these thoughts, a feeling came over him he had never felt before, a small humming sensation, a buzzing tranquility between his throat and his heart—small, but growing. Like an inner heat from an intense flame, it emanated outward, stretching from his center. It was peaceful, but powerful; a feeling of strength, affirmation, and a quiet energy source all in one.

He had never consciously felt anything like it before. Was this feeling, teeming all around him and through him, somehow confirming his thought about being part dragon? He felt that it was.

If so, then how was this possible? Marc only hoped the answers would arrive sooner than later.

In all the stories Marc loved most, there often appeared a mentor character that helped guide the hero. Luke Skywalker had Obi-Wan Kenobi and Frodo had Gandalf. Marc reasoned that if he was "born to this," as the dragon in his dreams had said, these supernaturally life-like dreams, and even the dragon himself within them, were a strange kind of mentor to guide him. Still, he was grateful for them. They not only pointed him to a gradual understanding of all that was happening to him, they also kept him from going completely crazy.

Am I going crazy? he wondered.

Thinking of what had happened downtown the night before, Marc replayed the moment in his mind. How did the car do that? It just *happened.*

He had felt something when the car turned, but if he was somehow responsible for the car turning onto its side, he wondered anew how he had come to have these powers, and whether or not he would be able to move something with his mind again.

Marc decided to test it.

The same self-doubt with his father's voice crept in, but he tried to push it aside.

Sitting in his bed, reaching in his mind for the name of the ability to move physical objects mentally, which still sat stubbornly on the tip of his tongue, he looked over at the light switch on the paint-chipped wall near the door to his room.

He stared at it, then closed his eyes and focused.

Light illuminated his room.

"Yeaaaah! Telekinesis!" Marc said aloud to himself, proud he remembered the name, but then he opened his eyes to see his mom with her hand on the light switch.

"Oh," said Marc, disappointed. "Hey, Mom."

"Practicing magic?" she asked.

"Uh, sort of."

"I heard sounds. Why are you up at this hour?" she asked.

"I just woke up from a dream."

"Was it a good one?" she asked.

"Yeah," Marc said. "It was about dragons."

"Very nice. Now ask the dragons nicely to let you sleep," she said.

"Okay," he said, the word drawn out with a yawn.

When his mom left, he sat up and tried to move a pen on his desk. He thought hard, but it wouldn't budge.

Confused, he wondered how it worked, how a big thing like a car could move, but not a pen or a light switch. Maybe it wasn't telekinesis after all.

Falling asleep, Marc smiled about the future. Of all his homework, of all the knowledge out there he could discover, the most exciting to him were the possibilities that lay within himself.

The problem now was the possibility that lay outside him.

He awoke the next day with severe acne.

When the sun rose, Marc faced the first day of ninth grade. The swamp cooler in Marc's small home sounded like an ethereal version of a great, rushing river. It had always woke him when it turned on. Marc scratched his head and sat up, already knowing that his mom had already gone to work. Soon, Marc and Luke were in Marc's room, skipping first period, debating what to do.

"Does it always appear this fast?" Marc said, looking into the mirror, staring horrified at the acne all over his face and neck, down his back, down his arms. Marc had gone from nary a zit to acute acne overnight.

Socially, he knew he would be an instant pariah at school.

"I've never heard of it happening this fast," said Luke, his face twisting in concern for his friend. "Well, at least you were never that popular to begin with, right?" Off Marc's look, Luke added, "Sorry."

"I just don't understand," Marc said. "The first day of school? Why now?"

"Maybe it's your new powers, Donk," offered Luke. "A reaction, maybe?"

Marc nodded, his brow furrowed because he knew this had to be the reason. What else could it be? No one else in his family had acne this bad, ever.

"Great," said Marc, staring into the mirror. "It's like the universe is telling me, 'You have dragon powers, kid. Oh and uh, here's some chronic acne to go along with that. Enjoy.'" Marc's disappointed, hopeless eyes examined the red leprosy.

"Well, Donk, just remember. The only thing anyone will look at or think of all day is you and your acne."

In the second or two that followed, Marc looked at Luke's expression and laughed. His best friend knew just when to make fun of a situation, and he actually felt better. Acne isn't the end of the world.

"Yeah. Let's go," said Marc, to school, it was understood. "Whatever social rejection is waiting, well, okay. whatever."

TEN

Social Outcast on the First Day of School

It was a classic first day of school: kids cramming the hallways, some pushing, some looking up, squinting at room numbers, opening their lockers with all the concentration of bank robbers, other kids laughing together about different things.

Besides the social outcast state of anyone with severe acne, Marc was convinced that everyone he saw knew that he was different. He was convinced of it. He told Luke about this insecurity, and Luke smiled. "No, buddy. It's *you* who aren't used to being both human and, uh, the other thing." Luke said this as two other boys walked past, their shoes squeaking against clean linoleum. Luke told him not to overreact or worry, and that seemed to help, though Marc saw Luke as a sort of security blanket. He watched Luke run to his second period class like a boy starting kindergarten watches his mom leave after dropping him off.

This first day hadn't started too badly, even though Marc had to endure the pain of the outcast: uncomfortable stares, averted gazes, even full-blown teasing, though only by one person.

"Four-eighty-two, four-eighty-two," Marc mumbled to himself as he waded through the hallway full of students with backpacks looking for their own lockers. His eyes found the 480s bank of lockers, but as he approached them, he felt a hand on the back of his head, then a searing pain.

Purple fuzz and tiny pinhole stars clouded his vision, the pain from his forehead rushing through him, the acne making the pain five times worse.

Marc's favorite frenemy showed up, a permanent stain on his life since they'd moved to Rifle, who had pushed his head hard into the lockers as a friendly 'good morning.'

Toshua Zuskie was a stocky kid with short, dark hair and a brash personality. Everyone called him Zoosh, though Marc and Luke called him a name that rhymed with it behind his back. He considered himself the most popular ninth grader in the seventh-through-twelfth-grade school—as popular as a ninth grader could possibly be, at least—and he sauntered through the halls with his posse of bad seeds.

"Hey, Mondragon, love the new look."

Marc said nothing. He felt cold inside, numb; a big, red welt appeared on his forehead.

"You must love pepperoni pizza, bro," Zoosh said with his trademark passive-aggressive smirk. "'Cause it's all over your face!"

Besides pushing kids 'harmlessly' into lockers as a daily friendly greeting, he never actually physically threatened anyone. It was always implied, especially if he wanted something the other person had.

Marc had only planned on enduring the teasing, the verbal abuse. He could take that, as he always had, but this was different. This was the first time in a while Zoosh had thrown Marc into a locker, causing physical pain, and Marc was furious. When Zoosh noticed the look in Marc's eye, he pivoted to avoid any entanglements with the administration. "Hey, I'm kidding! You're too sensitive!" Zoosh said, slapping Marc on the shoulder as if he were patting the cheek of an emotional child. The final insult was when Zoosh mussed Marc's hair with his hand and walked away, his friends cackling with delight.

Every student at Marc's school had sat through the anti-bullying rallies and assemblies many times, so of course Zoosh was careful to package his teasing as 'humor.'

Anger welled inside Marc as he watched Zoosh and his friends continue down the hallway 'welcoming' others back to school, marking their territory.

Something clicked inside him, a level of anger he hadn't felt before, an anger toward Zoosh but also himself for never really standing up to the kid. He tried to contain it by throwing a dismissive but forceful hand in Zoosh's direction, a get-outta-here gesture, and what happened next took a second for Marc to register.

From down the hall, it looked like a huge, invisible hand grabbed Zoosh's entire body and slammed it six feet across the hall to the bank of lockers, leaving a slight dent in one of them.

When Zoosh sunk down unconscious to the shiny lacquered concrete, gasps of panic and light pandemonium blossomed in the hallway surrounding him. Mr. Dorfin, a moustached physics teacher, stepped out of his classroom and told everyone to back away and go to class, then sent a student running for help.

Marc stood in shock. The noise in the hallway fell mute for a moment as Marc looked at his hands, a disbelieving gasp escaping him.

In the days that followed, the rumors as to what happened to Zoosh were many; some kids thought he fell hard, others said his friend pushed him, others said he slipped or was tripped, and still others said the hallways were haunted or it was a punishment from God for all of Zoosh's bullying.

Marc knew the truth.

It was him, and he didn't even mean to do it. These new powers thrilled and bothered him all at the same time.

ELEVEN

ENGLISH CLASS AND WAX SANDWICHES

Marc quickly went to his second period English class. What happened to Zoosh should have felt like a victory, but it didn't, not to Marc, not after the initial thrill wore off. Nothing ruined a party like someone getting hurt and not knowing the reason it happened.

Because the school had been built in the 1960s, the English classroom looked like every classic public school classroom one might imagine: sunlight pouring in from the windows on one side, desks and chairs connected by metal tentacles in neat little rows that faced a blackboard the school hadn't yet converted to a whiteboard.

The teacher was nice: a bright-eyed, bespectacled African-American woman named Mrs. Tenakin.

She started the class by asking about the books the kids had read over the summer, and soon J.R.R. Tolkien's *The Hobbit* was the topic of conversation. Mrs. Tenakin seemed like a teacher who never let an educational opportunity pass by, and soon after discussing the best parts of *The Hobbit*, when Smaug the dragon came up, she asked the class, "What are some of the dragons you have had to slay in your own lives? For instance, when you're overwhelmed or frustrated with homework, do you take a break for five minutes, and then come back to it? Is that how you slay that dragon? Or what about your parents? What dragons have they had to slay?"

A couple of students answered her question, and the more they talked, the more Marc slid down in his chair.

He felt eyes on him. He was sure they somehow knew his secret.

"Mrs. Tenakin?" Marc finally asked, raising his hand.

"Yes, uh, Marc?" she said, her eyes glancing down at her seating chart.

"Why do we always talk about dragons like they're something bad? I mean, aren't there, uh, like, any good dragons?"

She smiled. "Well, yes, I guess you could say that the dragon metaphors we often find in Western culture are often negative ones. Lucky for you, Marc, you're not a dragon, despite your name." She chuckled at her own joke, and though her attempt at humor only got a few pity smiles, Marc was self-conscious, his eyes quickly darting to the right and back.

She gave the long list of mythologically historical reasons why dragons were to be feared, and why they should be seen as evil, or bad, but then she talked about how differently Chinese dragons are viewed in that culture. "So I guess the answer to the good-or-bad dragon question really depends on where you live in the world. But thanks for that, Marc. Your etymological inquiry has spawned some good thought—helped us with a bird's-eye view of our topic, if you will." Many tenth graders had warned Marc and others that Mrs. Tenakin often used words that none of the kids understood, like some kind of Greek, but she never explained what they meant—in this case that etymology means the study of word origins—and by the end of this first class, it got frustrating. Yes, the kids could ask, and one blonde kid did during the hour, but it seemed no one could keep up.

"Moving on," she told the kids who just stared at her. "Okay, kids, let's talk about your reading assignment for this week. Yes, we're jumping right in. Please take out your copy of *The Strange Case of Dr. Jekyll and Mr. Hyde* under your desk . . ."

As the class filled with the groans of academic torture and the sounds of books moving from the wire basket beneath each seat to the top of the desk, Marc's certainty that others could tell he was different subsided somewhat, but not completely.

Later, Marc sat at a table in the back of the cafeteria alone, talking to no one, since Luke had been assigned to the other lunch period.

Congratulations, you're even weirder than you were before, said the voice of self doubt in his mind as he unwrapped his peanut butter sandwich. Marc was alone, but he tried to push the self-pity thoughts out of his brain.

Lunch was normal, but certain foods tasted weird. Lemonade tasted like kerosene, and the peanut butter tasted like wax. Marc wondered why, but figured it had something to do with his insides-on-fire sore throat that wouldn't go away.

The normal school moments he'd had that day made his surreal dragon experiences seem so distant, as if none of it had been real. He thought of his newfound powers and where they would lead. The changing pains were definitely painful, but sometimes the pain veered from annoying to holy-crap-please-make-it-stop.

He knew that his acne didn't make him worthless. Sure, he was a leper now, and not knowing how long it would last was the worst part, but he was hopeful that it would only be temporary.

The bell rang.

He had a lot on his mind, which he knew would make doing homework a bit tough. It frustrated him. The thought of seeing disappointment in his mom's eyes made him sad, knowing how hard she worked at her job. She always said school was his job.

"Shouldn't you be off to class, Mr. Mon*drag*-hine?" asked a passing teacher. Marc nodded, not bothering to correct the pronunciation of his name. It happened a lot.

As he left, the teacher suggested several home remedies to clear up that acne.

"Thanks," was all Marc said, his backpack heavy on his shoulder.

TWELVE

How to Embarrass Your Spanish Teacher

Spanish class had started innocently enough. A cute girl in his class with hair the color of wheat in the sun caught his eye and he shrank in his chair to hide his face. Marc had noticed Katie O'Hannon the year before, when they first exchanged furtive glances, and he had thought of her when asked to write an analogy in English class. He wrote, "Her smile is to a face what the sunrise is to a horizon." Plus, she always seemed smart and nice, but he wasn't about to say "hi" to her now with his acne in full bloom. When each member of the class was forced to say their full name, Marc did it, but was horrified to have to show his leprosy to all eyes in the classroom, especially the pretty eyes of Katie O'Hannon.

The class was taught by Mrs. Kessler, a mean lady with gray hair, neither fat nor thin, who had obviously taught middle school way too long, because she always made the kids who didn't know Spanish feel dumb. Marc didn't care if she was strict, but what really made him angry was she made kids feel bad about themselves just because they talk too much sometimes. That wasn't cool. He had no idea it would turn out the way it did. It all started when three kids behind Katie were being loud and obnoxious, their rebellious giggles punctuating the wadded paper they'd throw. Sitting like perfect angels when Kessler faced them, they got disrespectful when Mrs. Kessler's back was turned as she wrote something on the board, just to see her get angry.

She warned them once. "You kids better knock it off!" She yelled angrily, her large mouth and padded cheeks snarling like a rabid basset hound. When Mrs. Kessler turned back again to the board, one of the kids who sat behind Katie threw another crumpled-up piece of paper at the chalkboard.

Kessler lost it. She turned on Katie, rushing to the front row of the class. "Miss O'Hannon, get up here this instant!"

"B-but, I didn't—" Katie attempted.

"Now, I said!" Kessler bellowed, sprinkling the front row with her canine saliva.

Katie looked around, then began to tentatively rise from her chair, but that was when Marc stood.

"Stop it," he said with authority to Mrs. Kessler, his jaw muscles tight with indignation.

A hush fell over the stunned students. No student had ever dared stand up to Mrs. Kessler before, least of all when she was angry, but Marc had had enough. His anger at the injustice far outweighed the embarrassment of having this much acne.

"What did you say?" Kessler asked.

"I said stop it. Katie didn't do anything. You're not even trying to find out who really did it," Marc said, his eyes firm with purpose.

A self-satisfied smile slid onto Kessler's face during the pause, like a lion playing with an insolent mouse.

"You sound sure of yourself, young man," she said with her big lips, then paused for dramatic effect. "You seem to know a lot, don't you?"

"Yes, ma'am. I do about this," Marc said honestly, but firmly.

"Well, then," she said. "I suppose you could teach this class, couldn't you?"

"Better than you," said Marc, and a collective *I-can't-believe-he-said-that* gasp came from the other students.

"Is that so?" Mrs. Kessler asked. "Tell me, then, Mr. Mondragon. What's the subjunctive, third-person plural form of the verb *to sneeze* in Spanish?"

Panic set in, as well as his good friend self-doubt.

A nagging feeling at the back of his skull yelled, *you have a hard time confronting Zoosh, but you're picking a fight with a teacher!? You idiot!* His mind raced with thoughts of the trouble he'd get into, his worried eyes looking down. But then, like a fog in his mind had suddenly lifted, Marc stood straight, looked her right in the eyes, and spoke. "Is that a word that's supposed to stump me?" said Marc, but when he said it, everyone's eyes widened in amazement and turned in his direction. "You have no question more demanding than one the answer to which is *estornuden*?" Marc had no idea where these words were coming from.

It was only after Marc said it, only after he saw the incredulous gaze of his classmates, only after he noted Mrs. Kessler's mouth agape, completely speechless, did he realize that he had said all of the last two sentences in perfect Castellano, or 'Spain' Spanish.

Katie's eyes went from afraid-for-Marc's-life to wide-eyed with a light smile.

"Is that all you wanted to ask me, or has the verbal exam ended?" Marc spoke again in perfect, even regal, Spanish.

Kessler, who had learned Spanish at University and had never set foot in a Spanish-speaking country, was completely aghast. Her throat made a sort of noise in the pause.

"How—eh. What—" she stammered, and finally blurted, in English, "Get—get to the office, Mr. *Mahn*-drugg-ihn. Now!"

The words had just come to his mind, as easy as English. Marc had no idea how such Spanish, *any* Spanish, had come into his mind, nor did he know how he had summoned the guts to do what he did, but Luke loved it. It was one of the few times that Marc saw Luke speechless, his face lighting up like it was Christmas morning.

In the waiting room of Principal Jenkins's office, Marc sat in a chair beneath a poster with the photo of a smiling professional golfer with a golf club over a shoulder. The look in his eye was a confident *don't you wish you were me?* and the caption in white letters beneath read *Be a PRO-active Student!*

Marc's eyes, on the other hand, did not look very confident. *Great,* he thought. *Right when I thought my secret was safe, this happens.* Marc stared at the pale green plaster where the wall met the floor, overhearing Kessler and the office manager talking one room away.

"He's not even from Mexico?" asked Kessler. "Are you sure?"

"No," said the office lady.

"Oh! Colombia. Their Spanish is good down there."

"No, Barbara."

"And not even his home language is Spanish?" Kessler asked.

"Not for several generations, anyway. I think his surname is from Spain."

"I—I don't understand, eh, how—" the frustration and emotions choked up Kessler's voice and stopped her words.

"Barb," said the office lady with a compassionate voice, "maybe it's time to take a break."

There was silence, then Marc heard unintelligible, heartfelt whispering. The whispering contained a slight whimper in the voice, and the next thing Marc heard was, "I'll talk to Jenkins." Marc suddenly felt bad for taking it too far, though he didn't know how that Spanish came out of him. All he meant to do was stand up for Katie. He looked up at the clock on the wall and sighed.

Katie.

Marc thought of her and the look of amazement on her face. He could survive on the you're-my-hero gaze she gave him for a hundred years. No food, no water, just that memory. *Okay, fine, maybe* some *food and water.*

That's when Marc looked down.

Fire.

At first, he started on instinct, but then realized it wasn't normal fire. This fire wasn't yellow and orange, but purple and blue, with flickering finger flames of an aqua-green color appearing now and then. It had poured out of his nose and mouth as easy as air, and he hadn't noticed it until he looked down. The flames of purple and blue were bright and translucent, like regular fire, but they weren't causing any damage. The flames covered him like a bright, colorful carpet, and some of it had pooled on the floor at his feet. The fire made no distinguishable sound. At first, a panicked Marc looked around and saw that no one had noticed this. He was alone in the waiting room outside Jenkins's office. He began trying to put the flames out with his hands, until he realized that they still weren't burning anything—not him, not his clothes, not the floor, nor the hard plastic school chair he sat in. A giggle escaped him when he tried to put them out with his hands, but in this regard they again didn't act like normal fire. The flames seemed almost playful, dancing around his hands before disappearing, saying goodbye before they left, almost as if they knew they might be embarrassing him. It took a bit longer to put out this fire, but he did it just before he heard Principal Jenkins call his name.

Marc's brows were wrinkled and his eyes were question marks. He sheepishly shuffled into the principal's office, and the visit turned out to be the usual drill: the lecture about talking back to and disrespecting teachers, questions about his future, what he wanted in life, and a rundown of Stephen Covey's *The 7 Habits of Highly Effective People* and that Marc's actions didn't exemplify any of them. Marc decided it best not to argue that he was, in fact, being proactive, which *was* one of the Seven Habits. The principal even accused Marc of pretending not to know Spanish just so he could get an easy A. Marc's protestations and attempts to explain were taken as empty lies.

At least they didn't call his mom since it was the first time he'd ever been in trouble at school. As Marc walked to his locker, breathing the air that smelled like floor cleaner, he thought of the strange-colored fire. What had caused it? He had been thinking of Katie at the time—could she have something to do with it? Why didn't the flames burn anything? He had to get to the bottom of this.

THIRTEEN

KATIE AND THE HALF-BURNED HOUSE

Nothing shocks a quiet kid like a pretty girl paying him any attention at all, especially when he has severe acne, which is why Marc didn't say much at first when he found himself walking home with Katie, wishing Luke weren't there.

Katie's and Marc's backpacks dangled from the handlebars of his bike. As they walked, Luke rode his bike slowly around them, like a bee that won't leave a picnic, his 'funny' remarks thinly-veiled expressions of jealousy. Marc tried not to stare at the way Katie's blonde hair shone in the afternoon sunlight.

"Come on," Katie said. "You have to know some Spanish. How did you talk like that with Kessler back there? And how did you do that with your eyes?"

"My eyes?"

"Yeah, you know. When you were talking to Kessler, your eyes did something. It was really sick."

"You mean . . . you liked the way I blinked or something?" asked Marc with a smile in his voice.

"No. It was inside your eyes. They were—it was—I don't know," she said, her voice tentative.

"It's his magic powers," Luke said, passing behind them.

Marc coughed a nervous laugh. "Eh, yeah, well, I probably picked up more Spanish than I thought I did," he said, his eyes shooting a *what-are-you-doing!* glare at Luke, which Luke ignored.

"How many classes have we all had together?" Luke asked.

"A lot," Katie said sincerely, never for a moment acting like Luke was a pest at all. It was one of the many things a lot of the guys at the school, older guys included, loved about her. Her face broke into a big smile. "Remember when Luke got kicked out of Stringham's science class in the seventh grade? That was so funny."

"Hey. I was only trying to keep Jeff from retaliating against my awesome powers of flammable flatulence!"

Though Marc was jealous that it was Luke and not him making her laugh, he loved seeing her smile, no matter what the reason. But never mind that. Marc had to focus. Yes, Luke was being a ridiculous pest, and doing it on purpose because Katie had been so impressed with Marc coming to her rescue with his Spanish-power-smackdown, but Luke was still winning the 'attention' war, an unspoken game of sorts between him and Luke. The rules were clear—whoever could keep her attention the most won. *Yeah. Okay, Luke.*

Marc was going to say something, but didn't. *Why try?* he thought miserably. He knew that Luke was funnier than he was. *Great. I impress her, I'm the reason we're walking home together, but he gets her attention.*

The repeating whistle of a lark bunting sounded when they turned the corner on Birch Street. Green weeds collected around the light and power poles, searching for a lawn to populate, beneath a canopy of blue sky.

"You haven't seen the half-burned house? It happened a week ago," said Katie.

"That's what everyone calls it? 'The half-burned house'?" Marc asked.

"What else would you call it?" she asked, and pointed to a house that from their angle looked completely burned. They went quiet, nearing the house as if approaching the grave of a respected leader, and when Marc got a better look, there it was. The house was almost literally half-burned down. Exactly one half seemed untouched besides a smudge or two, while the other half was a mess of charred remains. A piece of insulation in the ceiling waved from a light breeze, like the mournful flag of a forgotten country.

Finally, Luke broke the silence with a tentative, "Did anyone die?"

"No," said Katie. "Thank the Lord."

"Yeah," is all Marc said with an absent voice, his eyes fixed on the house's burnt half.

As Luke kept playing his 'who has Katie's attention' game, Marc was only half listening. With his eyes on the charred black beams, Marc felt a yearning he couldn't describe. It was a mixture of feelings. One of them was anger that he was too late to see the fire with Katie first-hand. *What good are fire-proof powers if there isn't a fire around to impress a pretty girl?* The other feeling was sadness. So much fire had been here at once, and Marc felt this in a way that he usually would never have thought about before. It was a strange kind of sadness, one that comes when someone enters a room with the lingering smell of a long-departed family member. Marc felt a kinship toward fire he never felt before. As he stared at the blackened remnants, it wasn't the burned-to-nothing-garage that he yearned for, but the house's assailant. In his very pores, a new relationship was forming with the gaseous alien called fire that ate and breathed as he did, and somehow he knew this relationship would change his life forever.

The charcoal-gray dragon in his dream was solemn this time, its wise, thoughtful voice contemplative; it waited a while before it spoke.

"Who you are and what you must do may not be the path you sought," the dragon said. After a moment, the voice came back stronger, louder, the words struggling against some unseen force, like a fluid form of static, fading in and out, but undeniably demanding to be part of Marc's dream. "And though your life be fraught with dangers, though at times you may wish to beat these stars into submission, to an alternate, more effortless path..." A pause as the

voice faded, then, quieter, "...you must accept this fate. You must fulfill the extent of your life's purpose."

He never interrupted the great dragon. He only listened, his ears transcribing the words with fire, searing into the flesh of his mind.

"You must learn and grow in stature and wisdom," the dragon continued. "You must learn the unknowable language, the invisible fire. You must become what I know you to be."

Marc awoke in the middle of the night again, but his covers had stayed on the bed this time. What was this unknowable language the dragon spoke of? What was the invisible fire? He felt a deep desire to do what this dragon commanded, to fulfill the 'extent of his life's purpose,' *but what did that mean?* He wanted to prove himself. Would he be ready when the time came? He sighed heavily, his mind awash with the same self-doubt like a moat around his soul.

FOURTEEN

DRAKESEL FINDS A CLUE

James Drakesel had a lot on his mind: the shareholders' meeting coming up on the seventeenth, the tax fraud and domestic assault lawsuits he was fighting, the nice dinner that he'd promised his mistress they'd have at their favorite restaurant, the children's rights advocates protesting his factories' working conditions in southeast asia. *Infernal brats*, he thought of the children, wishing he could automate every factory he owned. And his sister's Doberman Pinscher named Mimi that he was stuck babysitting for the afternoon. He was more than annoyed, and wished he had a spare secretary who could take it for a walk, but his secretary, as well as Jonathan, his right-hand man, were swamped with work he needed them to finish.

Lost in reviewing expense reports, James got a call.

It was Stone Stajinski, whom he never felt completely comfortable speaking with.

"This is James," Drakesel answered.

"Mr. Drakesel. Stone Stajinski. We have something."

"You do?" said Drakesel with the excitement of a boy in his pajamas being told he has an extra candy egg from the Easter Bunny.

"A huge lead, sir. The most promising in weeks."

"Uh, well, great," said Drakesel.

"Do I have permission to pursue the target, sir?" said Stone.

"Eh, okay."

"I need definite confirmation from you, sir. A simple 'yes' or 'affirmative' will suffice," said Stone with a driver's-ed-instructor monotone voice.

Remembering that the line was secure, Drakesel said, "Eh, then yes. Pursue the target. Do we have a name?"

"Negative. Working on that, sir," said Stone.

At that moment, Mimi the doberman began snacking on the armrest of one of Drakesel's expensive leather chairs that faced his desk.

"No! Stop—aauughh! You're not supposed to—" Drakesel began, getting up from his chair, realizing the dog didn't speak English.

"You want us to stop the operation, sir?" asked Stone with a flat voice.

"No, no, not you," said Drakesel. "Eh, continue operation. Proceed with, eh, extreme prejudice," he added tentatively, grabbing at the dog's collar as it growled in protest.

"Very well, sir," said Stone. "We need to mobilize a team, but our gear is ready. I'll update daily via text."

"Yes, yes, and eh, where is it?"

"Colorado," said Stone.

"Good job, Stone."

"Sir," is all Stone said and hung up.

FIFTEEN

THE BULLY OF THE BULLY

"What happened to your face?" Jenny Mondragon shrieked.

Mom's reaction to his acne the next morning was typical for a mother prone to worrying, especially when she knew that her family didn't have a lot of acne in the gene pool.

"Gee, thanks, Mom. I feel better now."

Jenny backpedalled. "I mean, I'm sorry to make you self-conscious, but honey! What happened?"

"I don't know. Probably an allergy?" That's all Marc said. He learned that sometimes the less you say to parents, the better.

His mom rattled off the things she would do for his acne as soon as she got home, but he only half listened.

School was as normal as Marc could have expected. He should have been happy, since his mom gave him a five-dollar bill for lunch—a rare luxury—but Marc felt as deflated as a fifth-of-July balloon. His mind had sat in a puddle of guilt since he heard the news that Zoosh was at home in a cast that wrapped around his torso and ran the length of one of his arms.

"He must've fell hard!" said one kid. Mrs. Tenakin would have corrected him—fallen!

"Naw, I'm tellin' you, the hallway's haunted!" another said.

Marc told Luke he would ride his bike home alone, which surprised Luke, though he tried to understand. As he walked his bike home, Marc's eyes were crestfallen, tired from beating himself up inside his own mind. *I'm no better than a bully,* he lamented to himself. On his way home, he stopped at the Colorado River just to think and feel bad for a while.

Sometimes it felt better to feel bad all alone, and Marc imagined there were others somehow watching him, someone aware of all that he was going through, someone who understood; he wished someone could let him know it would be okay, but he knew there wasn't anyone.

His mom told him he had a 'self-communication' problem, that how you talk about yourself to yourself matters, and sure, that sounded great and all, but it wasn't easy when self-doubt seemed always there beside him, a shadow weight on his soul. As he stood there with his bike, watching the water move with a pace as slow as the town's, he felt as low as cell waste or a fatty deposit on the side of the river's artery that flows away from its heart, a tiny lake high in the Rockies. He thought it strange that something so natural as a great river would rush past, completely oblivious to the boy standing at its banks with the unnatural abilities to hurt people.

When he got home, his mother asked if something was bothering him, but she didn't push it when he said "no." She only asked him to come to the store with her, and Marc knew that she did it as a distraction to take his mind off whatever burdened him. She was great.

When they got back from the grocery store, Steve was there with a brand new longboard. Jenny took the two bags of groceries from Marc's hands and left them both on the front porch with a mother's *aww- he-made-a-new-friend* smile.

"You weren't kidding," said Marc.

"I told you I could get it," said Steve with a proud grin.

"It's beautiful," Marc said, his eyes taking in the longboard's features. "How much did it cost?"

"Who says I paid anything?"

"You stole it?"

"Naw. I borrowed it," he said with a mischievous grin. "Forever."

"Oh, so that's how it is?"

"'Take what you can get' is my motto," said Steve.

"Right, unless someone has the same motto about your stuff, right?" said Marc with a chuckle, but he couldn't read Steve's expression when he said it.

After the uncomfortable pause, Marc said, "You wanna see the backyard?"

"Sure," said Steve.

They brought the new longboard to the back fence, and as Marc opened it, he apologized. "Just to warn you, it's not an amazing backyard, I just thought I'd show you around."

"No worries," said Steve.

As the gate to the backyard creaked open, stubborn overgrown weeds making it difficult, Marc said, "I think it's been two years since I've been back here."

Steve smiled, but Marc couldn't tell whether his eyes held judgment or not. Marc's backyard was an empty, small sea of dead grass with only an old Weber grill and a cracked kiddie pool to keep it company.

They talked about stuff, mostly their favorite teams in the NFL and the MLB pennant chase and their favorite baseball players. Marc was aware that Steve was a year or so older. He sat down and watched him inspect the patio and felt happy that a cool guy wanted him as a friend.

Steve opened the old grill, curious.

"You won't be able to light it. Propane tank's been empty for years," said Marc.

"You sure?" asked Steve, and with that, a strange, orange glow emanated from beneath the skin in his upper chest and throat. Marc's eyes had a hard time registering what they saw. *Was it some kind of a trick?* Marc wondered. Steve wore an odd smile. His eyes went from Marc to the grill, and when he spat into it, the grill's belly burst into flames, with what looked like liquid fire dripping down the side to the yellow grass.

Marc jumped to his feet, his eyes huge. If strange phenomena were a disease, there must be a pandemic going on.

Steve turned to him like a lawyer who'd just gotten a client off with a warning. "You didn't think you were the only one, did you?"

Marc was speechless. "H-how did you know?" Marc finally asked, not aware he was slightly out of breath.

"Been watching you," said Steve, putting out the small fires around the base of the grill with his hands. "If you're one of us, you know what to look for. Some say it has to do with the Vibe, but it doesn't."

Marc didn't understand the reference, but after a pause, he chuckled as an exhale burst out of him accompanied by a smile. "Wow! I've been wondering if I was some kind of freak!"

"No. You're not a freak. Have other things started?"

"Uh, yeah. Different foods taste weird, but I don't know why."

"Your body's changing in more ways than just puberty, bro. You'll notice things taste a bit different, but, like, you can still pretty much eat anything, same as always. Soda kills you, though."

"Soda kills me?" asked Marc.

"Ah—I mean, it hurts a lot when you drink it, so drink water and juices, even though they'll taste a little different at first; everything will, but you get used to it."

"Yeah. Lemonade tastes like kerosene smells," said Marc.

"Yeah. It's different for everyone," Steve said. "Like, for me? I drank soda a lot when I was little. And I used to love apple juice, but now it tastes like cat pee."

"You drink cat pee?" Marc asked, and Steve groaned.

"Funny," he said, followed by a contained chuckle. "Maybe for you apple juice will be good. Lemonade tastes a little weird for me, but it doesn't taste like kerosene," said Steve. He closed the grill cover and approached Marc.

"But there's more than just this. Have you felt your armor yet?"

Marc smiled. "My what?" Marc's head was spinning. He went through the rest of this conversation with disbelieving numbness, an entire new world opening up.

"Go ahead. Feel my arm," Steve said, a gust of wind flapping part of his hair. When Marc did, it felt like no other arm he'd ever touched. It was rough, the skin thick, more so than any farmer's handshake around town.

"It looks and feels like normal skin, only, like, harder, right?"

"Yeah."

"Check it out," said Steve, and he took the nearby two-prong grill fork and stabbed himself in the forearm, near the elbow. The fork stayed in the arm, not a speck of blood, and Steve didn't flinch at all. Marc winced, mindful of the bandage on his arm. "Take your bandage off," Steve said.

Marc tore the white tape from his arm and saw that his wound was gone.

"I tried it, too, before my skin changed," said Steve.

"You did?" Suddenly, Marc didn't feel so embarrassed about the incident at his mom's work.

"Yeah. It hurt," said Steve. As if on cue, they both laughed at the same time, a laugh of mutual understanding that lasted eight full seconds.

"It's normal to feel invincible, even when our skin hasn't caught up yet."

They chuckled again, and talked about similar experiences, until Marc finally said, "So, fire or hot things don't hurt us, and stuff, but, uh, what are we?"

"You don't know?" said Steve.

"I mean, are we really part, uh, dragon?"

"Of course. You haven't had the dreams?" asked Steve.

"Oh, sure. Yeah," Marc said, trying to believe all this was actually happening. "I, uh, just don't know *how* we're part dragon, or what it means," Marc said.

"I'll tell you all the history and the DNA and all that, but, like, for now, just know that our powers come out when we fully reach puberty."

"And here I was thinking my voice would just sound weird for a while. C'mon. Be serious. This is some big practical joke, right?" he said, his eyes as unsure as his mind.

"Hard to believe, I know."

"But, but . . ." Marc said, trying to wrap his mind around it all.

Finally, Steve spoke. "We call ourselves Dragonkyn. Our clan of Dragonkyn comes from the Iberian peninsula."

"Dragonkyn," Marc said with an amazed whisper, almost a chuckle. "Wait. There're more of us?"

"Lots more," said Steve. "Our specific group of Dragonkyn we call Sorceron. Our leader's name is Victor. He's just older than us, and he came up with our group's name. You'll meet him. We're all living in a place in the mountains outside Denver. We call it the Dragonlair. Some of us have adopted the nickname *dragonflies*, but Victor hates that. He says we can't fly yet, and we're not insects. He says we need to call the Dragonkyn who *aren't* part of our group dragonflies, because they're the annoying insects." Steve smiled at this.

As Steve continued, Marc was still amazed at all he was learning, but he couldn't help stifling a laugh, watching Steve talk with a barbecue fork sticking out of his arm near his elbow. Every time Steve gestured with his hand, the big fork waved with it.

"You uh, gonna take that out?" asked Marc with a smile.

"Oh yeah," said Steve, eyeing it as if it appeared there spontaneously. He yanked the fork from his arm with a swift jerk. "So, you can spew fire already, right?" he asked.

"Me? Oh, uh, sure," Marc lied.

"Yeah, every Dragonkyn can. It's sorta like getting the sore throat. All of us firespew. Some are just better at it than others. Oh, and we don't breathe fire. We spew it, or scream it."

"Screaming fire. That's cool," Marc said with a smile. After a pause, Marc asked, "Does the pain ever go away?"

"Ah, yes. The changing pains. Yeah, a little," said Steve. "You'll feel it for a couple years, but, like, the worst goes away after a few weeks or months."

"A few weeks or months?" Marc asked with panicked eyes, and Steve laughed at his reaction. "You know how much ibuprofen that's gonna take?"

Steve held his big smile. "Yeah. You may have to take the pain, but just remember. It sucks, but there's no need for the hospital. It's all part of the deal."

"So, what magic powers do dragons have?"

"Oh, like, different types. Each of us has a greater and a lesser power; and again, it all depends on natural ability. You'll probably be getting a sense of what your other powers are pretty soon. And everyone's different. Some are better for, like, battle, and some aren't. One girl is good at strategy, really good at it, but there are, like, other kids who can change their skin to whatever color or surface they're on. It's cool," Steve said. "Yeah. There's another kid who can move any kind of precious metal with his mind."

"That's sweet! Like gold and stuff? What're *your* powers?" asked Marc, and Steve looked away.

"Mine? Well," he said, drawing out the word, reluctant to say.

"C'mon. Tell me," said Marc.

Steve sighed in a way that seemed to suggest that he had come to the part where he knew he would come across as less-than-cool. "To be totally honest, the cool one is my lesser power. I only have it at the level of party tricks, and the other one, my biggest strength, is also sort of lame."

"What do you mean?" Marc asked, and Steve looked around.

"We're not supposed to show our powers until the war happens or while hunting and gathering, but I'll show you."

A war? What war? What have I gotten myself into?

Marc knew he had to sit down.

SIXTEEN

O'Leary Finds a Clue

"Not so loud," is all that Detective O'Leary heard at first, but, having been a New York City cop for so long, it was seemingly meaningless words like this that got his attention. O'Leary and his wife had finally gone out to eat at an expensive restaurant, something she insisted on at least once a year, and here he was, leaning against the wall next to the small corridor that lead to the restrooms. Over the sound of expensive chinaware and utensils quietly colliding, O'Leary heard the older, pepper-haired man on his cellphone, standing around the corner within earshot. O'Leary knew that the guy had obviously said it by instinct, because the "not so loud" was an odd thing to hear a person say to someone else on the phone.

The thing that made O'Leary really take notice was what the man said after that.

"Let's just say I don't want to end up extra crispy, okay? Order them. Yes, for Stone and me."

Extra crispy? O'Leary thought, recognizing immediately the exact phrase he'd used with the coroner. O'Leary stared, his eyes fixed on the back of the pepper-haired man's head.

"Our table is about ready," O'Leary's cheerful wife said, approaching from the opposite side in her floral dress.

O'Leary whispered, "Hold on, honey," and walked directly to the maitre d', a balding, thin, late-twenties man with gaunt features and a five-o'clock shadow O'Leary could tell was always there, no matter how much he shaved. O'Leary's wife watched him for a few seconds, looked around, put her purse under her arm and walked to her table. Their evenings had always been interrupted with something.

"Excuse me," O'Leary said, flashing his detective badge at the host. O'Leary's wife looked around and—

"Yes, Officer? May I help you?" asked the maitre d'.

"I need to know the name of the man standing near the bathrooms in the dark suit, dark orange shirt. Do you see him? He's on the phone."

"Uh, yes. I see him."

"You know which guy I'm talking about?" O'Leary asked.

"Yes, I think so," said the maitre d', shifting uncomfortably. "What is this about?"

"You know his name?" said O'Leary.

"One moment, sir," said the maître d', turning to a similarly dressed woman. "Staci, could you take this to section four? I need to take care of our guest here." The lady nodded, took the tray he held, hurried away without a word, and the maitre d' turned back to O'Leary.

"The man in the dark suit on the phone, the only one near the restrooms?"

"That's right," said O'Leary.

"That's Mr. Drakesel," the maitre d' said.

"How do you know his name?"

"I'm surprised you don't know his name, sir. He's the head of a large conglomerate. Dines here at least twice a week. One of our honored guests."

"I see," said O'Leary, the smell of rich food and expensive linen wafting through the air.

"Is there a problem, Officer? Is he some kind of suspect in—" asked the maitre d'.

"No, no problem. I just want to ask him a couple of questions."

"What's his first name again?" O'Leary asked.

After a few more questions about Drakesel's identity, O'Leary returned to his wife at their table and dined on exotically prepared food surrounded by people with whom he never socialized.

SEVENTEEN

Changing Pains

Back in Marc's back yard, Marc sat bewildered on the plastic lawn chair.

"A war's gonna happen?" Marc asked.

"Yeah. It's inevitable. When regular humans discover who we are, we're going to be, like, lab rats, bro. That's just fact. That, or killed off out of fear, just like our pure dragon ancestors all that time ago, and it's that reality that makes us face the fact of a coming war, with some of them, anyway. With powers like we have, we're not going to be able to just live and be free. It's not like they're gonna let us get driver's licenses and stuff." He looked down at his feet as he said, "Kind of weird, being in America and all, huh?"

"Well, when is the war going to be exactly?"

"Victor decides that," he said matter-of-factly, "but we're preparing."

Marc sighed heavily. He averted his gaze but said nothing.

An old plastic clock faded by the sun on the back patio wall suddenly lifted from its rusty nail and floated across the space between it and Steve, as if carried. After wavering in the air for a moment, it dropped into Marc's hand.

"Whoa. You're telekinetic?"

"Yeah, but that's about the heaviest thing I can lift. There are others who can move a lot heavier things and more things at once."

"So, what's your strength power?"

"It's sort of lame, man, I'm not kidding," said Steve.

"No, c'mon. Show me."

Steve sighed like a parent being asked by a three-year-old to play peek-a-boo again, then took out a tiny canteen from his pocket. He took a swig and put it back.

"What's that?"

"It's lix."

"Lix?"

"Yeah. Just a nickname we have for it. It's a drink we came up with that helps Dragonkyn with their powers. It helps you focus, but it also relaxes you."

"Is it magic?" asked Marc.

Steve laughed. "No."

"What's it made of?" asked Marc.

"Uh, I think there's pear juice in it, and a bunch of other stuff. Here, try some."

Marc did, and it tasted like syrupy fruit with a kick.

"It's strong," Marc said, a cough escaping.

"Oh, yeah. I don't notice that anymore. Different, huh?"

"Um, yeah," said Marc.

Without another word, Steve held his hand out, firm and steady. "I don't wanna rupture the pipes under your house, so I'll try to focus it . . ."

After a moment, Marc heard a low rumbling sound. He looked around, wondering what was happening.

Suddenly, nine fragments of metal, from tiny bits the size of a pinhead to others the size of golf balls, covered in dirt, emerged from the ground, lifting into the air as if an earthquake were loosening them from the earth's grasp. The fragments came together in mid-air, heated, and melded into the shape of a crude-looking, small sword.

It fell to the ground smoldering and smoking, parts of it still red hot, and Steve lowered his hand.

"Steve! Wow! You're Magneto—"

"No, no, stop. I wish. All I can work with is iron. It's the only metal I can manipulate, and it's, like, mostly the stuff inside the ground. I can take it out, heat it almost to liquid, mix it together, and I can even swing it around, but it's the heaviest thing I can move. I don't know why. It's like I have a connection with it or something, especially when it's in the ground."

"So, can I meet the other Sorceron?" Marc asked.

"I was hoping you'd ask. We came to recruit you."

Marc gave a weak smile. Though his newfound friend was a thief, it was nice to know that he was honest in other ways. "Recruit me?"

"Yep. I bet you have a million questions."

"I do!"

"All in good time, newbie," said Steve. "Like, if you told your mom that my family invited you to Denver, could you come for, like, a week?"

"I guess I can ask," said Marc. "My mom let me go for a few days with a friend's family when I was eleven. She's pretty laid back about stuff like that. She thinks that public schools should have more field trips anyway."

"Cool. Tell her we leave tomorrow night," Steve said, leaving the way he came in.

Marc still felt unsure about it, but let his mom's choice be the deciding factor.

Marc hoped that convincing his mom wouldn't be hard. Jenny would be more than happy to have a break from trying to keep him entertained as the summer ended, he figured; plus, his teachers would probably let him make up the work. When he asked her, however, she debated it, considering how early in the school year it was.

"Please, mom?"

Finally, she agreed. "Okay. Fine," she said with a tired sigh. "You can go, but I , need to meet this Steve-boy's parents before you do."

That same day, Steve brought his parents over, a genial couple in their late forties, and though Marc watched them occasionally with untrusting eyes, Jenny liked them enough to entrust her son to their care. She called the school and got it all set up.

However, Marc knew that his mom had another reason for letting her son go on this trip.

Money.

Not having to feed him for a week (even with the diner providing a couple of meals) would give her extra money that she could use to buy him more school clothes and supplies. She was embarrassed that this fact played into her decision, and this was why she kept it to herself, but Marc knew, and wanted to relieve this burden from her, if for only a week or so. Marc knew she had a lot more on her mind besides a job that didn't pay enough. Marc figured that providing for him was only one of the reasons for letting him go on the trip without putting up too much of a fight. He also knew that she harbored her own fears that she would die alone in this little town without having found someone special she could spend the rest of her life with, and perhaps with Marc away, dating would be less awkward.

Jenny also made it very clear how much she would miss him, despite how supportive she was that Marc was making friends. She had told him, "The only man I ever loved is you, half-boy, half-man."

That night, as they sat at the dinner table that held their pork chops and peas, Marc was in a trance, the enormity of it all consuming him. His mother asked him what was wrong, but he said nothing.

"You've just been so quiet the last couple days."

"It's nothing, Mom, really," he said. Then, watching her reluctantly return to her meal, he added, "I love you, Mom."

Her face creased with a smile. "I love you too, honey," she said, then paused. "You know you can tell me anything, right?" she asked with pleading eyes.

"Mom, I promise. If there were anything important for you to know, I'd tell you. It's really nothing."

"You're all the family I've got," Jenny said, taking another bite of her pork chop.

"And you're all the family I've got," Marc said, a little embarrassed.

"Honey, there's a bill collector who might be by tonight," she said after a pause. "If he shows up, just pretend we're not home. I parked our car down the street again. I can't believe they'd come by this late, but if they do, don't answer it, ok?"

"Okay," Marc said.

That night, anxious to learn more, Marc decided to learn all he could about his dragon ancestry online.

He liked stories about dragons, but he liked lots of different stories. Never before did he ever think that he would be doing research for something he was a part of, something the entire world thought wasn't real.

Many cultures had some kind of mythical history about dragons, and the word itself meant "great water snake." Marc's eyes scanned his computer screen, peering at the many drawings and paintings of dragons. One showed a large and powerful dragon, probably from a Tolkien book. Its chest puffed out and its long neck curled up and back as it guarded a vast treasure of gold.

Well, that explains my obsession with money, Marc thought, trying to cheer himself up, but it didn't work. Dragons were intelligent creatures, and though much mention was made of people's fascination with their magic, the more Marc read about them, the more his eyes turned confused and sad. The large majority of stories and information involving dragons that he saw depicted them as horrible enemies to mankind. The men who killed them were considered heroes.

His gaze dropped from the computer screen, and he said to himself, "What am I?" He didn't even realize it had come out as a whisper. His thoughts spun all around him. *Am I good? Am I evil?* Marc felt a renewed guilt about what happened to Zoosh. He'd been sort of excited to start his training with Steve and the leader of the Sorceron Steve told him about, this Victor guy, and to do something interesting this early in his life, but now he was filled with doubt about all of it.

Am I all the things humans hate about dragons?

Of course you are, his dad's voice in his mind responded. *And you're probably all the things dragons hate about humans. Not the best combination.*

His sad, thoughtful eyes searched the air in his room as he pondered all he didn't know about this new world of which he was now a part. *Who is this Steve guy? Why would the Sorceron go to the trouble to find me?*

Before long, the thoughts of self-doubt that seemed to so easily attack him and his self esteem opened the door to a searing resentment about information withheld from him.

He thought of the number of years his mother had lied about how his father died. Lying about the ice cream truck was nothing compared to that, a hurt they never brought up anymore. She had told him for so many years that his dad had died a hero, battling forest fires, spinning yarn after yarn, the lies coming so easily for her. Marc remembered the day a year or so ago that he had Googled his father's name, expecting to see headlines of a hero fighting to protect people's lives or homes. Instead, he saw the truth.

"I did it to protect you," she had said when he confronted her.

"To protect me? From what?" he raged. "From the fact that my dad died a drunk in a jail cell, instead of fighting fires? What do I care? He wasn't the nicest guy to us, but he's still my dad. What matters to me is my mother telling me the truth. But I guess that's too much to ask. Lies and a fake hero are more important."

The memory of his mother's hurt face faded, as did the feeling of resentment.

Marc sighed heavily.

He stared at the phone, thinking about calling Steve to cancel this trip to wherever he was going. Maybe he should figure things out on his own.

Pain gripped him. His throat burned, but his chest and intestines had a strange mix between sharp burning and an ache that weighed as if the top and bottom half of his body were rebelling against each other, wanting to split apart in a violent, bloody secession. The pain was worse than anything he'd ever experienced before, his insides burning like his hand should have burned when he first discovered his nonflammable self. The urge to scream pulled at him, but instead, he grabbed his leather belt within reaching distance, bunched it up, and bit hard on the leather, yelling into the mattress of his bed. He tore his t-shirt off and scratched at himself as he agonized, a low, seething growl coming from deep within him, tears running from squinted eyes.

Calling out as he fell to the floor, he tried to focus on what Steve said, that the pain was never dangerous and that he had to take it. Though the intensity of the pain seemed like a hospital was necessary, he tried to remember the advice. His mom couldn't know about it, not yet anyway.

"Honey, you okay?" his mom called.

"Yeah!" he half-yelled, his voice cracking from pain. "Videogame! AAAAAAUUUGH!" he screamed.

"Addiction to that thing is real," he heard his mom say as she moved away from his bedroom door.

Marc heard the doorbell ring, but remembered he wasn't supposed to answer it. Not that he could, since he was paralyzed with pain on his bedroom floor.

Meanwhile, in the front room, Jenny carefully peeked out the front window of the house. She saw the bespectacled bill collector on the porch and stood quiet, waiting for him to leave. The man wore a disheveled suit. His face was the shape of a balloon, wide at the top with a tuft of light brown hair, no chin at the bottom.

"Uh, Mrs. Mon*drag*-on, I see your car down the street," said the bill collector with smug superiority. "I know you're in there."

Jenny heard a noise. A growling dog? The bill collector turned to the right and started. "Who the hey? What do you w—?" he said. Jenny's eyes narrowed as she watched, perplexed, and put a hand to her light smile when she saw the bill collector turn and scamper back to his car like a nervous chihuahua running from a rottweiler.

What Jenny didn't know was that Marc had simply decided to use the extreme pain he was in to help his mother. He was desperately in pain anyway, so, thinking fast, he crawled out his window without a shirt on, the belt still in his mouth, and agonized in front of the bill collector with blood-shot eyes, his mouth almost frothing from all the pain. Marc's torso was red from the deep welts and scratches he gave himself from the pain he was in, his body contorting from wave after wave of it. Luckily, it worked. The bill collector was so freaked out by seeing this kid growling and shrieking at him that he ran to his car. After the man had left, Marc, feeling good that he had helped his mom, but dizzy with exhaustion, crawled back into his bedroom window and collapsed onto the floor, unconscious.

He'd never before fallen unconscious because of pain he was experiencing, but his life had been filled with many firsts lately. The things he dreamt of as his body changed scared him way more than he had scared the bill collector.

EIGHTEEN

A Pleasant Welcome

I can't believe you're ditching me," said Luke with a smile.

"I'm not ditching you! It's just that only I was invited," said Marc.

"Yeah, well. Leave room in those selfies to photoshop me in later, to make people think you brought your best friend," Luke said with a bitter smile.

"C'mon."

"Donk, I'm happy for ya," and at this Luke went into his 'wise, fatherly' impersonation, something he did, complete with squinted eyes, like he was sixty years older. "I sometimes forget . . . you're not a child anymore," he said, thick with melodrama. "You're just . . . growing up so fast . . ."

"Shut up," Marc said, holding in the laugh.

"But I'm serious," Luke said, the 'fatherly squint' replaced by a grin. "I want a full report."

Luke had come by in the morning to see him off, and it meant a lot. Marc could tell that Luke was sad he couldn't go. The last thing you want to do when you realize your best friend has super powers is to stay home from an adventure, but Marc wasn't worried. His secret was safe with Luke.

The good news was that Marc's acne had cleared up, except for a few small zits on his nose and neck. However, feeling better about his looks would have to wait. The bad news was how excruciating the drive to Denver was because of the changing pains that attacked him ten miles north of Glenwood Springs.

As the white, unmarked passenger van made its way through green meadows and blue sky, Marc shook uncontrollably—even with a thousand milligrams of ibuprofen in him—as the worst of the pain came in waves. Marc thought he passed out twice on the way up, though he wasn't sure if it was from lack of sleep or the pain itself. At one point, trembling in pain, looking through dark hair hanging into his eyes, he saw Steve give him an understanding, pursed grin.

They drove up to the Dragonlair in the van with Steve's "father and mother," who turned out to be his Uncle Stan, a balding, unmarried forty-five-year-old with no children of his own, and a lady named Diane, about Stan's age, who sat in the passenger seat and talked nonstop for the first hour of the journey. Nobody seemed to pay much attention. Diane was an aunt of one of the Sorceron, sympathetic to their cause. She seemed a nice, talkative lady. Stan was quiet, keeping to himself as he drove, with a nearby Styrofoam cup full of chewed sunflower seeds. After the pain subsided enough for Marc to think, he could tell Diane had eyes for Stan, something Stan seemed oblivious to.

"So, how's the drive up so far?" she asked the boys even as she cast occasional glances at Stan.

Steve mumbled a tentative "good," trying to prevent a long conversation.

"Sure would be nice to have someone to talk to, since we have a couple hours until we get to the Lair," she said, never taking her eyes off Stan. Marc figured it didn't take a brain surgeon to see whom she really wanted attention from, but Stan just watched the road, probably thinking about baseball scores and little else, munching on those sunflower seeds.

"You sure love those seeds," Diane said with stifled annoyance, looking out to the passing trees for the first time. When no one engaged in her appeals for small talk, she slept, holding her novel under an arm like a blanket.

As desert shrubs gave way to increasingly taller pine and spruce trees and the white van climbed from the high desert plains to the mountains, Marc realized they were closer to where they were going and he hadn't asked any of his many questions.

"So, tell me how we got these powers. What's up with that?" asked Marc, and Steve spoke as if he had said the same thing to several 'newbies' before him.

"More than fifteen hundred years ago, dragons weren't in hiding, and they weren't just myths and legends like people think they are now," said Steve. "They fought for their right to live among humans, but humans were, like, kinda freaked out by the fact that dragons not only could think and talk just like people, but that they were bigger and had magical powers. So, humans, being insecure and, like, fearing death and all that, they started hunting dragons."

"So, did someone way back then decide that humans would have the same powers as dragons or something?"

"Nah. Like, you know all the stories of dragons attacking villages? That only happened *after* the dragons were already being hunted down and killed off by humans. Humans started it all. Some dragons got angry and pissed off because, duh, they were, like, being attacked and slaughtered. But others came up with a plan to survive. So, clans from all around the world decided to become genetic stowaways on the DNA of the only creatures they *knew* would survive. Humans," he said, louder.

"'Genetic stowaways'? You mean, literally fused to human DNA?" asked Marc.

"Yes," Steve said loudly, above the noise of the van's engine.

Marc took a moment to let it sink in. Finally, all that came out of Marc made him sound like an actor in a surfer movie: "Whoa."

Steve continued. "They utilized the few human allies they had and decided—for their descendants' safety—that the magical dragon genes would stay dormant in the DNA of their human hosts until the seventy-seventh generation."

Steve let this sink in before adding, "Our generation, as soon as we reach puberty. Your father, and seventy-five generations before him, carried the dormant gene. Wait—" said Steve, digging into his pocket. "Victor wanted me to read this to you word for word." Steve took out the latest high-tech phone from his back pocket and tapped the screen a few times. "Hold on," he said, focusing, scrolling a bit with an index finger. "Okay. Right here. Look."

As if in slow motion, Marc took the cell phone from Steve's hand, and read:

You are one of the seven and seventieth generation, the children whose dragon power from the ancients will finally be made manifest. Our fathers, from the Iberian Clan, live on within us. We honor them by learning our gifts . . . and using them.

Steve watched him, gauging his reaction as Marc read. Marc looked up at him and handed the phone back quietly, thinking of all the times he sat in his 'boring' house with his 'boring' life, dreaming of anything else. Never in a million years did he think those wishes would deliver themselves in the form of such a strange reality.

"More questions?" asked Steve.

"But, why so many generations?" Marc asked.

"Well, safety, for one," said Steve, "and also, they probably hoped that by now our age would more enlightened, you know? That hopefully they, like, wouldn't have to go back into hiding again."

Pain seared through Marc's body, and Steve noticed. "Changing pain?" he asked.

Marc nodded. "Get my mind off it. Tell me more."

"Well, uh, our skin-armor that forms when we turn twelve to fourteen is tough, see, but like, not indestructible. That's why we gotta be careful," said Steve, not knowing what else to say.

As they drove, the pain subsided a bit to the point that it was only annoying, but Marc got increasingly nervous. Who was this Victor guy, the leader of the group, and why had Marc so quickly agreed to a trip to meet this guy when he didn't know who he was or what he would want from Marc?

Marc opened the window of the van a crack, and his mind and soul felt restored when the smell of pine and juniper flooded his senses. He closed his eyes, leaning his head against the window and letting the fresh air into his lungs and memories into his mind—among them, his first camping trip with his mom and dad when he was young, pine needles strewn everywhere.

After driving farther on a remote mountain road, the van pulled into a dirt-road entrance and stopped. A hundred feet farther up stood a massive cabin, and the boys got out to stretch their legs.

Marc stood away from the others, behind the van near the property's entrance, admiring the forest and the fresh mountain air.

From out of the trees, across the remote mountain road, a thin, older man in his sixties with a crooked nose approached on foot. He had little hair, wore dark pants, and his hands were stuffed inside the pockets of a hooded sweatshirt, concealing something.

As he approached, Marc looked at the man, whose eyes were filled with a pained, crazed desperation that Marc had only seen in movies. Marc heard the sound of two loud, echoey cracks. He just had time to register the gun in the man's hand before dizziness tipped him off-balance, and when the pavement slammed into his cheek, it was only then that he realized he was on the ground, unable to move.

His eyes struggled to stay open, but they drifted back under their lids.

"Marc!" he heard someone shout. "Marc!" he heard again.

He felt a pair of hands clutch at his abdomen where the pain was.

"Feel cold," Marc said with a weak breath.

People shouted and shrieked all around him, and as purple fuzz swirled around his field of vision, unconsciousness pulling him into oblivion, there was a strange sound he had never heard before.

NINETEEN

Revenge for the Sorceron

The seven Sorceron stood in a large storage shed, surrounding the shivering man in the grey hoodie. The large, drafty shed made of fireproofed sheet metal was mostly empty, tucked away from the meadow behind the main building.

Marc wasn't there.

Victor was tall, and his dark, intense eyes looked like those of Chopin in Eugène Delacroix's famous painting. Though he was only seventeen, Victor behaved as though he were much older, a gentleman of the highest order, even when he administered death to a deserving enemy.

Seven Sorceron dressed in dark clothing surrounded the man in the grey hoodie who had shot Marc. Each Sorceron stared him down, shifting their weight, silently deliberating while they waited for Victor's orders.

The man in the grey hoodie knelt before them, his bloodstained hands lifted weakly in front of him as if he expected someone to strike him at any moment.

Victor stared him down like a lion considering its prey.

"Please," the man in the grey hoodie said. "I—I need the blood for my daughter. I was desperate."

"You know who we are?" Victor asked.

"I heard stuff. I dunno. I just heard stuff. I had to try," grey hoodie said sadly, his face creased with the knowledge of impending doom.

Victor waited before continuing. "And how did you expect to get away with his blood?" he asked patiently.

"I had to, had to try," the man repeated feebly, his voice trailing off to silence.

"Not a very good plan," said Victor, but the man in the grey hoodie said nothing, only glanced up with pleading eyes at each of the Sorceron.

Victor continued. "You're fortunate. You get to decide how to die, and the seven Sorceron who surround you have talents in these arts."

The man didn't seem to be listening. He babbled for a moment about nonsense, but then, as he did, the man's downcast eyes became sharper, his nonsense switching to Latin.

"*Et dedit illi draco praecipitabitur*," the man said.

By the time someone noticed the flash of light that glinted off the steel, the dagger the man hid in his boot was out and he lunged at Victor.

Quickly, however, an unseen force knocked the breath out of him. The man cried out, dropped the dagger, and his knees hit the cement floor again, hard.

Victor stared at the man, and translated what he said. "'*And the dragon shall be cast down,*' you say?" Victor chuckled with mirthy disbelief at the man's chutzpah. "So, all of this about saving your daughter was a lie, meant to elicit pity from us. Hmm..."

Though it was visibly difficult for him to speak, the man labored through it. "I know the fires of hell await me for failing," he said.

"Why should you wait, when I can deliver them now?" Victor said with a purposeful-yet-detached voice. He said this turned away, his eyes staring elsewhere.

Victor walked away from the circle.

As his footfalls echoed against the concrete of the large storage shed, Victor said under his breath as he reached the exit, "Let it be fire."

The man inside the circle disappeared inside a bright kiln, an inferno of seven sources.

The screams of the man grew fainter with each stride as Victor walked from the large shed toward the main building, a light smile on his face, his eyes bright with purpose.

TWENTY

Dragon blood Is Just Blood to Dragons . . .

Before he opened his eyes, Marc heard unintelligible voices conversing. The first clear voice said, "An ultra religious group or something?" to which another, more authoritative voice replied, "It seems we have a new enemy, then."

When Marc opened his eyes, he was in a large, four-post bed, the frame of which was made of dark, rich mahogany. And from the many people who stood around him, the only one he recognized was Steve.

"And he's back," said a young man, taller than Steve. When he said this, the others smiled, and three even clapped. Marc thought this was odd, but his mind was busy taking in the spacious room he was in where white curtains framed two big windows.

"Where am I?" Marc asked.

"You're at the Dragonlair," said the tall young man with dark hair and dark eyes; he spoke with a confidence and authority that Marc had never seen before in a teenager. "You had quite the welcome party," he said, and the others smiled knowingly. The tall young man, who clearly seemed to be in charge, neared the large bed where Marc lay. "I'm Victor. Victor Ferrer."

"Marc Mondragon," Marc said, introducing himself. "What happened?"

"You were shot," said Victor.

"Shot? Like, with a gun?" asked Marc.

"Yes," Victor said with an amused voice spiced with *did you think you were shot with a harpoon?* "Twice."

"Twice? Why—shouldn't I be in pain?" Marc asked, and they smiled.

"If you had been fully human, yes. But you're not. You're one of us," said Victor.

"Who shot me?" asked Marc.

"Someone—someone desperate—must have found out who we were or heard the rumors," said Victor.

"Why would anyone shoot us?"

"For our blood, most likely. Dragon's blood has healing properties for humans. It's said to be able to cure all kinds of maladies, and this man obviously needed it for someone."

Maladies? What teenager talks like this? Marc thought. *He must really be taking his role seriously as the leader of this group.* "Where is he?"

"Don't worry about him."

"Did I hear clapping just now?" Marc asked, sitting up, and Victor smiled.

"Yes, because it's exciting," said Victor.

"You see," a kid Marc's age said, excitedly interjecting. "Dragon blood is just blood to dragons, but since we have both dragon and human DNA, we wondered how it would affect us, as Sorceron. We heal faster than normal humans. We know that. But you're the first of us to be shot, let alone heal this quickly from being shot—"

Victor finished his thought. "Your speedy recovery is proof that we're just beginning to see the extent of our powers."

"How long have I been here?" Marc asked.

"About ten or fifteen minutes."

"I was shot in the stomach *twice* ten minutes ago?" When Marc asked this, everyone in the room was smiling, as if Marc had just spoken the winning numbers of a lottery.

"Yes," Victor said. "Your body spit the bullets out four minutes after you were shot. If you'd like them for a souvenir, let me know. But that's why we didn't rush you to the hospital. When your blood pressure began to rise, we could tell something was going on with you, something only possible with Dragonkyn."

Marc had no words. He just stared forward at the smiling strangers.

Then a girl with brown eyes, dark hair with auburn highlights, and a smattering of freckles entered the room in worn jeans and a white, long-sleeved shirt.

"What'd I miss? The new kid wake up already?" she said. She seemed winded as if she had been doing some kind of training.

"Hi. I'm Jen. Well—Jennika," she said, "but call me Jen."

"I'm Marc."

"Have we given him a nickname yet? Because it should be Lucky," Jen said with a smile.

"No, we haven't given him a nickn—"

"Well, we should. We should call him Lucky," said Jen.

"Jen," Victor said.

Marc could tell she was being annoying on purpose; he guessed it was some game between her and Victor, and Victor didn't like it.

"Thank you, Jen," said Victor and turned to her. "That's enough."

He then turned back to Marc. "More tests need to be done."

"So, if someone else like us was shot, they might heal faster than me?" Marc asked.

"Or slower," said Victor. "We don't know at this point."

"But, like, what if someone shot me with an Uzi, or an AK-47? Would I heal just as fast?"

"Well, like I said, you're the first of us who has ever been shot, so we need to find out."

"Oh." After a pause, Marc added, "you don't need to use me to test that. I was just . . . wondering." His weak smile made a few of them chuckle. "Can I ask another question?"

"Of course," said Victor.

"If the guy shot me because he desperately needed it to help someone who's sick, did we give him some of the blood so he can help whoever he knows who's sick?"

"Why do you care about the man who shot you?" asked Victor, his eyes slightly narrowing.

"I'm just curious. I mean yeah, he shot me, but I'm fine now, it's all good, so I figure, since the guy was that desperate and my blood helped me, why not let it help someone else?"

A smile tugged at Jen's mouth.

Victor exchanged a look with a few of the others, and then turned back to Marc. "I'm glad you value life. This is a good thing," Victor said, his face now serious. "But the man who shot you didn't care at all whether you lived or died."

"That's true," said Marc.

"Don't worry. He's in custody, in a jail somewhere."

"Oh," Marc said. "So, Steve said we exist because ancient dragons put their DNA into our ancestors."

"That's correct," said Victor.

"So, I was also wondering something else, about the name *Sorceron.* So, we're all Sorcerons—" Marc began.

"Just *Sorceron.* It's the same for the plural, too," said Victor, then at Marc's look, he added, "more than one—I am Sorceron, and you are Sorceron, but we are all Sorceron," said Victor.

"Oh. Oh, right. Yeah. Sure," Marc said, unsure. "Well, I actually looked it up. Do you know that the dictionary says that sorcery is magical powers that come from *evil*? The dark arts?" Marc said.

"You really say what's on your mind, don't you," Victor said.

"Yeah. I've always been that way, especially when, uh—"

"You've been through a lot," said Victor.

"—Uh, but, um, I mean, why would you choose that name for your group of Dragonkyn? Why not just, I don't know, call us 'seventy-sevens' or 'Victor's Dragonkyn' or something?"

"You're right, Marc," Victor said. "Some dictionaries say that, yes, but other dictionaries say that sorcery is synonymous with wizardry, with magic in general. And if there is a hint of 'evil' in there, as humans call it," Victor said, then paused for effect, "good."

Another pause, and no one said a word until Victor continued.

"Marc, you will find that loosening yourself from the chains of what humans believe to be moral is an indispensable freedom that you must possess to continue with us."

Marc suddenly felt a weight collecting in his chest, but nodded slightly, his eyes scanning the room.

Victor continued, "The Bible itself uses the word *dragon* synonymously with the word *devil* or *Satan* many times. Even their most 'moral' people see us as evil. And yet the Bible also sees serpents as healers, synonymous with God Himself. In the Old Testament, all the Israelites had to do was look at the bronze snake on the pole and they were healed." When Victor spoke this, with unmistakable authority in his voice, everyone was quiet, some nodding solemnly. As if feeling the mantle of his authority lessening everyone's doubt, the corner of his mouth raised into a knowing grin. "Humans can't make up their minds what they believe us to be."

"Makes sense, I guess," said Marc.

"I want to hear you say it, Marc," said Victor, his eyes darker, intense.

Marc looked at him, surprised at Victor's sudden change in tone.

"Uh, we uh, shouldn't care what humans think of us?"

Victor smiled wide. "Exactly. Now that you're here and have helped us know more about the extent of our blood's healing powers, we have work to do. But first, some introductions."

Victor was almost eighteen, the eldest of all the Sorceron Dragonkyn. He pointed at Steve. "You know that one," and everyone smiled. Then he gestured to a girl with a lock of white mixed into her dark hair. "This is Marah. And these two," he said, pointing to two twin boys, "are Jaden and Jake Muñoz. They're our resident warriors. You'll meet the others later."

Marc figured that Victor surrounded himself with members of the seventy-fifth and seventy-sixth generations who functioned as counselors, and no doubt to give the illusion to outsiders that adults were in control. Three of the four adults in the room were men in their forties and fifties who barely cracked a smile. The fourth was Susan, the sixty-something grandma of one of the Sorceron who smiled so much Marc wondered if she wore it while sleeping.

"I'll be happy to show him to his room, Victor," said Susan, and Victor shook his head.

"Thanks, Susan, but he'll be staying in this room for now."

"But this is—"

"It's okay, Susan, it's okay," Victor said and turned his head to look directly into Marc's eyes as he spoke again. "I trust him."

Despite the new weight on his heart squeezing his insides like a vise, Marc pursed a smile in response to Victor's reassuring grin and steady eyes.

Marc looked around, not knowing what to say.

TWENTY-ONE

Victor Explains the Vibe

Victor had asked Marc to dine with him that night, and there he was, his mind still in awe of watching the different Sorceron use their telekinesis and other powers as he made his way to dinner.

"I imagine you're already Firespewing well," Victor said.

"Firespewing? Oh, right. Firespewing," Marc said.

"It's something we practice doing, but I'm sure you've already been practicing."

"Yeah," Marc said, insecure about those abilities, his usual self-doubt tugging at him. He didn't mention that up to this point he'd only been able to burn a cake.

Marc sat in an ornate, high-backed chair that seemed like it belonged in a castle and wanted to laugh at the formality of it all. *This Victor guy really takes all of this super seriously*, Marc thought.

"Something funny?" Victor asked, and Marc was struck by the fact that he hadn't hidden his smile as much as he'd thought.

"Oh, nothing. Just thinking of something my mom said."

Victor smiled. "I wish I could remember my mother," he said, lifting his glass of lix. "Welcome, Marc. I do hope you find your accommodations satisfying."

"Yes, yes, I do," Marc said.

A pause, and Victor stared at him.

"Marc, this is the dawn of amazing things for our people, and I want us to be friends."

"Great," Marc said. "I wondered if friendship was one of the moral codes that the humans made up. It's good to know it isn't."

Victor smiled stiffly. "We do have a code. And there are excellent reasons why we break the moral codes of the humans. We do it for our own long-term survival. It's what our ancestors wanted us to do. It's what they sacrificed everything for. *Us.* We are their resurrection. The seventy-first through seventy-sixth generations have prepared for this for decades. They've sought our kind everywhere, and though there is another group of Dragonkyn, we believe the Sorceron were chosen to truly lead our people."

Marc was quiet at first, but then he spoke. "There aren't a lot of us, are there? I mean, it makes sense that we would be friends and stick together, right?"

"That's right. There are more than we know of out there, a clan for every region in the world, in different countries, but we are still a very small part of the population compared to humans."

Marc noticed that Victor was only eating raw fish on a metal plate, sipping his crystal glass of lix. Marc looked around at the maces and other older weapons on the walls that made up its decor and figured that Victor was so proud of the pre-medieval source of his powers that he was doing his best to surround himself with artifacts and decor that harkened to that period of time.

"We are not that different, you know," said Victor.

"Really?"

"No. I'm but a few years older than you. I grew up in upstate New York."

"Albany?"

"No, not *that* upstate. No, just a few cities north of Manhattan. A small town."

"Well, you talk like you're a lot older."

"It was necessary for me to grow up fast. Never really had a childhood, but I won't bore you with that stuff."

Marc filled his mouth with almost a fourth of what was on his plate, and with his mouth full, asked, "So, why did you come to Denver—eh, the mountains west of Denver? What's here?"

For the first time, Victor leaned back in his chair, his back still straight, poised, like the leader he knew he was and was trying to be, but for the first time, his eyes didn't seem to have some kind of guard up. "When I found out that I was destined to lead this group, and that the Dragonkyn I would lead were out west, I had to come."

Marc really wanted to ask how Victor came to *find out* he was destined to lead the group, but didn't want to come across like he was questioning Victor's destiny.

"Do you like your room?" Victor asked.

"Yeah. It's nice. It's spendy and spacious."

Victor smiled in a way that said he liked the phrase, and he repeated it under his breath before continuing: "Spendy and spacious." Then, louder, he said, "Yes. Well, it is nice to have money. We have quite a bit, and we're building up more to face our ancient enemies head-on."

Something unstable in Victor's eyes made Marc uneasy, like he was capable of doing something unexpectedly bad at any given moment. "That's cool," was all that Marc said, though he wasn't sure why he said it, and he felt dumb because he knew that it made him seem younger than he was. He wasn't sure what else to say.

Victor lifted a piece of his raw fish, sniffed it, breathed fire onto it, cooking it right there in his hand, and then ate it.

Marc marveled at it, noting that it was the perfect amount of fire. Victor didn't Firespew full-blast like some of the other kids might do. Based on how he cooked the fish right there in his hand, Victor seemed to be able to control his Firespew better than many of the others.

After licking two of his fingers, Victor said, "You will be a great asset to our team, Marc. There's something about you.

You're exceptional. And I know all about that." His lips pursed with a knowing grin as his plate magically lifted into the air and travelled into an adjacent room that Marc figured was the kitchen. Though Marc was impressed, he wore a half-smile, the weight on his heart persisting. "Yes," Victor continued, "it's true that you have yet to discover the extent of your powers and to understand the Dragon Order, but the Vibe is with you. I can sense it."

"Dragon Order? Is that a Sorceron thing?"

"All Dragonkyn know the Dragon Order. It's a way of organizing a pecking order among us. And whether you're a Wyrmling, a Draignor, or a Dragon Lord, deep down, we're all united in the region of Spain we hail from, despite our differences."

Down the hallway, Marc heard a loud crash, all the louder because of the quiet that came before it, followed by the sounds of struggle. Two people were sparing, but Victor ignored it.

"Your name is Mondragon," said Victor, pronouncing it Mon-dra-*goan*, with a regal tone, and Marc liked the sound of it when spoken with a Spanish accent. It was the first time in a while he'd heard his name pronounced that way, and a pride of his heritage filled him.

"Are you a Dragon Lord?" Marc asked.

Victor laughed. "That's good. That's rich, Marcos," he said, but Marc didn't get the joke. Victor noticed his lost expression and continued. "None of the seventy-seventh generation is older than seventeen or eighteen. The great ones are still being gathered throughout the world. None of us have reached Dragon Lordship, but there will be those who make it. We cannot truly face our enemies without reaching the highest, most powerful level of the Dragon Order—a Dragon Lord."

"So, what does it take to become a Dragon Lord?" Marc asked.

"They say you'll know when you become it, that others will sense it, too, when one's powers and connection with dragons past become complete. But it's not external. No one hands you a medal or a black belt. You feel it, as others do. Other

Dragonkyn can feel the rank everyone else holds in the Dragon Order. It's a knowledge that's wordless, like Erifice."

"Erifice?"

"You have much to learn, but one day at a time."

"And how do people just *know*?"

"They know through the Vibe," said Victor. "As long as the Vibe is clear, as long as they listen for the Vibe within them, others can sense your power, your rank. The Vibration, or the Vibe for short, is a power you'll begin to feel. It guides us, and connects Dragonkyn to each other and to all things. But it takes time to be able to read it and to be centered within it."

"The Vibe?" repeated Marc.

"Yes," Victor said. "You'll start feeling—"

"Oh, yes, yes! I've felt that before, yes! In my room, after the dragon dreams I had. It's a sort of peaceful, buzzing tranquilness?"

"Tranquility," Victor corrected him, smiling with recognition. "Yes. We believe it to be the source of all dragon powers. It will guide us as we face our ancient enemies."

"When you say 'our enemies,' you mean normal humans, right?"

"Yes," Victor said with a firm gaze. "We have to keep our eyes on what's important." After a pause, he said, "Speaking of eyes, we all have a birthmark that resembles a cat's eye."

"Uh, yes! I have one. It's on top of my head. My hair covers it, but it's dark. You can sorta see it if you look close. Where's yours?"

Victor stared at Marc with a sudden look of guarded seriousness, as if Victor was suddenly sizing up an opponent. This left Marc totally perplexed, not knowing what he could have possibly said to get a look like that.

Just then, the cacophony of fighting spilled into the chamber where they ate dinner. The twins, Jake and Jaden, were in full armor, and as they entered the room, Jake swung his mace at Jaden, who countered with his blunt spear. They reluctantly broke away from their battle when they saw Victor. Approaching him, they bowed, a fist held over their hearts.

"Honored Basilisk, permission to continue our sparring. He's really pissing me off."

"Permission granted," Victor said, chuckling at their childish squabbling.

"Basilisk," Jaden repeated, bowing again before Victor, a clenched fist held to his heart. Then he turned to spar with his brother. Visible between the armor, their muscles strained as they lunged at each other again. Jake, able to grab Jaden's spear, kicked him into the stone wall.

"You little tool!" Jaden yelled, struggling to stand.

"You're the tool," Jake said. "You can't take the punishment."

Fire erupted into Jake's face from Jaden's mouth, but all Jake did was laugh, shaking tiny embers out of his hair. Jake's hair looked a bit darker afterward, but nothing singed. "That's all you can do, huh?" he taunted, then threw his hand out, causing Jaden's feet to telekinetically come out from beneath him so he fell again, his chin hitting the stone floor hard enough for Marc to wince. Jaden threw his hand toward Jake, sending Jake back against the stone wall. He grunted and fell, but quickly got up.

"Tool!" Jake yelled with a laugh as he ran down the hallway.

"Aaaaaaaaaugh!" Jaden yelled in frustration as he grunted anew, scrambling to his feet and running after him, finally leaving Victor and Marc alone again.

"Where were we?" Victor asked calmly, his eyes down the hallway where Jake and Jaden disappeared. Victor straightened his button-up shirt, his demeanor the very presence of dignity.

"Why did they call you Basilisk?" asked Marc.

"Ah, only an honorable nickname they give me. It's the name of a lizard that runs on water, but it also means 'king of serpents.' Who am I to stop them?" Victor said with a self-satisfied, tight-lipped smile.

Marc nodded with a lift of his eyebrows, not sure what to say. He looked around the room for any interesting details he might have missed, but Victor's eyes stayed on Marc.

"You could do likewise," Victor said, his confident gaze penetrating Marc's eyes in a game of wills.

"What?" Marc asked, and there was a pause before Victor answered.

"Bow to me, fist over heart, and call me Basilisk."

The oppressive weight on his heart tightened into a commanding grip, almost as if his soul were tearing at his physical body.

"Really?" Marc asked with a faint smile, not sure if Victor was kidding. Considering how serious the guy was about everything, Marc got the feeling he wasn't.

"Really," he said. "Bow to me. Swear allegiance to me as leader of all Sorceron, and in return I will make you my right hand, my closest advisor."

Marc thought he smelled blood; he didn't know from where the smell could have come, but a part of him felt sick. After Marc's awkward pause, Victor added, "It's only a show of respect to me as leader." Victor's intense eyes stayed fixed on Marc, and his mouth was a straight line as he awaited Marc's answer.

What could it hurt? Just bow to the guy! said the side of Marc that wanted to fit in, to belong, wanted to do what the leader asked, wanted the discomfort of the situation to ebb. *It seems to be really important to the guy, so why not? Who cares?* However, another side of him, a feeling he couldn't describe, knew it was a manipulation tactic, a form of bullying, of control, and the side of Marc that rejected this, the side that refused to play that game felt as absolute as his own existence. Marc's eyes hardened, but he swallowed hard when Victor's eyes, never wavering from his, narrowed.

"I do respect you, Victor, as a leader, but I won't bow to you."

Victor stared at him for the longest seven seconds that Marc could remember. "Are you sure?" Victor finally asked, and Marc nodded, his eyes darting away but returning.

Another long moment of silence.

Marc felt like he was suddenly in a chess game but didn't know whose turn it was. Just as the tension of the moment reached its apex, Victor's face split with a smile and a manic laugh echoed through the chamber. He quickly composed himself.

"I'm just joking. Just joking. Not a big deal. I don't need you to bow to me to know that you're faithful to our cause and to me," Victor said, as if convincing himself. "However, I wasn't lying about you being my right-hand man. It's the greatest honor bestowed on any Sorceron."

All through Victor's uproarious laughter, Marc wore a half-smile, and now his eyes wore surprise. "Me? But, but I just got here," said Marc.

"Yes, but I'm the leader, and I'm deciding you're the one."

"Yeah, but I don't want any of the others to hate me because you chose me so quickly."

"Who would hate you?"

"Well, I know that Steve worships you in a way. He's the one who recruited me and told me all about you. Plus, isn't he your second in command?"

With that, Victor smiled. "No, I'll tell him in a few days. He will get over it. Don't worry."

That night, there in his nice room on the 'spendy and spacious' four-poster bed, Marc couldn't sleep. The changing pain had returned, but it was manageable. It was the most annoying kind of pain—just enough to keep him awake.

But there were more reasons he couldn't sleep. Though he battled his own feelings of inadequacy as usual, he also missed his mom. His self-doubt berated him for feeling like such a baby, but it was true. He thought that because he'd been on a sleepover for several nights with Luke's family when he was eleven, things would be even easier now that he was almost four years older, now that he could truly call himself a teenager, but they weren't easier. He hadn't accounted for the fact that he had barely met these people, this wasn't a vacation, and something in his gut felt uneasy about all of it. He tried to dismiss it, figuring that he'd never had changing pains before, and he was still unclear about what powers he would have, so why not assume the best? Still, something deep inside, a weight on his heart, gave him pause. The weight wasn't his self-doubt. That felt different. Marc wondered if the weight was the 'fate' the dragon from his dreams spoke of, or if perhaps it was a warning of something dreadful to come, something worse than getting shot in the gut. *I wouldn't have minded getting some kind of warning about that,* Marc thought, trying to smile.

TWENTY-TWO

THE DOCTOR ISN'T HAPPY

The doctor's office was strewn with papers and broken glass containers. The place looked like a normal small town Colorado doctor's office with a fake-marble top counter and a waiting room, but its nurses and assistants were replaced with men in black riot gear holding guns, and it looked like a bomb had gone off minus the smoke. Overturned broken furnishings and debris were everywhere.

Dr. Frenz was in the middle, his heart racing, looking at the tough men in his office with a defiant, you-better-pray-those-guns-are-loaded glare in his eye. The broken glass on the floor clinked and squeaked beneath one of the mercenaries as he shifted his weight. Dr. Frenz was born in a tough part of Baltimore, had clawed his way to the education he attained, and wasn't a man easily intimidated. He knew he lived in a country of laws, and as a respected pillar of this small community, there was no way anyone was going to come into his workplace and do *this*. Dr. Frenz stood in anger. "Give me my phone back!" he shouted to one of the soldiers. "Are you deaf?"

The soldiers said nothing, only stared forward, standing at attention. Dr. Frenz turned to another one. "Are you going to tell me what is going on, or what?" he asked loudly, but the soldier to whom he spoke stood silent, staring forward with shielded eyes and a mouth as hard as granite. Dr. Frenz lunged at one of them, but the man brandished his gun at the doctor with a quick, decisive move and, understanding the law of the gun, Dr. Frenz stood down, his eyes blazing their own helpless bullets.

Finally, Stone Stajinski stepped through the door with the cool demeanor of a general taking a tour of a city he'd just conquered.

"Dr. Frenz," is all Stone said, and Dr. Frenz turned to him.

"So, I take it you're in charge of these heathens? These, these, *cretins* who trashed my entire office?"

"Yes," said Stone cooly.

"What the hell do you want? And where are my assistants?"

"They're fine, Dr. Frenz. They're all in that back examination room, they're unharmed, and they'll probably return tomorrow, business as usual."

"You have a lot to answer for, pal, you know that?" Dr. Frenz yelled, the last word a high-pitched screech.

Stone ignored Dr. Frenz, still surveying the damage like a critic examines an art gallery.

"I'm sorry, Dr. Frenz. I'm having trouble understanding your tone." With this, Stone neared him, staring down at him with lifeless eyes. "You still believe you're the one in control here, don't you?" Stone said methodically. He didn't move, his eyes as firm as fifty steel fences, letting Frenz stew in his new situation.

The good doctor looked around, his breathing slowing; he blinked a couple of times, then sank heavily into a chair, ignoring the bits of glass in its folds, the sounds of traffic outside oblivious to his plight.

"What could you possibly want?" Dr. Frenz asked, but in his gut he might have guessed.

"You made two reports about unidentified cellular activity in a patient after swabbing his throat," Stone said with machine-like precision. "You communicated these reports to two different people online. You remember this?"

The doctor seemed stunned, and now it was his turn to be silent.

"Do you remember this?" Stone commanded, the words more assertive this time, pronounced slower, with menacing enunciation.

"Y-yes," Dr. Frenz finally said, nonplussed and amazed that sending out a report of any cellular abnormality would have any chance of causing a small army to attack his office.

"Good," Stone said with a tone as straightforward as his gaze. "Tell me the patient's name and information, keep our visit to your office a secret, and you'll never see us again."

"And if I don't keep it a secret?" Dr. Frenz asked weakly.

Stone turned in the doctor's direction without meeting his eyes, wearing a light, sadistic smile. "I assure you, Doctor. You don't want to see us again."

TWENTY-THREE

FIRESPEW DESTROYS, ERIFICE BUILDS

The sun was bright on his first day of training, but clouds, huddled in the distance, threatened rain. As Marc walked to the meadow behind the cabin where he was told the others were practicing, he thought of the Vibration within him, or the Vibe, as Victor labeled it the night before. He wanted more of it, even yearned for it, but all he currently felt was the same weight clamped around his heart. He didn't know why. Somehow, deep within him, he immediately knew a few things about this Vibe, though he had no idea how. He knew it was a special source of power that one needed to be 'in tune' with in some way. As he walked, he searched for the Vibe within him, the invisible fire, and there it was. It wasn't burning from within his center like before, but it teemed all around him like a quiet friend.

When Marc felt the Vibe, his spirits lifted, and a reassuring peace filled him despite the oppressive feeling in his chest.

The cabin was surrounded by acres and acres of forest. Firespewing practice happened in a tightly controlled meadow behind the cabin, a two-hundred-foot perimeter dug out as a fire line to protect the trees.

When Marc approached the meadow, everyone was talking in different groups of two or three, waiting for the others to show up. Jen and Steve were there, as well as two other guys who couldn't have looked more different. One was named Felipe, a short, wiry-but-muscular Latino kid who smiled a devious grin more often than a sincere one, and a tall, bigger, pasty-white guy named Taymor that Marc wondered was albino or not. The twins were also there, Jaden and Jake, sipping lix from small canteens, as well as eight or so other Sorceron Marc hadn't met yet. Some of them spoke Spanish to each other, some didn't.

Jen was the only one wearing bright clothes. Her loose-fitting blouse was a bright, pale yellow, and she wore some kind of apparatus with strong, black cords wrapped around her shoulders and neck, looking like something one would wear to a dragon-person archery class. *Perhaps it's more fashion than anything else*, he wondered.

That was when he noticed a group of three Sorceron engulfed by the same purple and blue-green fire that had fallen out of his nose and mouth at Principal Jenkins's office.

He was fascinated. They didn't speak with their mouths. They only smiled at each other occasionally as the strange fire enveloped them. Marc noticed that the fire looked slightly different depending on who was spewing it. One of the three, an African-American kid, had more green in the fire he spewed, and the girl's fire was more blue, but the different shades of purple were a constant for both. One of the Sorceron in the group nodded, and the girl jerked her head back in delight.

What *was* that? He wondered.

Marc approached them with wide eyes, like a young boy watching a grown-up juggle three little bean bags for the first time. "Okay, you guys gotta tell me what's going on with that," said Marc.

The African-American boy looked at Marc with a knowing smile one would give to a newbie. "This? This is party fire," he said with a laugh, but the girl with the lock of white amidst brunette, collar-length hair, said, "Don't listen to him. It's called Erifice."

"Your name is Marah, right?" asked Marc and she nodded.

"Marah Vivas."

"Nice to meet you again.

"I was just messin' with ya," said the boy. "Name's Demitrius. Demitrius Villanueva." Marc shook his hand.

"Hi. Uh, so, um. Eriff-iss? It's spelled with an *s*?"

"No," said Marah. "It's spelled with *i-c-e* on the end, but you pronounce it Erif-*iss*. We also call it Eriflow, especially when we use it as a verb—Eriflowing, you know. Some even call it Erifspeak, or Dragonvey."

"Wow. A lot of names for one thing."

Demitrius was already resuming his erificed conversation with someone else, bored with the tutorial.

"Well, it's the purest form of communication among dragons. Ironic that something that communicates so wordlessly has so many names."

"Yeah. What do you mean when you say it's the purest form of communication?" Marc asked, and he could tell she wasn't the most comfortable talking to someone she didn't know.

Marah wore black leggings, brown boots, and a white, comfortable-looking blouse. "It's wordless. Um, pure. Here," she said, and with her mouth still smile-shaped, she blew the purple-blue fire all over Marc's face. By instinct, his eyes closed as she did this, but in his mind, pictures came alive. Marah stood near a home, talking to an older woman near a sign, and without any words exchanged, Marc immediately knew she was from Montana. He also knew that she was introducing herself. Marah Vivas had been with the Sorceron a year, and Steve's uncle had found her when he sensed through the Vibe that a Dragonkyn was in her small town in Montana as he had passed through on I-90. Marc immediately knew this information without a single spoken word.

"Wow!" was all Marc said to her, his eyes and mouth flying open, smiling at once. She only smiled, and with the purple-blue fire still dancing around his shoulders, wisps of aqua-green flames appearing now and then, he felt her thoughts say, *Yeah. It's cool, isn't it?*

Marc also knew how normally shy and reserved she was. It wasn't anything she was overly concerned about. She just had a harder time trusting people. He knew how vulnerable she felt, and her bravery in speaking Erifice to him, a stranger, made him like her that much more. Soon, the same purple, blue, and green fire fell from his face. When the Erifice he breathed enveloped Marah, her tentative, reluctant smile grew to a warm one. She got everything he had thought, and she stared at him through more trusting eyes.

An immediate connection of friendship formed between Marc and Marah, a closeness that would take people much longer to achieve through conventional language.

"See? You're getting it," Marah said. "Yeah, looks sorta weird when you first see it or speak it, but Erifice is central to all communication. It's usually used for positive, even intimate exchanges. Sometimes for neutral exchanges, but we usually just speak verbal English, Spanish or Welsh for that stuff."

"Welsh?"

"Of course. A little bit anyway. None of us are fluent, but Wales is the birthplace and Welsh is thus the birthlanguage of all dragons."

"Makes sense," said Marc. So, what about *negative* exchanges?" Marc asked, and she gave a pirate's smile. "Well, that's Firespew—which has lots of other names, too, like Tali`o or firescream. It burns things, but to us it also communicates negative emotions and anger. Erifice is the opposite. Firespew destroys, Erifice builds."

"So, we only Firespew when we're angry at someone?" Marc asked, and she laughed.

"No, we also use it as a weapon, but it's sorta the same thing, isn't it?" she said.

It made perfect sense. "Yeah. I guess it is," he said.

"Don't worry if you can't do it sometimes. Like all emotional expressions, it takes time to learn."

Marc thanked her and moved away, feeling much better than he did during his first impression of the place, with two bullets in his gut. He waded through the you-must-be-the-new-kid stares and finally wandered over to Steve, the only other person he knew.

"Hey," Marc said. "So, now what?"

"Well," said Steve, "now it's target practice. We have to learn how to master the powers we're discovering, and that begins with Firespewing."

"Ah, right. Firespewing." Marc said, looking at the others who were talking among themselves.

"It's, like, different for everybody. Some are better at firespewing than others."

"Makes sense," Marc said, suddenly aware of how much Steve said the word *like*. Marc knew that he himself said it too, but now he felt self-conscious. Did he say *like* as much as Steve? And why would he notice or wonder about this? *Maybe all this is putting me into some kind of emotional shock*, he thought.

As Marc contemplated, Steve continued. "See Jen, that girl in the yellow shirt? She's the one who was there when you woke up. She can spew fire, like, thirty or forty feet," Steve said. "She's our flame thrower."

"Wow," Marc said, watching her, genuinely impressed.

"Most Sorceron can only spew fire eight to fifteen feet. Plus, she's cool too."

"Is she able to do that because she accesses the Vibe better than anyone?" said Marc, to which Steve scrunched up his face in disgust.

"Look. Don't believe everything everyone tells you about the Vibe, okay?"

"Why?" said Marc, surprised.

"Some people believe in the Vibe, that it's some kind of mystical force that connects all Dragonkyn to all matter, but *it's not.*"

"It's not?"

"No. Look," Steve said, looking around before looking back to Marc. "We're all part dragon, and dragons had magical powers, and that's why we have those powers. And lix enhances those powers. It's that simple. I don't get my strength and power from anything else. Forget it." Just as he said this, Steve's eyes went wide. He lifted two feet off the ground as Felipe wandered past and stopped.

"Let me go, Felipe!" Steve said, frustrated, floating in the air as if pinned to an invisible wall.

Felipe, his arm extended toward Steve, said with a mock-dramatic voice, "I find your lack of faith disturbing," followed with laughter. As Felipe dropped his hand, Steve fell to the ground.

"Give the kid a break. *Déjelo en paz* already. It's his first day here," said Felipe, and Marc smiled. He liked Felipe immediately.

"Shut up. I'm serious," said Steve with a grunt as he stood again.

Turning his head in Marc's direction, Felipe held out his palm for a handshake. "Whussup, bro," he said.

Taymor, the albino-looking kid, never smiled and never said hello. He barely looked at him, and when he did, his gaze looked demeaning, as if Marc were a lower life form.

Jen was first to start practice. She stepped up, took a swig of lix from her side flask, and faced a circular target three feet in diameter on a large tree. She smiled as tiny orange venules in her neck glowed. They went from almost invisible to bright orange on her neck and upper chest. Fire burst from her mouth and the circular target was engulfed in flames. Marc heard a smattering of applause and shouts of amazement, since her target was thirty-five feet back, while the other targets were fifteen or twenty feet back.

"Nice trick," Taymor said.

"How'd you make it go so far?" asked Felipe.

Marc's eye caught the look that Marah and the other girls had—just a smile that said, *Jen makes all women proud.*

"Got anything else, babe?" Taymor had barely gotten the words out of his mouth when Jen turned, and a thin, straight line of pure fire shot like a laser from her mouth. Within two full seconds, the crude, dark spelling of the word *idiot* was pyrographed into Taymor's target, smoldering with wisps of white smoke.

"Yeah, *babe*," Jen said sarcastically.

Marc couldn't help but laugh, and Taymor looked at him with cold eyes, though everyone else was smiling too.

"Hey. It's funny," Marc said, defending his reaction to Taymor.

Clearly cheating, Taymor ran twenty feet closer to his target. Fire flew thickly from his mouth, lighting up only half of his target, the ground getting most of it.

He then gave Marc another cold stare and walked away.

"Geez. Nice meeting you too," Marc said aloud as Steve approached him smiling.

"Don't worry about him," said Steve. "He's grumpy when a girl proves she's better than him at anything."

Jen's smile was wider now.

Marc still grinned at Steve's comment until Jen stopped it. "Your turn," she said with a smile.

"Wait. Mine?" said Marc.

"Of course," said Jen. "Let's see what the newbie can do."

"Yeah. Let's see what you've got," said Steve with an everyone-loves-to-watch-a-train-wreck smile.

"But, uh, I haven't practiced," Marc said.

"This is practice," Jen said, still wearing a sarcastic smile.

"Here. Have some lix," Steve said, handing him a bottle of amber liquid. "It enhances your powers."

Marc took the bottle and drank a few gulps. It burned a little, but he was determined not to embarrass himself.

Handing the bottle back to Steve, he stepped up to face his target and looked around nervously. He coughed weakly, because that was how it happened before with his mom's birthday cake, but nothing came out. Marc put a hand to his mouth to feign real coughing.

He tried it again; a bit of fire dribbled out of his mouth and onto his shoe, turning part of it into a goopy hole. Forgetting he was fireproof, Marc put it out with his other foot, looking like he was doing some kind of foot-on-foot twist dance. Self-consciousness formed like a bubonic plague in his mind. He heard a couple of the kids openly laugh.

"The guy's not even a Wyrmling!" one of them said, but he didn't look around to see who it was. "This is Victor's wonderkid?" Marc heard another whisper loudly.

I'm horrible! Marc thought. Frustrated, he tried it one more time, but only a feeble puff of smoke came out of his mouth.

"Wow. You're gooood," said Jen sarcastically, and Marc wondered what he did to deserve such a snarky attitude from a girl he barely knew. Steve and the others stifled laughter, trying not to make him feel bad, but Marc heard it and felt embarrassed.

This is worse than middle school!

TWENTY-FOUR

Dancing with Fire

"Don't worry about them," Marah said later on when she gave him the tour of the place. "They've just never seen Victor rave about anyone like this before."

Marc gave a guarded smile as they walked to the back of the spacious meadow in the middle of the compound, away from the main building. "It never works when anyone tries to cheer me up," Marc said, "but when you do it, I actually feel better."

She waved him away. "C'mon," she said.

"It's true!" He said. "You're like the sister I never had."

"Well, I never had a brother," she said. "The job's open, so you're welcome to it."

He smiled. "Even without Erifice, I don't think I've ever bonded with anyone so fast. Wait. No, that's not true. I did once."

"Really?"

"Yeah. My mom," he said, but he said it dry as flour, looking away, which made her smile.

Marc was impressed with how self-sufficient the infrastructure of the compound was. It really was a lair. At first, Marc thought it was a cute word they used to describe the place because of its association with dragon habitats, but no. They not only had a weapons stash, but they also had their own mini-hydro-electric dam on the river, a power plant, and four wind-turbines that powered the entire complex, completely off grid.

The compound held underground sleeping quarters complete with running water, hotplates, and even its own sewage system.

"This is amazing," Marc said. "Next you're gonna tell me that you have your own grocery stores," he said, and she returned a knowing smile.

"You're kidding me," he said, and she chuckled.

"There's another property where we grow crops and different grains. It has its own mill and even a grain silo," she said.

This place is legit, he thought. "All this was built by the seventy-fifth and seventy-sixth generation?" he asked.

"Some of the seventy-first through seventy-fourth generation laid the groundwork. They were just as aware of the prophecies about our generation, and they wanted to help.

They walked on, and while walking past the stables in the very back of the property where they kept free-range chickens and two horses, they began sharing their memories and experiences of their lives before they discovered they were Dragonkyn.

"Whoa! You have a 'Zoosh' in your school too! These guys have to get together and go bowling," said Marc.

As they walked, Marah shared an oddity she had. "I've always thought that the word *togetherness* was weird," she said.

"Like, it looks weird?" he asked.

"Well, everyone says the word that way, but when I look at the word, I can't help reading it like *to-get-her-ness*. I look at words in a weird way sometimes." Marah said. Gauging his reaction, she added, "See? It's weird. I'm weird."

He chuckled, but countered. "No, it's great! Stay weird, then," said Marc, and pointed at her hair. "Is that white part natural?"

She smiled a shrug. "Yeah. One more odd thing about me. I've got tons."

"I like it," he said, his accepting eyes making her stifle a grin.

The shadows grew longer and the sunlight turned the color of honey as they walked across the expanse of lawn in the middle of the property where eight Sorceron were playing a pickup game of Ultimate Frisbee. The background noise of their laughter and shouts somehow comforted Marc.

After a pause, he asked, "So, do you believe in the Vibe?"

She nodded, her eyes more solemn.

"Why does Victor swear by it, and yet Steve thinks it's all superstition? Is Steve the only one who doesn't believe in it?"

She thought for a moment, blew her lone white lock of hair out of her eyes and said, "I dunno. I think Dragonkyn are just like people. Some believe in things they can't see, and others don't."

"Why do you believe in it?" asked Marc.

Again, she looked pensive, but then her eyes met his. "To me, that feeling is as real as anything physical or emotional I've ever felt, and when I use my powers, or sometimes when I don't, there it is, guiding me."

"So, for you, it's something that guides you?" asked Marc.

She looked right at him. "I think if you listen for it, really seek the Vibe and nothing else, it'll awaken powers that you never knew you had."

She said it with such conviction that Marc just stood there, looking at her.

"Ow!" Marc said when a frisbee bounced off the side of his head, followed by a chorus of laughter and apologies. He felt a sharp pain, but it didn't last long.

Marah's eyes never left him when he threw it back to the others.

"Yeah," he continued, rubbing his head, his eyes looking concerned. "I mean—seeking the Vibe, listening for it, how it connects to our powers. There's just so much to know and learn. I wonder if I'll ever be good at it. I know I want to. I've been trying," he said, then looked back at the others playing. "So, explain again why the Vibe doesn't warn people about badly thrown Frisbees?" he said, and she smiled.

They talked of other things as they walked. Marc found out that her greater power wasn't telekinesis like many kids had, but strategic skill. She could out-think any opponent in any game, could have given Bobby Fischer tips on playing chess. Marc noticed she was very shy about this information because he had to coax it out of her, using Erifice.

"So, what's the deal with this upcoming war against the humans that Steve told me about?" Marc asked, and she nodded pensively. "I mean, how are you comfortable with that? Aren't humans just like us, since we're half human?"

"I like to believe that Victor wants to prepare for a war if it happens, but the main point is to face humans from a position of power, to force them to accept us."

"Yeah, maybe." Marc remained skeptical of Victor's true intentions. The tightness in his chest eased when he was with Marah, but it never went away. He changed the subject.

"So, are there other kids here who train for a week and then go home?"

"A few," she said, "but others live here full time, like me—for, well, different reasons."

Later that evening, Marc sparred in a hand-to-hand combat training battle with Demitrius Villanueva, the funny kid with the wide smile who had called Erifice 'party fire.'

They were in the same spacious basement (*tall ceiling for a basement*, Marc noted) where Marc had dined with Victor.

Demitrius's huge advantage in battle was clear to Marc the moment he stepped into the 'space,' which is what they called the seven-foot-in-diameter painted circle on the floor, since they had no elevated boxing ring for sparring.

Marc was head to toe in sparring gear. *Padding in every crack*, he complained in his mind. He held a padded pair of nunchucks, and at his feet was a padded staff with what looked like stiff boxing gloves on each end.

They were the third to spar, and by the time they started, Marc was already sweating in his padding, a rush of heat blowing up from beneath it all. *When does the training start that actually involves making my powers better?* Marc thought, annoyed. *This is some dumb initiation for the new kid,* he guessed.

When facing him, Marc saw that the only padding Demetrius had was a blue helmet and boxing gloves, whereas Marc's helmet and pads were red.

"So, uh, what's your power?" Marc asked Demetrius, trying to shake the nerves away.

"You'll see real soon," he said.

"What—?"

"Ready, go!" someone shouted. Someone gave Marc a light push and that was when Marc realized they were now both in the circle, with every other Sorceron surrounding it, thirsty to see Marc's humiliating defeat.

When Marc looked back at Demetrius, his brain couldn't exactly grasp what he was looking at. Had someone put up a mirror in front of him?

Marc was facing himself.

There he was, wearing blue sparring headgear, smiling back at him. Marc threw a quick what-do-I-do-now expression at Marah, who stood with the others around the circle, all wearing a yes-he-can-do-that smile.

Demetrius (as Marc) hit him with seven blows before Marc could process what was happening, and before he knew it, Marc was on the ground, face up, with a chorus of cheers, jeers, and applause erupting from the other Sorceron. Marc hitting the floor was the punchline everyone was waiting for.

Marc wanted to sleep for at least an hour, but he didn't pass out. Marc looked up with dazed eyes, and Demitrius looked like his dark-complexioned self again. Marc realized that his biggest advantage wasn't that he could simply trick an opponent's mind into thinking he had morphed into looking like the opponent, it was the few seconds that the shock to the opponent bought him.

"Good thing he can't actually transform into someone else," Marc heard someone say, "'cuz that'd be freaking everybody out."

Demetrius helped him up. "Don't worry," he said with a gracious but mischievous smile. "I always win the first time I spar anybody."

Later that night, just before they all went to bed, Marah and Marc sat together in the large, stone gathering room where all the Sorceron watched a talent show like none he'd ever seen before.

"It was Victor's idea," Marah whispered to Marc. "He doesn't want us entertaining ourselves with the same things humans do—movies and video games and stuff like that."

"Isn't that a little overboard?" Marc asked.

"Of course," she replied. "Why do you think half the Sorceron only train for two weeks at a time and go home?" she said, lips together, fighting a smile.

Marc prepared his mind for a less-than-great show, but he was shocked at all the talent. Jake and Jaden sparred with an athleticism he could only hope for, a Sorceron named Talec with brown hair and brown eyes telekinetically turned himself upside down, and, with his head near the floor, juggled three wooden balls on fire. Even Demitrius tried his hand at comedy, and when two of his jokes failed to land, those on the front row screamed fire at him to show their displeasure. Bright cinders danced where his blue shirt used to be, but he laughed along. A tougher but warmer crowd Marc had never seen. But the highlight of the show was when a girl with long, frizzy dark hair named Carmen danced with Erifice. Marc knew that it lasted longer than fire, that it seemed to have a personality all its own at times, but until he saw Carmen dancing with it that night, he wondered if he had ever seen anything more beautiful.

Everyone clapped to the beat, embraced by the strings of a Spanish guitar.

Wearing a burgundy gypsy dress, she was pure grace as she moved, fluid and precise; Marc had never seen any kind of fire dance with someone before, but this dance was to movement what a sonnet is to words.

With Erifice in sync, she rose and fell.

When she sank to the floor, the flames bid farewell, and everyone erupted in applause as she stood.

"Gracias," she said with a timid smile.

Twenty-Five

Beware the Black Dragon

That night, the entire main building of the Dragonlair was still and dark. Marc had slept little, and his antsy mind convinced him that it was six-thirty or seven in the morning when he woke up, but when Marc looked at the clock, he was wrong.

1:37 a.m.

Across the spacious room stood a large oak cabinet, much larger than any other cabinet he'd ever seen. Was it a wardrobe? Did it have a television inside? Marc wasn't sure. He stared at it. *Well, might as well take the tour*, he thought, quietly getting out of bed and nearing it.

He tried the ornate left handle.

Locked.

As his hand reached the right handle, he thought of what Victor had said earlier when Susan protested that he allowed Marc to stay in that room. "I trust him," Victor had said.

*Right handle's probably locked, anyw—*Marc thought as he tried it. It moved freely, and now Marc was faced with a choice.

With no words exchanged between his conscience and his mind, he simply knew that doing this would change something.

He felt the cold, dark hardwood floor beneath his feet, and his breathing was shallow. His eyes narrowed, his mouth a straight line of concentration, weighing the options.

Lightly tapping the ball of his right foot on the floor as he pondered, he became aware that his throat was dry. *If I look in here, I'll be snooping,* he thought, *and if I do that, I will have broken the trust of this new friend.*

On the other hand, he reasoned, *if I don't do it, I won't find out something I feel that I need to find out—something important that may help me understand better not only who they are, but maybe who I am also.* He thought of the trust Victor had placed in him, but then thought of the longboard Steve had stolen.

That's when he turned the handle and opened it a crack.

Darkness inside.

He opened it wider.

Nothing. Just a bare, empty cabinet, its cavernous shelf accompanied by other smaller shelves.

Marc exhaled relief.

He turned, looked around the room, and kept turning until he faced the opposite wall. Then came the feeling that the room itself was watching him. He stared at the dark windows framed by the white curtains, their color now muted by darkness.

"Hello?" he whispered, with a half smile, half mocking the ridiculous notion he had that the room was somehow alive.

Marc felt the Vibration in his chest again. The feeling that Victor had described was, yes, peaceful, but it was also powerful, five times stronger than how it felt before in his bedroom.

He felt he could do anything in the midst of this invisible fire that filled him. The feeling wasn't physical, really, but it felt as close to physical as any feeling could.

Tears leaked from his eyes involuntarily. He wasn't sad, he wasn't in physical pain, not to the point of tears, anyway, yet there they were. Tears. The Vibe emanated stronger from within him than ever before, and Marc felt a light illuminate behind him.

It was a blue light, coming from the open cabinet, lighting up the wall of windows in front of him. It was the color of harsh moonlight, a subtle blue. When he looked down, he saw the light on the back of his hands.

Had it been any normal light, he would have simply turned around immediately to see what it was, but this time, with this light, he felt the powerful, peaceful fire that burned within him somehow fighting against the blue light behind him. Marc felt calm, protected, no doubt because of the tranquil strength of the Vibe he felt, yet he didn't want to turn around. Should he wait until the silent war between the Vibe and the blue light subsided?

He turned, the tension between the Vibe and blue light at an apex, the light blinding at first, but no longer blue.

A whiteness shone so bright it overtook everything else in the room.

He could no longer see the cabinet, couldn't feel his feet on the floor, and all he saw in front of him was a large dragon, its color a polished, gleaming black, as if perpetually wet, like a beetle dipped in crude oil.

Marc started, then forced himself to exhale and take another breath. He knew it wasn't a dream, or was it?

This can't be real, Marc thought with wary eyes never leaving the dragon.

The dragon's long, thick, scaly horns on its head pointed like the coarsest of hair in the opposite direction of the gaze its eyes cast. When the dragon spoke, it did not open its mouth, the words coming like a strange form of erifice, the dragon projecting its thoughts.

Marc stared in amazement at the majesty of the dragon, whose body seemed crouched, ready to strike, its face ten feet from Marc's.

Do you know why you're here? the dragon asked sullenly, the voice resonating all around him.

Gone were Marc's tears, as well as the Vibe that he had felt so strongly not moments before.

"Uh, uh, to train?" Marc finally said, and the dragon continued to stare at him, its eyes two almond-shaped lanterns.

Do you know who you are? it asked.

"I am Sorceron?" Marc said with a tentative voice. He couldn't keep his voice from shaking. "One of the seventy-seventh generation. A dragonkyn." Marc said these answers sort of like a question, as if to ask, *isn't that right?*

A pause followed, but the dragon's gaze never wavered from his. It blinked.

Is that all you know? the voice asked.

"Uh," Marc's voice box grunted. He wasn't sure how to answer it. Why did the dragon ask this? As Marc searched silently for an answer, the question came again, stronger, more adamant this time.

Is that all you know?

"Yes," Marc said, and there was a long pause.

When the dragon spoke again, it was barely a whisper. *Wonderful*, the voice breathed through clenched teeth, as if not meaning to say it aloud.

Marc heard laughter, a smug, mocking chuckle from the dragon, as if it held an inside joke it would never part with.

As the deep-voiced chuckling turned to simmering laughter, the large, black dragon before him continued staring forward, with no smile, no open mouth, as if it were separate from the words the voice made, its studious eyes never leaving the boy before him.

"Who are you?" Marc asked, more assertively this time, but the dragon was gone. All Marc saw was whiteness in front of him, but the basic shapes of the furniture of the room began melting back into view as the room began spinning like a whirlwind all around him,

"Who are you?" Marc shouted into the wind.

As Marc squinted, his face turned away from the wind, he heard the dragon's faint but deep voice one last time.

I'll ask the questions, Marc thought it said, as pain tore through Marc's body, twice the intensity of the changing pains, as if his insides were literally on fire. Marc screamed into the wind, but it had no effect.

The details of the room were a blur as it all spun around him. Images superimposed themselves over it all—images of blood and fire and dragons of different earth-toned colors battling themselves, clawing at each other.

It was too much. Marc felt dizzy, and with his feet still not on the ground, he didn't know what was up or down. The weight on his chest deepened, and for a moment he thought his heart would burst. He cried out into the wind, but nothing changed.

Still more spinning, Marc's eyes squinted into the wind. He saw more dragons fighting each other, some screeching, some screaming a soul-rending howl, others dying.

Marc cried out again for it to stop. "Please!" Marc shouted limply into the tumult, his voice a high-pitched screech. "Please make it stop!"

A few more interminable seconds after he yelled this, it stopped; all of it, including his consciousness.

TWENTY-SIX

Test of Loyalty

Marc awoke on the floor, blank eyes staring at the large, sturdy, squat legs of the cabinet, as if there to welcome him back from the crazy hallucination he'd just experienced. How long he'd been there on the floor, he wasn't sure, but he knew by the darkness it was still the middle of the night. Cloudy and foggy, his head felt like it weighed three times more than it did, and he sat up quickly.

No. Not a good idea, Marc thought, as the top half of him slowly fell back to the floor. He felt okay on the floor, besides the slight nausea.

Exhaustion encircled his mind like vultures, but he knew he had to get to the bed, so he slid across the floor, his feet pushing himself backward. He'd been enough of a problem already. He didn't want anyone coming in and finding him on the floor, finding out that he'd opened the cabinet.

The last thing he remembered before sleep stole him again was getting his torso and one of his legs onto the bed.

When Marc woke up, he felt a lot better. Morning light poured from the windows, and somehow he'd finally managed to get his entire body onto the bed during the night. The door opened and in came Susan, the nice lady who always smiled.

"Sleep well?"

Marc's eyes went to the large cabinet, the doors of which were closed. "Uh, yeah," Marc managed, rubbing an eye with a finger. "Interesting furniture you have here."

"Say again?" the nice lady asked, turning to hand him a towel for the shower.

"Eh, nothing. Thanks," he said.

After eating breakfast in a darker-than-usual basement with no one he knew, Marc made his way to the meadow behind the main building where they all gathered each morning for roll call. After a nod or two to a few kids, he saw Marah. They exchanged timid smiles. Something warm and wonderful welled up inside him when he saw her. She already felt like family.

Marc moved through the small crowd of kids to stand next to Marah. She asked how he was and he said fine, not wanting to mention the previous night's drama to anyone. A couple more Sorceron waved to him, and after a while, he started wondering where Steve was. Usually, everyone met in the meadow at 10:00 a.m. when Steve took roll call for Victor, but after conversing for some time, everyone started realizing how late it was getting. At 10:20, Marc asked Marah where Steve was, and she said she didn't know.

"He's usually the first one here," she said.

"Steve seems really dedicated to doing whatever Victor says," Marc said.

"Yeah. But then again, everyone is," she said, as Jen joined them.

"They agree on every little thing?" asked Marc.

"Naw," said Jen with a faint voice, looking across the meadow to see Steve coming from the main building, and then her full volume returned. "They agree on everything but the Vibe. Victor believes in it, and Steve doesn't at all. He's the heretic, but Victor doesn't force it on him."

Finally, Steve approached and called everyone to attention. A loud whistle sounded.

He addressed them all in a loud voice. "Victor and the others were called away this morning, but they wanted us to continue without them," Steve said, and Marc assumed that Victor hadn't yet told Steve that he planned to make Marc his second-in-command.

Jen raised her hand to ask a question, and Steve said her name.

"He never said exactly what was going on? Not even to you?" asked Jen.

"No, Jen," said Steve, whose eyes then gauged Marc's reaction, which Marc thought was odd. "Nothing's wrong, okay?" Steve repeated. "Victor decided that he and a few members of the seventy-fifth and seventy-sixth generations would do some research on their healing powers so they can plan and strategize accordingly. He said we're supposed to, like, do some Firespew practice and then the standard ritual when a new recruit shows up."

All eyes and smiles turned to Marc. This was the first time Taymor smiled, and Marc asked what it meant.

"You'll like it," Felipe said. "The last one was two counties away, but today's is a lot closer to the Lair."

"Yeah. Listen to Phil," Jen said with a mischievous grin.

"Don't call me that, Jen," said Felipe.

After practice, during which Marc again felt horrible about his Firespewing abilities, they gathered gear and were on the road.

"Don't worry. We've cased it out for at least two weeks. Between 1:00 and 3:00 p.m. is their slowest time," said Felipe with a mischievous *I'm-hiding-something* look in his eye.

Cased it out? Marc still wasn't sure where they were going. He only knew about the almost physical weight he felt in his chest, the same weight he felt during the visit with the black dragon apparition the night before and during his dinner with Victor. His hazel-green eyes tried to hide the thousand-pound worry and doubt that sat in his mind.

Jen, Steve, Taymor, Felipe, and Marc rode in one of the sleek black SUVs that Victor preferred to other cars.

They were at least thirty miles out on a small highway, and the other five wouldn't tell Marc where they were going. The knowing smiles were cute at first, but the dumb secrecy annoyed him.

The slowing tires crunched the gravel near the mid-sized market as it came into view around the next bend in the highway. Dingy and run down, its fresh coat of tan paint couldn't hide the age of its building. Marc already felt a little carsick from the winding roads that brought him there, but a new nervous tension settled into his pores, accompanied by an erratic heartbeat when they told him their purpose.

"We're hunting for resources," said Steve.

"What?" Marc said, indignant.

"It's not a big deal," Taymor said smoothly with the lowest, most casual voice he could.

"So, it's an initiation?" Marc said.

"It's not like we're going to haze you, bro," Felipe said, "but it *is* something you have to do with us."

"A hunt for what again?" Marc asked, still wrapping his head around the assignment.

"Resources," Steve and Taymor said at the same time, both dramatically, like they were starring in a political thriller.

"A robbery. You're stealing from people?"

"*We're* stealing from people," said Taymor.

"Call it what you want, bro," Felipe said, looking down.

"Call it what I want? Steve—" Marc began, but their faces were all serious as cancer. "I mean," Marc continued, "stealing a longboard now and then is one thing, but, but—armed robbery?"

"No one is armed, Marc," said Felipe.

"We have powers, Felipe. Call it what you want, *bro*." Marc said.

"Marc, we need to know you're with us one hundred percent," said Steve. There was an awkward pause.

"I am, you guys, I'm with you," Marc said, unsure.

"Are you?" asked Taymor, his cold voice now dipped in annoyance.

"I am," Marc said more assertively, his fierce eyes on Taymor. "I *am*."

"Okay, then it's settled," Jen said. "Here's the plan."

Marc hated the situation he was in. He had never wanted anyone to be there more than he wanted Luke or Marah. Why hadn't Marah come? No one answered when he asked.

Let me out! He wanted to scream. *Give me a phone, I'll call mom, and I'll be outta here!* he thought, but how could he? He felt torn between his duty to his newfound tribe and his conscience.

Soon they all stood behind the gas station dressed in dark clothing. Steve closed his eyes and held out his arms. A slight tremor in his hands as the ground shook. Marc heard glass breaking, then more glass, and the deep, unnerving sound of the earth tearing itself. Shouts were heard, and two Hispanic men, early twenties, came running out of the store toward a gray late-model Ford sedan yelling, "*Terremoto*!" They both got in and drove off.

"They think it's an earthquake," said Felipe. "Perfect."

Steve dropped to his knees, exhausted, and Jen was there to steady him as Marc, Felipe, and Taymor ran around to the front of the building.

When they entered, the store Marc imagined wasn't what he saw. The inside looked like a zombie apocalypse movie. The floor was torn open in big chunks with large, iron pipes and cables of different sizes bursting out of it like evil, invading snakes. Almost a foot of water covered what was left of the floor, and Marc heard a gushing sound.

Reluctantly, but determined to prove his allegiance, Marc jumped over the counter, opened the register, and collected the cash. The other two stood guard. Felipe was just outside the building. Taymor was inside, by the door, on the other side of the counter from Marc, and just as Marc had the cash in a paper bag, an older man spoke up from a doorway in the back.

"Can't let you do that, son." The stout man in his sixties meant business. He stood knee-deep in the water with a crowbar and a crew cut, wearing soaked jeans and a flannel button-up over a t-shirt, next to a small freezer that floated nearby.

What happened next happened fast.

Marc saw Taymor's determined eyes. Orange venules in his throat glowing through his skin, Taymor gathered air into his lungs, preparing a fiery end to this human that stood in their way.

As if in slow motion, Marc's eyes registered what Taymor intended.

"No!" Marc yelled and put out his hand in Taymor's direction. As if Marc had punched him, Taymor's face flew to the side, just as fire erupted from his mouth.

Dropping the crowbar, the older man yelped, more out of surprise than fear, for some of Taymor's Firespew caught the left sleeve of his flannel shirt below the elbow, which he extinguished in the small lake that made up the floor. Other pools of fire sat atop the water as well. Holding the paper bag full of cash, Marc jumped over the counter and pushed Taymor up the three stairs to the entrance and out of the store, leaving the bewildered owner with a wet sleeve and a million questions.

TWENTY-SEVEN

Different from the Others

Meanwhile, back at the Lair, Victor stood in a dark robe, his black hair disheveled, staring into the mystical white light of the open cabinet, in the same room where Marc had slept.

The dragon's liquid-black scales shone in light as he lifted his head, staring forward with a grave expression, a weary bitterness in his baritone voice.

Your new favored recruit, the voice said, emanating from the dragon staring forward.

"Yes. The one called Marc?"

The dragon only nodded solemnly, its eyes turned away, thoughtful. *What are your thoughts on him?*

"He is earnest," Victor said, but a silent pause followed. "I believe his powers will improve. It's interesting. I cannot quite sense what the great Vibration would—eh, I sense something. Something familiar?" Victor chuckled. "I do not know, bisabuelo. Perhaps he can help us—" His words stopped with his breath when the dragon turned its eyes of fire to meet his.

Hear me now.

"Y—yes, Lord Prencheret, mi bisabuelo," and with these words, Victor bowed before him.

The dragon waited long enough for Victor to look up.

"Bisabuelo?"

The dragon paused, prefacing the importance of his words with another patch of silence. *He is...different from the others . . .*

Victor listened with intense eyes, slightly narrowed.

The longer the voice of the black dragon spoke, the more the resolve in Victor's gaze went from tentative to steel.

TWENTY-EIGHT

A CHANGE OF PLANS

In the car on the way back to the Dragonlair, they argued.

"I can't believe you were about to kill that guy!" Marc yelled at Taymor, but Taymor sat with hard, angry eyes.

"You ruined it! I had 'im!"

"I ruined your kill. You're nuts, you know that?"

"You have no place here!" Taymor shot back.

"Unbelievable," Marc muttered.

"I said calm down, Marc!" said Steve.

"Next time we go out, I don't want this dill weed coming anywhere near us!" yelled Taymor.

"Dill weed? Wow. That's spicy talk for a guy who looks like a glass of milk," Marc said.

"Fight each other when we get back, you guys!" Jen yelled over Taymor's angry shouting, turning the steering wheel sharply to interrupt their arguing. "Do I need to remind you that this is a getaway!?" Felipe was in the back seat silently laughing at both of them.

Marc's heart beat fast. He felt nervous, but also sort of proud that he had the guts to argue this much with people who were practically strangers. He knew right from wrong, and this, he knew, was wrong.

"Victor says that if a human dies in any of our quests, then too bad. The ends justify the means," said Taymor.

"Yeah!" Felipe said in solidarity. The SUV took a sharp turn, the wheels moaning as they skidded, and the inertia sent them all leaning in the opposite direction.

"Oh, that's nice," said Marc, his voice dripping with sarcasm. "Convince ourselves we're better than those 'other' people. Hey, it worked for Hitler."

"Shut up!" said Taymor.

"Doesn't anyone remember that we are *also* part human?" asked Marc.

"They've always seen us as creatures that only lust after their gold anyway," said Jen.

"Gee. I wonder where they got that idea," Marc interrupted, but Jen finished.

"So we are only doing what they think we've done for centuries. But this time there's a reason. The chance for our long-term survival!" Jen yelled over the noise of the SUV's downshifting transmission.

"I can't believe that Victor is so willing to kill to find the money he needs for his plans. You already built the Lair. Aren't there any more rich people in the seventy-fifth or seventy-sixth generation?" asked Marc.

"You're no Sorceron," Taymor spit the words like they were the ultimate insult.

Jen stopped all the arguing with a sharp turn that sent Taymor's head and a swearword into the window without breaking it. Steve quieted them all as Taymor rubbed his head.

When they neared the entrance to the Lair, Marc knew there was trouble when he looked out the window. Police cars clogged the main entrance. A man from the seventy-sixth generation waved an arm in some kind of secret emergency code, which obviously meant to keep driving past the main entrance and turn left into a dirt alley on the other end of the property, because that's exactly what Jen did.

When she turned the SUV into the alley, Marc wondered why the police had been at the entrance. How could they already know about the robbery? Maybe it wasn't related, he figured. A couple hundred feet down on the left, Marc saw a white, unmarked van sitting on a rich, dark patch of dirt and stubborn grass.

These guys are organized. "Where—?" Marc began to ask, but before he could finish the sentence, the SUV stopped and they all got into the white van and drove away, Felipe behind the wheel.

For the first couple minutes of driving in the white van, Jen, Steve, and Taymor were on their phones, and the heavy feeling in Marc's chest tightened again. Was it the Vibe, somehow warning him of something? Considering all that was happening right then, he knew it could have meant any number of things.

It was only as Marc sat in the van near the window, watching trees fly past as fast as his thoughts that he noticed how hungry he was. All he'd been able to grab that morning before practice was a piece of toast; there'd been no time for eating since then. Marc was in the back seat, and in the tense moments before anyone spoke, Marc saw Felipe, Taymor, Jen, and Steve all lift in unison when they hit a bump. They all looked a bit somber, but Marc figured it was because they had their own questions.

Jen turned to Marc. "The Sorceron are hiding for the day. Vic—"

"Hiding for the day?" asked Marc.

"Well, let me explain, please," said Jen, who then turned to Steve. "Does he always repeat what you say?"

"Always," said Steve with a monotone voice, without missing a beat.

"Hey. I don't always repeat—"

"Victor says things are too hot with the cops showing up, asking so many questions." said Jen.

"But why? Because of the robbery? Um, I mean, the 'search for resources'?" asked Marc.

"Something about a man who went missing in the area. All Victor told me on the phone is that we're supposed to lay low for the day. Don't worry," said Jen, but then, seeing the worry in his eyes, she added, "When we saw the cops there at the Dragonlair, we went into emergency evac mode. That's why we're in this van right now."

"So, where are we going?" asked Marc. Jen and Taymor exchanged a cryptic glance.

"We have to stick to Victor's orders he just gave us on the phone," Jen said, casting a glance at Steve.

"But why—?"

"I think the cops are onto something, and Victor doesn't want to give them any reason to come back to the Lair."

They drove in silence, and all the while, Marc couldn't get all that he had experienced out of his mind: the shocked, vulnerable face of the man with the crowbar and the burning sleeve, the Vibe he felt just before the vision he had from the cabinet, the unsettling look in Victor's eyes when he said certain things, the consistent weight on his heart about all of it. Who was the black dragon he'd seen? Why had he said what he said? Why had he laughed that mocking chuckle after he answered? *Great. The one power I'm good at is seeing and hearing mystical black dragons inside of furniture. Wonderful.*

His stomach growled, and Marc sighed.

TWENTY-NINE

DITCHING DEATH IS DIFFICULT

The gas station they stopped at, with its large mini mart, sat like a white and red buoy in a sea of green trees. Jen had the bag of money from the robbery, and though he was hungry enough to use that money to get something to eat, he still felt bad about robbing the store and didn't want to ask her. Marc only had money for a candy bar, which he'd devoured even before going into the bathroom.

As Marc stood at the urinal, expressionless, watching the empty cleaning bottle surf the overflowing garbage can to his left in the corner, his thoughts turned to something his mom would often say as they watched a scary movie together. "Everyone's afraid of the unknown," she would say, ever the armchair psychologist. He felt a tug of a smile at the memory, but the words only confirmed the way he felt. He wondered what Luke was doing right then, and felt a pang of jealousy toward him and his normal, boring family; all these thoughts and feelings happened fast, like songs on the internet changing as fast as a click.

The weight on his chest persisted. If a feeling could scream, it was this weight. He desperately wanted to know what it meant. *Is it a warning? Feels strong enough that it could be*, he thought.

A wave of emotion struck when he thought of his mom, the look of unspoken worry in her eye the last time he saw her when they drove away toward the Lair. Marc still wore the dark jeans, shirt, and jacket they gave him for the robbery. After washing his hands, he leaned on the sink with locked elbows. Looking into the scratched-up mirror, Marc wiped a welling tear from his eye as if trying to hide it from his reflection.

So many unanswered questions.

He scowled at the blurred reflection, angry at the barrage of things out of his control. *How many almost fifteen-year-olds had ever had to deal with this?*

When Marc came out of the bathroom, the soft 'elevator' music playing across the store, Jen was there with a shushing finger to her lips.

"Just listen, okay?" Jen whispered, eyes intense, and Marc nodded.

"You're in serious danger. You—"

As if in slow motion, Jen looked to her left and pushed Marc hard into the chips stand.

"Wha—" Marc asked as he fell back with the different-colored bags, but his eyes went wide when a big, Arab-looking sword embedded itself into the wall where his neck had just been.

The place erupted into chaos.

As Taymor struggled to get the big sword out of the wall, a hundred plastic cups and ten cans of Fix-a-Flat came flying from out of nowhere, hitting Taymor hard in the face.

He fell, a shout and two shrieks bouncing off the walls when the cans ricocheted off his head, and his body sprawled awkwardly on the floor.

"Hey!" someone from the front of the store shouted, but flying debris and shouting drowned out any more discernible words, except for the one Jen screamed at him.

"Run!"

Marc scrambled to his feet as loud, deep whooshing sounds enveloped his ears.

He suppressed the panic exploding inside him. He wanted to look back, but decided to obey her and dash for the first exit he saw, ignoring the fear that yelled in his mind like a man on fire.

An unseen force pulled Marc's metal necklace back in the opposite direction. His feet flew up from underneath him and he crashed back to the tiled floor. Coughing from being telekinetically choked and ignoring the pain in his shoulders, he spun to his hands and knees and looked up to see Steve reaching toward him with an intent hand and a mad glare in his eyes Marc hadn't seen before.

Marc tore the necklace from him as he scrambled to get away, his panicked eyes staring in disbelief as an older, green sedan came crashing through the main window of the convenience store *sideways,* taking out two or three aisles of the mini-mart. The deafening sound made Marc wince as debris whizzed past his face. He couldn't see Steve, but in his breakneck hurry to obey what Jen yelled at him, he launched himself toward the side exit.

Seconds after Marc ran out of the mini-mart, he looked back and saw fire erupting inside. When Jen broke from the same door in a sprint, she ran to the van and grabbed a backpack out of it.

"Jen!" Marc yelled.

Ignoring him, she stopped and turned, facing the van. Using her telekinetic powers, Jen lifted the van six inches off the pavement all by itself. As Marc watched in awe, the van turned in the air, as if on huge marionette cables, and Jen sent the van crashing into the side of the mini-mart near the door she had just come out of, the sound of groaning metal and shattering glass echoing off the nearby trees. The tires of the van faced Marc and Jen, and a laser-like line of fire shot out of Jen's mouth, hitting the van's gas tank. Just before it exploded, Taymor reached the door inside, his determined eyes fixed on them.

The blast wave knocked Jen and Marc to the ground, and had Marc not been fleeing for his life, he would have really appreciated the beautiful mushroom cloud of fire that bloomed toward the sky above the mini-mart, before disappearing like a smoky phantom.

The smell of gasoline and melted plastic was intense as burning debris rained down.

Marc looked to his left to see two employees running from the store.

Before he knew it, Jen appeared behind the car where Marc was hiding, as calm and focused as he was out of breath.

"See that hill?" she asked, pointing to the small mound of grass behind the store, a curtain of forest beyond it. Marc nodded, but as they crouched to run, the same big sword Taymor used came flying toward them and Jen screamed. Marc turned, put up an arm as a feeble attempt to protect himself, and the big sword suddenly changed course, flying upward, but slicing him as it did. Marc cried out and grabbed his arm, crumpling to his knees. Instead of falling to the ground, the sword magically hovered in midair, pointing at him like an accusing, metal arm.

Who had it? Marc wondered, then he saw Felipe facing Jen, who stood her ground to protect Marc. She hissed at him, snake-like.

"I have orders, Jen," Felipe said, breathing heavy, a sheen of sweat on his dark face, blood on his shoulder from a gaping wound.

"It's wrong, Felipe," Jen said. "You don't just order the death of someone when we were celebrating his arrival two days earlier. Something's going on, Felipe, something we don't know about. Don't you see?"

"Victor has his reasons, Jen. Now get out of the way!" screamed Felipe, and as he did, the gleaming sword hovering in the air inched closer to Marc, who turned away, sure that it would stab him at any moment.

"Phil," Jen said to Felipe, her voice suddenly more calm. "You're going to put down your sword."

"Stop calling me that!" Felipe said.

"In fact, Phil, I think you *want* to put down your sword," she said.

"Your little mind tricks aren't going to work on me, Jen," said Felipe, his voice unsure. "I know it's your lesser power," he said.

"Phil, it's yourself that you want to hurt, not Marc," Jen said, and the sword swung around to face Felipe. His eyes widened in panic and consternation. "No, it's not!" Felipe yelled, struggling with his own thoughts and powers to block her mind control.

"No, it's not!" Felipe yelled again, strain in his voice, trying to convince himself.

"No, it's not!" Jen volleyed, turning it all around, and the aggression with which she said it tipped the scale in her favor. If the mind control Jen exerted on Felipe were an arm-wrestling match between his will and hers, Jen threw him over the table.

"Yes—wait! No!" Felipe yelled, and the sword that hung in mid air flew toward him, plunging deep into his thigh, staying there.

"Aaaugh!" Felipe cried out in pain and dropped to the ground, agonizing.

"My lesser power is still able to best you, ya stupid half wit," Jen said, her breath still a bit out of reach. She and Marc took off, running a half-mile into the forest. They left Felipe hoping that yelling curse words in Spanish would somehow stop both the pain and stop them from running away.

THIRTY

A WALK THROUGH THE WOODS

Later, crouching behind a clump of dead trees a half-mile into the forest, looking nervously in the direction they came, Jen explained the best she could. "I don't know how any of this happened, but one second, you're the hero of all Sorceron with your healed bullet-wounds, and next, we're ordered to kill you."

"What?" Marc asked.

She nodded, still out of breath. "Over the phone, just as we got into the white van, Victor ordered us to kill you. I've never known him to do that. Not since . . ."

"It happened before?" Marc asked, and she nodded.

"Only once, for the good of the group, he said, but that was someone Victor's age who directly challenged his authority, someone who had been there before Victor arrived, not a new arrival." She sighed, still winded from the running. "It was a year ago. His name was Alex. Some of us still think he could read minds, or he sought the Vibe, because right after the order was given, Alex took off before anyone could do anything," she said, unzipping her backpack and checking something inside. "All Victor said was, 'he won't be bothering us any more,' to make us think that he killed Alex, but I still think he got away." At this, her eyes seemed unsure. "I think," she repeated, clearly upset, but then her eyes turned willful when they met Marc's. "I haven't liked a lot of how Victor leads the group," she said, "but this was the last straw. I wasn't going to let it happen." She looked at Marc with a determined stare, but then her eyes softened a bit after giving a hard exhale. "You okay?" she asked, gesturing to the blood seeping from his forearm.

"I think I'll live," he said. "Thank you for saving me," Marc said, and even he was surprised by the guileless, unguarded sincerity with which he said it. A line of sweat had worked through the dirt on the side of his face.

She smiled, looking down. "No worries."

"I didn't know one of your powers was mind control," Marc said. "That's wicked cool."

"I like to keep that one a secret, but the other Sorceron know," she said. "I'm usually the one who has mind clean up duty." At his confused expression, she explained, "Whenever people in public witness some of our powers, I'm the one who suggests to their minds that they didn't actually *see* what they saw," she said. "They only thought about it. The mind can imagine anything. Most usually accept it right away. There are only a few that I need to work on just a bit more."

"But don't you have to follow everyone around and make sure that your suggestion stays in their mind?"

"No," Jen said with a grin. "I can tell. Their own mind takes in the suggestion. They themselves keep the illusion going, because it's a thought that makes sense to people. Magic is too unrealistic to most people. They don't know where to put it in their reality, so my suggestion to their mind is something they're actually looking for anyway. They take it and continue on with their lives."

It made sense to Marc, his eyes pensive. "Last night, Victor asked me to be his right-hand man. I don't know why he would suddenly want to kill me," Marc said.

"For whatever reason, you became really threatening to him really fast," she said. "It's so weird. Did you ever argue with him?"

"No," said Marc, thinking of the cabinet episode the night before, wondering if snooping around large furniture and seeing a black dragon was a good reason to kill someone. There was a pause, and Marc changed the subject. "Do you think they'll find us?"

"I don't think they saw the direction we went," she said.

Jen's brown eyes looked up, scanning the sky.

She sighed heavily. "So, here's our sitch. We're here in the woods, sundown is a couple of hours away, and half the Sorceron are probably looking for us by now."

"Not the funnest afternoon," said Marc.

"No," she said, a begrudging appreciation on her face for his attempt to lighten the mood. "Probably the best thing we can do is hike to Fairplay, only about ten miles from here."

"Sounds good, even though it's ironic," said Marc, and they started back in the general direction of the road.

"What's ironic?" asked Jen, matching his pace.

"That after getting ambushed by three Sorceron, we're walking to a town called Fairplay."

She chuckled, and Marc was sure that it was a courtesy laugh. She was a year and a few months older than Marc, but acted like she was twenty-five. Marc was a little in awe of her, aware of his every action, wondering if he was sounding like an idiot. He thought about what had just happened. It was all still a blur.

As they walked, their bodies making a rhythmic symphony of snapping twigs underfoot and clothing against leaves, Marc finally asked, "So, what actually happened in there?"

A smile tugged at her mouth, but he didn't notice because she walked in tandem behind him. "It's my greater power. Telekinesis."

"Really? Like Steve?"

"At least half of us have some form of telekinesis. You know how Steve can move iron as his greater power?" she said, and Marc nodded. "I can move any kind of petroleum-based product."

Marc exhaled a laugh, amazed. "You mean, like, plastic?"

"Yeah. Anything petroleum based, which is why I could throw around most of what was in that store back there."

"But what about those cars you threw into the store? Those were metal," he said.

"So, you're saying that the tires and the plastic in them were metal, too?" she said with a grin. "I moved everything else. The metal just came along for the ride."

"I thought Firespewing was your greater power," he said.

"Naw," she said. "I just have more practice at that than the others."

Marc walked with a look like someone had proven to him the existence of unicorns. He looked back at her, the late afternoon sun through the trees lighting one of his eyes. She saw his expression and spoke with a laugh in her voice. "I forget you've only been with us a few days," she said. "You're sort of getting the telekinesis thing."

"Not really," he said, gesturing with his bloody forearm, "but thanks," he said.

"It's better than your Firespewing."

"Ouch," he said, again wondering what the sarcasm was for.

"Sorry, but it's true," she said, a loud bird squawking above them.

"No, you're right. I'm horrible at it," he said.

"Maybe I'll teach you a few things that will help."

"Thanks."

"Maybe not," she said, and Marc was taken aback by her hot-cold attitude. She seemed annoyed with him for some reason, and Marc noticed, but didn't call her on it.

They continued walking, the quiet forest sounds taking the place of their conversation for another mile.

Marc broke the silence first. "So, Victor said there are more groups of Dragonkyn besides the Sorceron. What's up with that?"

"Yeah," she said, passing a hand over the bark of a tree as she passed it. "Some with their own agenda, some even within the same nationality. There are three groups of Iberian-American Dragonkyn. The S—"

"Iberian?" asked Marc.

"Yeah. Where Spain is? Your ancestral home?" she said sarcastically.

"Oh, right. Yeah. I knew that."

"Uh, huh. Sure," she said. After a moment of walking, she seemed to forgive his ignorance and continued. "There's the Sorceron and another called the Taneen. The third isn't exactly *organized*," Jen said, her voice rising, putting verbal quotation marks around the last word. "The last group we call Rogues. They're crazy. There aren't many of them. Most of them live back east, and they exist in, like, every type of clan from around the world—though I haven't met any yet. Not sure I want to. There aren't nearly as many Rogues as the rest of us, but they're the juvenile delinquents of all Dragonkind. Completely unpredictable. They just want to destroy stuff for the sake of it. I heard there are three Dragonkyn with mind-control powers back east who do nothing but clean up what these Rogues do, trying to keep our powers a secret from normal humans."

"Well, should we talk to the Taneen group? Marc said.

"No," she said. "They don't allow any Sorceron near them. They would always fear that we're spying on them for Victor. It's happened before."

"So, you know someone in Fairplay?" asked Marc.

"No. But I still have the money from the robbery, so I think we'll be fine for a few days," Jen said, holding the backpack open. Marc peered inside. The robbery had happened so fast, he hadn't paid attention when he was stuffing the bills in the bag. Now he stared, amazed. Outside of movies, TV or the internet, he'd never seen more than a hundred and twenty dollars cash at once his entire life, and as he stared speechless at all the twenty and ten dollar bills, Jen studied the look on his face, amused at the spell the money cast.

THIRTY-ONE

Marc and Jen's First Fight

They walked back to the road diagonally, away from their original direction, bypassing the gas station.

"Why did Taymor try to kill me with a big sword?

"He probably did it because they knew that you can recover from bullets easier and faster than most," said Jen, and it made sense.

"Hard to recuperate when your head is separated from your body," said Marc, and he thought of the old movie *Highlander*, about ancient, immortal Scots, in which the only way to kill one was to chop off their heads with a special sword. "Oh, hey! I almost forgot. Do you have any lix?" Marc was growing to like the taste of the stuff, and he liked the idea that it enhanced dragon powers—something he needed a lot of.

"Here," she said, digging a small metal flask out of her pocket and throwing it to him. "Take mine. You're uh, you're gonna need it more than me." She chuckled. "I mean, how threatening can you be with that Firespew of yours?" she said sarcastically.

Marc put the flask in his pocket, but as she said those last words, he stopped.

"Wait, wait a sec," said Marc.

She continued a couple feet more before stopping, turning.

"This isn't going to work, Jen."

"What isn't going to—what are you talking about?" she asked.

"What's all the sarcasm for?"

"I'm only teasing you, Mr. Sensitive," she said, turning again to continue walking.

"No. I know friendly teasing, and that's not friendly."

"Geez. I'm sorry," she said, again, sarcastically, throwing the nonchalant apology over her shoulder without looking back. "Happy?"

"What's going on?" Marc asked.

She sighed loudly, not hiding her irritation. "Nothing," she said.

"Jen, be honest. There's a reason you're all sarcastic with me sometimes but you barely know me. What is it? I don't like tiptoeing around others. I'm already stressed out as it is, so tell me."

She looked astounded at the accusation. "You sure have some guts. I just saved your life and now you're lecturing me on manners?"

"Say it," Marc said, more assertively.

"It's just the way I am, okay?" she said. "Don't be so offended. Just deal."

"I don't like unspoken stuff, okay?" he said, louder. "What'd I do? Just say it."

"Nothing," she said, matching his intensity, continuing her walk with a pouty stomp. "Look, I understand you're paranoid, but don't throw it on me, okay? I've got enough to have to figure out right now," Jen said, defensive.

"C'mon! What's going on?" he insisted.

"Nothing!" She turned back to him. "They're gonna hear us! Shut up!"

"They will not! We're far enough into the forest, okay? Now say it!" Marc yelled.

Jen ran at him with angry eyes and swept his leg, tackling him to the ground. He fell hard against a fallen branch the width of his wrist. He let out a sharp cry, but her hand was quickly over his mouth. "Shut up!" she whispered intensely, practically on top of him. That's when Marc thought he heard something in the surrounding trees, and his angry expression changed to worry; he froze, no longer trying to pry her hand from his mouth. Jen's dark eyes scanned all around them, searching deep into the trees for movement, any movement. Finally she pulled her hand away from his mouth and pushed Marc away, scooting herself against a tree. "Idiot. They're gonna hear us," she said. After sixty full seconds, she sighed heavily and, quietly, with begrudging resignation, said, "I can't read you," followed by another sigh. "I can't read you, okay?"

Silence.

Marc didn't know what to say.

Finally, she looked up at him. "Now you know. Happy?" She asked. Marc waited for her to explain, and though she did, Marc could tell it was the last thing she wanted to do. "My mind powers," she said, standing, brushing dead leaves from her coat. "Besides some light mind control, I usually can get a sense for what people might be thinking. Nothing specific, just a sense. It's, like, a way for me to check how well people are taking my thought suggestions. But none of it works on you, and it pisses me off," she said defensively.

Marc looked at her, a grin on his face. "Uh, I'm sorry, your powers don't work on me?"

"It's not your fault," she said, standing, and then let out a loud, frustrated exhale. "When people use their mind a lot, when they're smart, or educated, or good at math for example, my suggestions don't stick as easily."

"Well, there you go," Marc said. "I like math."

"No, it's more than that. Because usually I can at least pick up general readings, but you're a blank. Nothing. You and Victor are the only ones I haven't been able to read."

"But why does that make you angry?" Marc asked.

"Because! Because you're—you're younger than me," she said, annoyed, continuing her march.

Marc chuckled. "Only by, like, a year," he said.

"Just forget it. Never mind."

For three minutes they walked in silence.

Finally, Jen said, "I know it's my lesser power, but I always thought that when I had no power over someone's mind it was because they were smarter or older than me, and you're neither of those."

A pause. "Gee, thanks," he said.

"You know what I meant, okay?" said Jen, a softer edge to her voice finally.

"I was just kidding," Marc said and gave her a smile, which she volleyed reluctantly over her shoulder.

As they crunched their way through leaves and wild grass, the dusky sun bathing the tops of the trees with a honeyed glow, Marc got Jen to tell him her story and the first moment she knew she could move plastic. "I was at a picnic my mom dragged me to, and it started with a plastic spoon. Happened two months after I realized I could spew fire, about four or five years ago," she said matter-of-factly, her eyes darting around her, always watching for other Sorceron. "Little things happening, like the spoon, stuff I couldn't explain. Finally, I realized that it was only stuff like plastic. Once," she said, smiling, "I thought I could move people, because I lifted my grandma when she was asleep." Marc's breathing labored with silent laughter as she continued. "Seriously," she said, trying not to laugh also. "I had her sitting up in her bed. She never woke up once. But then I realized that I wasn't moving her. I was moving her dentures and her denture adhesive, which are petroleum products."

"That's amazing. So, you can move all sorts of stuff, right?" Marc asked.

"Yeah. Everything from shoes to stereo speakers."

As they hiked, she continued. She was from Topeka, Kansas, and her dad had left when she was young. Her mom disowned her when she found out she could spew fire. She shook her head sadly and added, "My mom thought I was possessed by the devil."

"Your own mom thought you were possessed by the devil?" Marc asked.

Jen said, "Yeah," with a tired, resigned tone. "She's an old-school religious fanatic, so she disowned me. My aunt tells me my mom never brings me up because she's so embarrassed and freaked out by it all. I only talk to my aunt every other year, and she begs me to tell her what happened, but I can't. We're not ready for humans to know about us. Not yet."

"Whoa," Marc said. He couldn't imagine his own mom doing that, and though he was confident sometimes, the thought of being on his own without his mom in his life sort of scared him. "You've been through a lot."

"Yeah. But it's not so bad. You've been through a lot too since you first realized you were Dragonkyn."

"Yeah," Marc said, still marveling at it all. "All this started with a grilled cheese sandwich," he mumbled in disbelief.

She smiled. "What?"

"Nothing," he said, too tired to explain it. When they got back to the highway, hearing the steady sound of cars and trucks whooshing by, they walked along the treeline.

They decided to stay at the first discount motel they came to.

Marc noticed Jen looking over her shoulder for Sorceron, so he looked around himself. "I know they tried to kill me, but does every Sorceron obey Victor no matter what order he gives?" Marc asked before they reached the building.

"No," she said. "A few are like me, I think, but Victor has most Sorceron convinced that the key to our survival is unity, and that anything that might drive us apart, including people who disagree with him, is a threat."

The spartan lobby smelled like stale cigarette smoke. The motel manager was an older, no-nonsense guy, whose puffy, tired eyes spoke of all of the pain and nonstop work it took to scratch out a living as a small business owner. Glancing occasionally at Marc, the older man seemed about to question Jen's age, but he never did. Jen's mind control sure came in handy.

They got a room with two queen beds.

THIRTY-TWO

THE DANGER-IS-COMING DREAM

Marc relished every bite of his two huge bison burgers that night. As soon as his mind was convinced that he was out of immediate danger, his appetite returned. The locally owned Burro Cafe wasn't the nicest building in Fairplay, but its bison burgers put nationally recognized fast food to shame. The Burro Cafe was about to close when they showed up, but John, the owner, was nice enough to keep it open just a spell longer.

Jen had already finished her chicken sandwich and sat nervously as Marc started his second bison burger. "Can you hurry up and finish that? I'd rather not be hanging out in public places any longer than we need to," Jen said, her gaze cast out the window for any familiar vehicles.

He looked at her for a few seconds, quickly chewing, then wiped away the bison sauce on his chin before saying, "Thank you for saving me."

"No worries," she said. "Wasn't about to let you get killed."

After a moment, she spoke again. "As we walked here, I asked myself why I saved you, and yeah, the reasons are there. I haven't liked how Victor has led the Sorceron, and I thought it was wrong of him to do that to any Dragonkyn, but it was more than that," Jen said, and sighed in frustration. "It was so weird. The Vibe's never prompted me to do anything that strongly before, but I guess it did then."

"Well, I know *that* ticked you off," said Marc through a full mouth.

"It did! I've never experienced anything like that. I mean, the Vibe and I are tight. I'm always trying to listen to it, learn to recognize what it's saying. But I'd never felt it trying to get me to do anything like that before."

"Was it always your plan to kill me at the mini-mart?" Marc asked with dry, dead-pan sincerity. As she coughed a laugh, trying not to choke on her soda, he added with a wry smile, "Now there's a sentence I never thought I'd say."

"No," she managed to say through giggles. "I think Taymor could tell I was trying to warn you and decided to take action right then and there."

Marc looked at her earnest face, which was also sort of pretty. Not wanting to dwell on it, he looked at a slow-chewing lady sitting next to them.

Out of nowhere, Jen asked, "So, what's your story. Any girlfriends in your hometown?"

Marc exhaled a short laugh. "Naw," he said. "Not really." Marc said this in self-deprecation, but he knew he was blushing and hated it. He wondered why he hadn't mentioned Katie O'Hannon to Jen. It wasn't like he and Katie were dating. It was only a crush, though Marc thought the attraction was mutual. Still, why didn't he mention Katie? And why did Jen ask him about it? It seemed an odd thing to ask him right then. It's not like they were talking about love interests before she asked him. A bit uncomfortable, Marc changed the subject.

"Uh, can I ask you a question?" Marc looked away for a second as she nodded. "Can every telekinetic move cars and stuff?"

"Some of us can, but only a few," she said, and then her eyes got pensive. "Most of the Sorceron think it's all set in stone, that whatever abilities you have are set, like they can't be improved. But that's not true. I haven't always been able to move cars, but I've been practicing a lot more than most." She got up from the table abruptly and added, "We better go."

That night, Marc was a bit weirded out. It was the first time he'd ever slept alone in the same room with a girl he barely knew, let alone one who was pretty in a 'tough' sort of way. Luckily, his exhaustion far outweighed his discomfort with the situation.

He dreamt, and the dream felt like the sternest of warnings.

Marc was tied to a post, immobile. Though he tried, he couldn't move an inch. The nylon cords pinched as he struggled. He found himself in a high meadow, and beyond it was an imposing mountain. A low rumble sounded, like an approaching force.

Indistinguishable sounds in the distance, getting louder.

Marc's eyes strained to see. There, the distant mountain began to change. It darkened somehow, but Marc saw no clouds to block the sun.

His eyes narrowed to see, and finally, he understood.

The mountain wasn't getting darker from a shadow, but with the swarm of men wearing black body armor, head to toe in paramilitary uniforms, assault rifles at the ready. He stared in alarm as they closed the distance, like frantic, hungry scorpions.

A steady drumbeat of war slowly rose in volume as they approached.

As the men quickened their pace, Marc's heartbeat did the same.

Marc struggled more against the cords that bound him, but it was no use.

He craned his neck to see behind him, the whites of his eyes bulging, but all he saw were the members of the Sorceron sleeping on the ground.

"Hey!" he called. "Wake up!" But none did. Though they were only sleeping, none moved.

"Wake up!!" he screamed.

Victor either wasn't there, or he was outside Marc's field of vision. Either way, Marc watched helplessly as the dark, armed militia came closer, running with purpose, bent on every Dragonkyn's destruction.

They were close, and getting closer.

One thousand feet.

The drumbeat was louder now, more intense.

Marc looked back at the sleeping Sorceron. "Wake up!" he screamed again.

Eight hundred feet.

Marc's throat constricted in fear. "Wake up!" his voice cried with diminished strength.

Five hundred feet.

Marc tried to scream louder, but all that came out was air.

Three hundred feet.

He could see them clearer now. Some held machetes at their sides.

One hundred feet.

Marc tried to spew fire at them, but all that came out was pathetic bits of fire dripping off his chin with tendrils of smoke. He yelled in frustration.

Fifty feet.

The first man to reach him slowly lifted his machete with both hands.

Thirty feet.

At once, he realized that it was all a dream. Like a light switch flipping on, Marc suddenly knew that he could choose the outcome of all this. The Vibe felt strong within him, so all he had to do was make that choice. He did.

"Stop!" Marc yelled, and as if pushing a pause button, the encroaching horde stopped, frames frozen, the closest man's machete poised to strike three feet away.

Marc's breath had flown away, but he finally caught it.

He stared at the men closest to him, whose eyes gleamed with bloodlust.

So determined, *Marc thought.*

Marc awoke to the sound of the cheap air conditioner in the motel room, its plastic mouth heaving out one long, labored sigh. Faint light came through the drapes.

The clock read 1:37 a.m.

Jen's motionless form lay under the covers of her bed, as still and slumbering as the Sorceron were in his dream, and a chill went up Marc's spine.

THIRTY-THREE

A CALL TO ARMS

"Mom, slow down! No, I didn't! Wait. Wait. Just slow down! Tell me again." Marc nervously wound the telephone cord around his finger as he spoke to her the next morning. He had planned to ask his mom if he could stay longer with Steve's family, but instead, she was frantic.

"These men just left. They were cops, and they told me you were in trouble and they had to find you, so I gave them the address Steve gave me. How are you in trouble all of a sudden? What did you do before you went to Denver?"

"Mom, nothing. I promise!"

"But, honey, how am I supposed to know—"

"Mom, Mom, back up. How do you know they were cops?"

Jenny's voice became uncertain. "Well, uh, they wore black and they flashed a badge. Why wouldn't they be cops?"

"I don't know, Mom, but I promise. It's probably just a big, elaborate joke that Luke is playing on me."

"Luke Rendat? Why in the world would Lu—"

"He probably—Mom, listen—he probably got one of his uncles to dress up like a cop, okay? Stop freaking out!"

When her son said this, she exhaled in a way that Marc knew she had just put a hand to her head. Imagining this made Marc smile and miss her that much more. Deep down, his heart ached to be in the safety of his little home with his mom again, and he hated this feeling, for Marc mistook it for some sort of inner weakness.

He missed her, yes, but he also knew he couldn't endanger her life by letting her know what was really happening; he knew how worried she would be.

"Well, this is ridiculous that Luke went to all this trouble just to play a prank, or find out where you are," she said. "I'm going to call his mother right now."

"Mom, no!"

"This is serious, Marc! What kind of a weirdo is his uncle, anyway?"

"Please, mom. You always tell me to start handling things. Let me handle this, okay? I know it scared you. Let me take care if it."

"Marc—"

"Please? I swear I'll find out exactly why he did it, okay? I wanna know what's going on as much as you," he said.

She paused, and finally gave in. "I don't know why God made me your mother. In the last few years, I always give in to what you want more than not."

Marc's mind was awash in the relief that she didn't push the issue further. He knew it was probably because she was tired, and a tinge of anger welled inside him about how much her boss made her work.

"Maybe it's because I don't ask for much?" he asked, and she sighed again.

"That's true, my boy," she said with a weary tenderness he missed. "Okay," she said, exhaling her last worried sigh. "Fake cops showing up and scaring the bejeesus out of me is the least of it." Then she whispered, "So many strange things lately," she whispered to herself, under her breath.

"Like what? Mom, tell me," Marc said.

"Oh, nothing, honey."

"No, really. Tell me," he asked.

"It's really nothing. The neighbors across the street still play their music too loud when I have to sleep, and I had a weird dream about your father, but it's—"

"What happened in the dream, Mom?"

"Such a random dream. It's not—well, your dad was there, in Spain, where his family is originally from, and we were talking, and then he turns into some kind of a serpent and tells me to stop worrying so much. So crazy."

"That *is* crazy, Mom," Marc said, a corner of his mouth tugging at a smile, his eyes mystified by it all.

"Well, enough of my dumb stuff. I miss you, honey," she said.

"I miss you, too, Mom, and don't worry. I'll talk to Luke and his mom for you."

"Yes! Tell him it wasn't funny; it wasn't funny at all!" his mom said.

"I will, I promise. He probably wanted some showy way of trying to find out exactly where I was."

"Well, he gave me a heart attack. Tell him I didn't like that one bit!"

"Okay."

"Okay, what?" she asked.

"Okay, Mom. I swear I'll tell him!"

"Yes, but don't swear, honey," Jenny teased, and Marc could tell she seemed happier knowing it was all just a joke. "Actually, no," she corrected herself. "Forget that. You have my permission to swear at him a lot this time!" They chuckled, talked about a few other things, like his mom's raise at work—an extra fifty cents an hour—and yes, she said it was fine to be with Steve's family for another few days after Marc lied about all the museums he was going to and how much he was getting out of the experience. He felt bad about lying, but felt it was worth her not worrying. Now he sort of understood why his mom lied about his father for so long.

When Marc got off the phone, Jen had just come out of the small bathroom dressed in the same clothes as the day before, a towel around her head. She turned off the light as Marc asked her the address of the Dragonlair property. She told him, and he and his heart sank together onto the unmade motel bed.

"What's wrong?" Jen asked.

"That's the same address Steve gave my mom," said Marc.

"Steve gave your mom the address of the Dragonlair? What an idiot!"

"It's a problem."

"Why?" Jen asked, dabbing her wet, shoulder-length hair with the towel.

"Had a dream last night, and I think it was a warning," said Marc.

"Yeah?" she said, her voice still a question mark.

"Yeah. Some military guys wearing black showed up at my house asking for me, saying that I was in trouble, but wouldn't say why, and she gave them the address."

"Wait. This happened in your dream?"

"No, this *really happened*. Some guys dressed like a SWAT team just left my house, and they were asking for me, saying I was in some kind of trouble, and my mom gave them the address to the Dragonlair."

"You really think they're going to attack the Dragonlair? How do you know what they want?"

"Well, I guess I don't, really. All I have is that dream last night and what my mom told me. But I know for a fact that they're not cops and they're not planning on giving every Sorceron a restaurant gift card," Marc said, and Jen fought a smile.

"Yeah," she said, then walked over to her bed and lay down. "It's good we're not there."

"We have to help them, Jen," Marc said.

"Help the Sorceron? Yeah, sure we do," said Jen.

"I'm serious, Jen. We have to help them."

"Wait. You want to help the same people who almost killed us?" she asked, her eyebrows bunched in confusion.

"I know it sounds weird, but I feel like I have to. The rest of the Sorceron shouldn't have to pay for Victor ordering my execution."

She looked at him like he had just farted green Jell-O out the top of his head. "Marc, you know most of them don't question what Victor says. They just do it. They're all trying to kill you now—kill *us* now!"

"But it's my fault that those guys are targeting the Dragonlair in the first place," Marc said. "I don't know who they are, or how they found me, I don't know at all, but I still feel responsible."

Jen sighed, and the bed let out a squeak when she sat up.

"Let me call. I'll warn them," said Jen, reaching for the motel's phone. There was a pause, and she cursed with an aggravated sigh. "Stupid Victor. He always changes the phone number. Hold on," she said, and dialed again. After a moment, another curse word. "I tried calling Marah, but Victor must have collected all the phones again. Either that, or she's just not answering, but since the Dragonlair's main line was switched, I bet you anything it's another one of Victor's paranoid things he does."

When Jen mentioned Marah, a sting of worry struck Marc's mind, but he pushed it away.

"I'll go by myself. I'll just do what I can to help, then I'll leave," Marc offered.

"No, you'll get yourself killed," she said, sitting on the bed, deep in thought, and there was a pause. "How long does it take to get from your house to the Dragonlair?" she asked.

"About two hours by car."

"So with all this talking, and you on the phone with your mom, that gives us just over an hour, and if you subtract the time it'll take us to get back to the Lair, it's right about an hour. So, if we're gonna do this, we have exactly one hour to teach you a couple things about how to seek the Vibe when it comes to using your powers."

"I'll drink some lix."

"Yes. That's good," she said, and sighed. "Well, I can't believe we're doing this, and I think you're insane. There. I said it. I'm blaming you if we get killed," she said flatly, her eyes serious.

Marc knew she wasn't joking.

Thirty-Four

Preparation for Battle

With the clock ticking, Jen and Marc stood outside next to a field, the surrounding forest beyond that; behind them was the parking lot to Jasper's, a local sit-down diner that served classic dishes in a building made of fading, grayish brown wood.

"Okay," Jen said. "Are you ready?"

"Yeah," Marc said, breathing nervously, eyeing a lonely, gray tree branch ten feet away they had picked out. "But what if I suck, like my Firespewing?"

"No one accomplished anything great while they were afraid of doing it," Jen said, and Marc resented her dollar-ninety-nine wisdom, even though he knew it was true.

"Just relax. And I'm not talking about falling-asleep relax. Just focus on your breathing."

"Wait. So, you mean, just pay attention to it?"

"Yeah. That's it. Breathing is the only thing you can do that's not only involuntary, but also voluntary."

"Well, I can jump around to get my heart going," Marc countered.

"Yeah, but you can't just sit there and make your heart beat faster by thinking about it."

"Ah, I see," said Marc. "And what does that have to do with this again?"

"You don't think about it. That's the point. So, if you're focusing on your breathing, thinking about it, you'll automatically start to relax because your body's always trying to stay balanced, okay?"

"Uh, okay," Marc said, and he stared at the branch, lifting his hand toward it.

Nothing.

"Oh, one more thing," she said. "Have fun."

"Have fun," Marc repeated flatly, as if she had just said *the way to drive a car is use the pedals correctly, and the steering wheel, and the buttons—Oh! And also make sure you bring cotton candy, because that's what makes the car go.*

Marc turned back to the dead branch with unamused eyes, concentrating. They waited thirty seconds, but still nothing.

Marc let out an exasperated exhale, doubt creeping into his mind. "What am I doing wrong?" Marc asked.

"Nothing," said Jen, looking around again. "Look. Maybe you're focusing too much on the end result," she said, but Marc still looked confused.

"It has to do with letting go—a playing kind of attitude. I'll tell you how it was explained to me, okay? You know when you first played basketball?"

"You were there?" asked Marc with a smirk.

"Shut up. No," said Jen, continuing. "But you know how you start shooting a basketball and suddenly you start making a lot more baskets than you normally would?"

"Yeah."

"Some people call it beginner's luck," she said. "Well, it's pretty much the same thing, but it's not beginner's luck. It's just that you know you're not good, so you relax and let go, and you don't focus on the end result, and suddenly, voila! Your shots are going into the hoop."

"Oh, cool, okay," Marc said. "Let me see," he said, as a distant car alarm sounded for three full seconds. Annoyed, Marc tried to concentrate, but after another thirty more seconds, the branch still hadn't moved.

The same self-doubt began to threaten his mind, taunting him, mocking how pathetic he was.

"Aaaaaaaauuugh!" Marc yelled in frustration, trying his best to fight against his dark thoughts. "What the—?"

"Just get in touch with what's inside you," Jen said.

"Maybe I need something outside me, because what's inside isn't working," Marc said, frustration in his voice and anger in his eyes.

"Maybe all this advice is just confusing you," she said. "They call it being in a Zen state. It's the best way to access the Vibe. Uh," she lingered on the word, thinking of a new way to explain. "In sports they call it being in the zone, and, um, in acting, they call it . . ." she looked up. "Something else. I can't rememb—"

"Being in the moment?" offered Marc.

"That's it! Yes. That's it for acting. So, be in the moment! Don't think about helping the Sorceron, don't think about anything. Stay in the moment and try it again. We have to get something to eat soon if we're going to get there in time."

"So, uh, let me remember what I have to do here: relax, focus, don't think of the end result, have fun—but we have to hurry?" Marc asked sarcastically.

"Just go!"

Marc turned back to the branch, closed his eyes, gave a harsh sigh to summon a best effort, and pointed his hand toward it.

After thirty seconds, still nothing.

He turned away from the log. "Aaaaaah! I suck at this!" Marc said, punctuating the sentence with an exasperated, angry wave of his arms.

When he did that, all twenty-seven cars in the parking lot lifted off the ground four inches and fell back down with heavy, groaning thuds.

Marc didn't see it, too busy staring at the ground in disgust, but Jen gaped in disbelief as if Elvis had just appeared.

Several car alarms going off at once made Marc look up. "Whuh—? Ah, great. I can make car alarms go off. Wonderful. That's my gift," said Marc sarcastically. "My Firespewing is for crap and I can't move anything unless it's an accident. I'm the worst Dragonkyn of all time in the history of Dragon, uh, people!" After giving his eloquent tantrum, he exhaled sharply and sat on the ground instead of whining any more in front of a girl whose opinion of him mattered. When Marc finally looked up at Jen, he couldn't read her expression.

Jen blinked, her face still looking like she just saw an infant dunk a basketball. A little out of breath, and starting the sentence with a higher pitch, she said, "I uh, I think you're going to be fine."

"Thanks," Marc said sarcastically, thinking she was just humoring or mocking him.

"No, really, Marc. You're gonna be fine." A pause, and then, "Uh, let's do a test," she said, throwing another glance back at the cars in the parking lot. "Try to lift me."

"Lift you?" asked Marc.

"Yeah. With your mind—and don't think so much! Just point your hand toward me and do it!"

Marc lifted his hand toward her, and as she lifted five feet, her body stiffened and bent slightly.

Marc gasped. "I—I did it! I did it! I mean, I'm doing it!" he yelled excitedly, his outstretched hand still pointing at her like a boy holding a kite with invisible string.

"Put me down before someone sees!"

Jen fell hard, splaying out on the dirt and grass. "You're gonna have to work on that," she said with effort as he helped her up.

Squeezing his hand, she faced him, her eyes burning with the momentous declaration. "Marc, you're an omni-telekinetic."

He waited for the punchline. "A what?" Marc asked.

"Marc," she said, her eyes still wide. "You can move more than one kind of thing! I've never heard of that before—at least not with any Dragonkyn around here! You not only lifted every single car in that parking lot, you also lifted something *alive!* Me!

"Wait. I lifted every—"

"Every car in that parking lot! Yes!" she said excitedly, enunciating it louder so he got it.

His constant self-doubt briefly left him alone. "Shut up," Marc said, his disbelieving eyes wide, with a smile. He threw a fist into the air in celebration. "Yes!"

"And even though you need a lot of practice," she said, "I feel a lot better about facing guys with guns now, that's for sure."

Even her backhanded compliment couldn't dampen Marc's spirits. He was psyched, thoroughly enjoying the fact that he didn't have to feel like a liability anymore.

THIRTY-FIVE

Long Lost Friend

It was at the peak of late breakfast rush when the waiter brought them their food at Jasper's, and Jen reminded Marc they had just over twenty minutes to eat and get outta there.

After most of their quick eating was done, Marc asked, "I seriously lifted every single car out there four inches?"

"Well, maybe there was a big truck or two that only went up two, but holy crimeny, man! Most Dragonkyn can't even lift one car, let alone thirty at once!" She whispered it intensely as she grabbed three fries, eating fast.

"Okay. Here's the plan," Marc said, his mouth still full from inhaling his food, but before he could swallow his food to talk more, an impatient Jen jumped in.

"The plan is," she said, still chewing fries, "when we get close to the Dragonlair, we ditch the car and sneak into the woods."

"We—Wait. The car?"

"Yeah. The one we're going to steal to get there," Jen said, a self-assured, sassy smirk on her face. At his look, she said, "I don't think we'll make it there in time if we hitchhike, and we don't have enough money to buy one, brainiac."

"Yeah, yeah," Marc said, feigning confidence. "I knew that, I just wish we didn't have to steal one," he said.

Jen chuckled at his boy-scout ethics, and just as she did . . .

Color drained from her face.

She stared forward, her mouth searching for the breath to speak. The look in her eyes alone scared Marc more than anything, and the hairs on the back of his neck stood on end.

"Jen—?"

"There's a Dragonkyn in here besides us," she said, her hands shaking.

"In here? How do you know?"

"I just know," she said with panicked breath, her eyes looking like someone just pulled a pin on a grenade she held in her hand.

Marc knew she was better at using the Vibe, and he immediately knew that this was how she sensed another Dragonkyn there in the dining area. Marc looked around, trying to figure out who it was, when Jen suddenly got up from the table, following a tall guy with sunglasses out to the parking lot.

Marc started to follow her, but when the guy at the cash register yelled at him, he returned and paid for their lunch.

Questions burned his mind. *Why did she follow that guy? Is she okay? Is she trying to attack him on her own?*

Outside the restaurant, the sound of an occasional car passed, and a light breeze teased Jen's hair. When she tentatively approached the young man in the sunglasses, he looked up at her with a reluctant grin.

"How you been, Jen?" the tall teen asked with a steady voice, and Jen's eyes were a blank.

"Alex," was all that came out.

THIRTY-SIX

Sorry for the Radio Silence

A few minutes later, Marc had joined them in the parking lot, the sound of passing cars giving way to the sound of the tall kid apologizing. "I should have contacted you, Jen, I'm sorry. But I knew doing that would have put you in the middle of it. That would have gotten you hurt, knowing how paranoid Victor is," he said.

"Victor made us believe that you were dead," she began, but emotion took the rest of the words.

"I know. I'm sorry," was all Alex said, taking off his sunglasses.

"Marc, this is Alex," Jen said, her eyes not leaving the tall, dark-haired guy. Marc and Alex exchanged guarded hellos, and Jen continued. "Where, uh," she said, biting a lip, "where have you been this last year?" All the while, as Marc watched them, Marc was self-conscious. He could tell Alex was older than Jen, by a year? Two? He wasn't sure. Marc's self-consciousness, however, didn't stop there. No, Alex was also *handsome*. Period. He was tall, and Marc could tell that the reason for his deeply tanned skin wasn't all from the sun. His intelligent, striking-but-mellow dark eyes peered out from beneath a mop of thick, black, wavy hair, parts of which flowed down to his collar.

"I've been around, spent some time in Arizona on the rez with some of my family," Alex said.

"Did you sense Victor was going to kill you?" Jen asked.

"Yeah. Vibe told me. I sensed he was going to turn everyone against me, and it's a good thing I did."

"But why are you back?" she asked.

Marc hadn't seen a guy this good-looking outside of a TV commercial, and it bugged him. He could tell that Alex and Jen had been something of an item when he was with the Sorceron because of the way she acted around him. As they stood and talked, Jen quickly fixed her hair more than once. It was the first time Jen ever gave any indication that she cared how she looked.

"I stayed in touch with my seventy-fifth," he said, leaning against his black Chevy Camaro. Jen quickly explained to Marc. "His grandpa," she said, her head leaning in, eyes not leaving Alex.

"He said he had a vision," Alex said, "that the Sorceron were in trouble, but that someone else had been found. Another Dragonkyn, I guess. Someone who would change everything."

"Change everything? What does that mean?" Jen asked, and Marc wanted to tease her about repeating people, but he didn't.

"Not my words. That's how Naali said it," Alex said, raising a hand in defense. "People never have a Vision Quest for someone else, Naali said, but he told me that the vision he had was meant to get me to do something about it, so here I am."

There was a pause, and then, his eyes never leaving Jen's, Alex continued.

"I'm so sorry for the radio silence, Jen. I am. But the Sorceron wanted me six feet down."

"I know how you feel," said Marc, and Alex looked at him suspiciously at first.

"Victor tried to kill you too?" asked Alex.

"It must be going around," Marc said, trying to be casual about it.

Alex looked at him, the first glint of confusion in his eyes, and Jen gave him a brief account of what happened. As she did, Alex looked at Marc differently, his eyes narrowing ever so slightly at times. He seemed to be studying Marc as Jen spoke of their adventure, and Marc felt uncomfortable, like a contestant on a game show when the announcer tells the audience his biography.

When she was done, Alex turned to Marc. "You must be a powerful Dragonkyn for Victor to target you."

"I guess," said Marc. After he said it, he figured Alex probably meant it as a genuine conversation starter about their powers, but Marc had taken it as a compliment one would give at a party.

"Jump in," Alex said, gesturing to the black Camaro, and soon they were on the road back to the Dragonlair.

They mostly talked about all that had happened in the year they were separated, and the only time Marc didn't feel slightly uncomfortable as they drove back to the Dragonlair was when Jen excitedly told him about Marc being an omni-telekinetic.

"This kid has more potential than any newbie I've seen at the Lair in a while," she said.

What brought back the discomfort was Jen speaking about Marc as if he weren't there. *Great,* Marc thought. *I'm just the third wheel.*

Get a grip, Mondragon, Marc told himself. They had something important to do here.

THIRTY-SEVEN

Defending the Lair

"What's the game plan?" Jen asked.

"Warn the Sorceron about these guys somehow," said Marc.

The Dragonlair was on a dirt road called Miner's Drive, across from a small ranger's station set back among the trees.

"But how? I've tried reaching Marah's cell phone and there's no answer. Same with texting."

"What about your mind control?" asked Marc.

"It's my lesser power. If they're more than fifty feet away, it doesn't work."

"Well," said Marc, "I say we just go there and warn 'em. If they try anything, we run, but hopefully they'll listen."

"Uh, guys?" Jen asked, looking into the rearview mirror. "I think the bad guys are behind us."

Marc looked behind him and saw a heavy-duty para-military truck forty feet behind them going the same speed. He waved to make them think he was younger, then spun and sank in his seat, his eyes wide, heart racing, the feeling of hundreds of pins against his skin

"Who are they?" Jen asked, her eyes still on the mirror.

"I have no idea, but they're not cops. They just told my mom they were," said Marc.

"Our plan to warn the Sorceron may have to switch to fighting these guys," said Jen.

"They outnumber us," said Alex. "We can't let them see us going into the Lair. We have to take 'em by surprise."

"I agree," said Jen.

Perpendicular to Miner's Drive, two hundred yards past the Dragonlair entrance, was another dirt road called Vallejo that led to other ranch properties away from Dragonlair, all carved up into parcels of undeveloped forest. Miner's Drive, Vallejo, and the two other dirt roads that connected them appeared to anyone visiting as a big square block of dirt road in the middle of the woods.

Alex's Camaro drove past the Dragonlair entrance and pulled left onto Vallejo. They flipped a U-turn and pulled over.

"Eyes?"

"On it," said Alex, his face still and stoic, his gaze fixed on the sparse trees that stood between them and the Dragonlair entrance. Marc's face said, *translate this cryptic lingo please?*

Marc looked through the trees and couldn't figure out how anyone could see the entrance to the Dragonlair property from this far away.

"Are they storming the Lair?" asked Jen.

"No. They're just sitting there—more than three vehicles, not sure how many more," said Alex.

"Let me know when they get out of their cars," Jen said, masking the fear in her voice. "Look, I know we're doing this, and we're committed to it, but if . . ." she said, her words trailing off. "I mean, I just wonder—if we kill others to defend our friends, I wonder what that makes us."

"It makes us Dragonkyn," said Alex, and Marc nodded in solidarity.

After a moment, Jen responded. "I know," she said, her eyes pensive. "I just wonder how it'll change us, and how much of that change we'll actually want."

They were quiet as Jen again tried calling to warn Marah. There was no response.

THIRTY-EIGHT

The Rogue

Every once in a while, a break in a case came through a crazy miracle of a coincidence, like the incident at the fancy restaurant when O'Leary overheard the guy named Drakesel talking on the phone. It had been at least a decade since a great lead in a case like that had plopped so effortlessly into O'Leary's lap, though the detective had to admit to himself that rarely had a break like this spawned so many more questions than it answered.

So, on a hunch, O'Leary decided to stake out random warehouses or businesses owned by Drakesel, a different one every night, for a half hour to an hour on his own time after work, just to see what he could find.

After a bit of research, he learned that Drakesel's family's holdings included a large variety of businesses across several industries. Most of the businesses his family owned created copycat products, cheap knock-offs of the brands that commanded the largest market share in a given industry. On this particular night, he sat in his unmarked police car, the one he'd been assigned to since becoming a detective, in the industrial section of Brooklyn at one of Drakesel's textile factories. The Drakesel family's position in the textile industry was one of the more respectable ones of their many businesses.

The building was old, built at the turn of the twentieth century, and the former swamp beneath it slowly tried to reclaim it through cracks in the pavement. It was hulking and nondescript, with all the curb appeal of an abandoned Soviet-era apartment building. *Looks like parts o' Patterson*, O'Leary thought with a chuckle, casting his eyes about, setting his thermos and camping gear on the passenger seat of his car: fire-proof blanket, his firearm, and several packages of sugary carbohydrates.

With its windows bleached a cloudy gray with age, O'Leary's nondescript, ten-year-old sedan was the perfect stakeout car for this task, perfectly matching the forlorn, abandoned look of the buildings in every direction. O'Leary positioned the car across the street from the small, gravel parking lot on the building's west side.

O'Leary felt an itch on his hip, and the car slightly rocked and squeaked as he reached to scratch it. Maybe nothing ever would come of it, he figured, but he had learned to follow his hunches, as boring or far-fetched as they might be—even if sometimes he only found petty crimes—and his wife was used to him staying late, chasing down clues at all hours. When his thoughts wandered, they would often turn cynical about the strangest things, and now was no exception. *Balloons*, he wondered. *What's up with giving people a balloon? Happy birthday. Here's a round rubbery ball holding my breath. Yeah. Nice gift.*

His cell phone rang. It was Frank, his friend and fellow detective he had known for years.

"Hey," is all the greeting he gave.

"Where you at tonight?"

"Brooklyn," O'Leary said. "At the textile mill, just down from the turnpike."

"Yeah, I know it."

"You know it?"

"Never felt a need to go there, but I know it," Frank said with a quarter chuckle. "How long you been out there, half hour?"

"About that," O'Leary said, and Frank laughed.

"Come on! Grab a beer with me already. How many times I gotta ask?"

"Yeah, yeah, okay," O'Leary said. "You're right."

"I know I'm right, war horse," said Frank.

That's when O'Leary saw them. Two boys. Couldn't have been much older than fifteen, who looked like they both shopped at the same ratty hoodlum outfitter, sneaking up to the perimeter of the factory's fence. *Great,* O'Leary thought. *Another petty crime.* But something was different with these two, and he leaned forward and narrowed his eyes to get a better view.

"I got a couple a prowlers is all," O'Leary told Frank with an exasperated sigh.

One of the boys sniffed the air like a dog, casting his eyes about, while the other was crouched, holding a small blowtorch near his face, trying to make a hole in the chainlink fence. O'Leary took the small binoculars from his car's glove compartment, and when he brought them to his eyes, his brain couldn't accept what he was seeing. He narrowed his eyes again.

The small blowtorch he thought the boy held wasn't a blowtorch at all. The flame came directly from the boy's mouth.

O'Leary lowered and raised the binoculars, convinced they were the culprit responsible for tricking his eyes. After watching a bit more, O'Leary finally swallowed.

"Frank, call it in for me, two-eleven in progress," O'Leary said.

"Seriously? A two-eleven? There?" asked Frank.

"Just call it in. Send me a car," O'Leary said.

"Okay."

O'Leary dropped his cell phone onto his seat, wrapped the fireproof blanket he had purchased around him, then put his firearm back into its shoulder holster.

And stepped out of the car.

A patch of fence glowed orange from the fire, and as he approached, the boy who had sniffed the air grabbed it with his bare hands, tearing it away. O'Leary let out a little snort of a laugh, the kind that happens when people witness something they can't make sense of.

The boys seemed to know that O'Leary was approaching, but they made no oh-no-we're-caught movements, as if what they were doing was perfectly legal.

"You boys lost?" asked O'Leary, and the sniffing boy looked up. His hair was greasy blond, his face oblong and asymmetrical, with large lips and gums, a perpetual sneer.

"Well," the boy said with a thick Cockney accent, adding to the surreal nature of the moment. "If it ain't the ol' Pot-n-Pan," he said confidently.

"What are you boys doin' at this hour, huh? What could you ever want outta this place?" O'Leary asked.

"We're takin' a bit of a tour, 'ere, guv'nuh," said the boy. "What are *you* doin' out 'ere?"

O'Leary's left hand was wrapped around one end of the fireproof blanket draped over his shoulders, and his right hand was ready to reach for his gun. "I'm a cop," O'Leary said.

"Oooooh," the boys mockingly cried, as if this was going to put the fear of God into them.

Blowtorch boy was dark haired, with a scar on his left temple. He approached with a disconcerting gait, trying to put O'Leary between himself and sniffing boy, but O'Leary moved with him, footfalls carefully stepping back, making sure both boys were in front of him.

"Can't you see we're busy?" asked the blond, sniffing boy.

"Yeah, we're busy, ol' hodger," agreed the other.

They continued creeping toward O'Leary and he continued backing up. For the first time in a while, he felt his life was in danger even though he was armed and they weren't.

O'Leary took out his gun, and the boys stared at it dumbly.

"You kids get out of here, ya hear me?" O'Leary said with a commanding tone, but their silent laughter sent a chill up his spine.

The gun magically came out of O'Leary's hand and, disbelieving, O'Leary weakly reached for it, eyes wide, as it hovered in the air. Seconds later, the gun was thirty feet away from him.

Just as Blowtorch began to speak, Sniffing Boy opened fire from his mouth, spitting it at O'Leary, but O'Leary didn't cover his face with the blanket in time.

The distant cry of a police siren filled the air, the shower of flame stopped, and after finishing him off, the boys ran away at a leisurely pace, not a care in the world. Sniffing boy threw a "Sod off, tossuh!" over his shoulder as they made their escape with a laugh.

A week later, at the funeral, there were lots of flags. Frank and other detectives served as pallbearers, and there were many tears shed for O'Leary. He'd been a good cop, a good husband and friend.

This was not the end he deserved.

Far from it.

As is always the case when a police officer is killed, the department spared no expense to find his killer, but despite best efforts, it would be several years before anyone figured out exactly what had happened to him.

THIRTY-NINE

The Best-Laid Plans . . .

Movement," said Alex.

"Attack mode?" Jen asked.

"No. Looks like they're waiting for final orders," said Alex, and Jen jumped out of the car before anyone could say anything else.

"Recon duty," she said as she ran from the Camaro toward Dragonlair through the sparse trees.

Alex shook his head with an admiring smile.

"She's going by herself?" asked Marc.

"She's a better shot than any of us," Alex said.

"But that's dangerous!" Marc said, his voice rising.

"That's Jen, bro. She's fearlessly loyal to her friends," Alex said. "Don't worry, Belegana."

Marc didn't know what belegana meant, but he figured it was some word in Navajo. After five tense minutes, Alex sat up straight. "She's motioning something—telling us to wait here."

Marc looked around, confused. "Where? Where is she?"

"Through those trees," Alex said, but Marc couldn't see anything from the back seat and couldn't imagine Alex being able to see anything either.

Unless . . .

"You can see a long ways away, right?" Marc asked, and Alex only nodded. "Is that your greater power?" Marc asked, and again Alex only nodded.

"How good is your eyesight?" Marc asked quietly.

"Probably twice as good as an eagle," he said. "I dunno, maybe better, but I can control it. Depends on what I need to see."

"That's awesome," said Marc.

"I can also see with others' eyes if I have to, but that takes a lot of energy," said Alex flatly, like he'd already explained this many times and was bored with it.

"Ever wonder why we have the different powers we have?" Marc asked. "It just seems so random."

"Well, the word *dragon* comes from a verb the ancient Greeks had, meaning 'to see strong.' Maybe that had something to do with mine, but who knows." Alex said this distantly, his eyes turning concerned, looking in the rearview mirror. Alex got out of the car as an armored Dodge Charger sedan the color of gray primer approached from behind. He stood inside the open door of his Camaro, facing the car when it stopped.

The cloud of dust in the sedan's wake arrived to greet them as it stopped. Alex stared at the driver as he got out, and darted a glance at Marc in the back seat.

Do something, Marc silently implored him, but Alex stood perfectly still. The driver, a toughy in his mid thirties clad in black tactical gear, wandered toward them with the keys to his vehicle dangling from a hand.

"Jen, you're beautiful," Alex muttered under his breath. Marc just watched, mouth agape.

Toughy seemed in a daze. "I'm supposed to give you these," he said, nearing Alex.

"Yes, thank you," Alex said, taking the keys. "Oh, and I'll take the gun, too" he said. Toughy undid his holster and handed Alex his nine-millimeter auto, including three extra clips. "Continue walking through those trees," Alex commanded, and the man obeyed, wandering into the forest in the opposite direction of the Dragonlair.

Jen returned a moment later, running. "Let's go!" she said, jumping into Alex's driver's side while Alex and Marc took the armored sedan.

When Toughy got a few hundred yards into the forest, Jen's spell over his mind must have faded, because as they turned around to regroup, he came storming out of the trees, angry as a scalding wound.

Marc heard the short chirp-zip-sounds of a pistol just as white stars appeared on the passenger side window.

Toughy had another gun, apparently.

The bulletproof glass of Toughy's passenger seat window was the only thing that saved Marc from a bullet to the head. Alex had the armored sedan already pointed back in the direction it had come from, and when Toughy came barrelling out of the forest, gun blazing, Alex had his driver-side window down. He jumped up on the driver's side door, and with his arm extending over the roof of Toughy's car, Alex shot him between the eyes with his own nine-millimeter. Marc heard himself involuntarily expel a short, shocked shout even before Alex fired, and his teeth pulsed with an ache when the gun went off. His mind spun when he saw Toughy drop like a limp doll into the dirt.

They drove around to the far side of the big dirt square opposite the Dragonlair to regroup. Both cars pulled around the corner in case anyone heard the shots.

When they got out to plan, Jen spoke fast. "There are seven vehicles total," she said, still out of breath. "Two heavily armored trucks, two jeeps, and three armored sedans, but now we have this," she said, gesturing to the gray Dodge she had used her powers to get. "They were all parked on the side of the road, all in a line, near the Dragonlair entrance, but I'm not sure how many men are in those cars. As many as twenty, as few as eight, I'm guessing. This sedan was in the back of the line of cars, and just as they were parking, I suggested to his brain that he come around these back roads and join us."

"Great job, Jen," Alex said.

Marc's eyes were still focused on Alex. "You—you killed him," Marc said in amazement.

"Yeah," Alex said, as if Marc asked him if he read left to right.

"You didn't see any of their equipment?" Alex asked Jen, gesturing to the four automatic weapons with ammunition in the back seat of the armored sedan.

"No, but I'm guessing by this stash that it's pretty severe. I would almost count on them having fireproofed everything," Jen said.

Before Alex could respond, his eyes went wide and he instinctively aimed the 9mm towards something over Jen's shoulder.

As soon as Marc heard Alex's gun bark once, he and Jen ducked behind the armored car and a cacophony of discharging weapons burst upon Marc's ears, eclipsing every other sound.

A millisecond later, Alex was crouched next to Marc.

"Three of them!" Alex screamed above the angry bullets digging into the sedan, seeking vital organs but failing.

It was then, when Alex's left hand took the nine-millimeter from his right, that Marc noticed a bullet had gone through Alex's right hand. Dark blood gushed from the hole in his palm, but Alex ripped off part of his shirt to put a tourniquet at his wrist, his lips curled into a painful smile.

"Spew fire! I'll bend it!" Alex yelled to Jen.

"Hold on!" Jen said. "Follow me first!"

Marc tied Alex's tourniquet, and Alex shook with pain, but then nodded. Their eyes darted around as the car moved. As if it were on marionette wires, the armored sedan slowly turned sideways, almost blocking the dirt road, pushing the gravelly earth beneath it.

The approaching three men in black ops gear were distinguishable by what they wore: the first man wore a beard. The second man wore sunglasses, or shades, and the third man, an older guy, had salt and pepper colored hair. The men paused for a moment when the armored sedan moved by itself. They continued cautiously, twenty yards from the car and closing in on it. Marc moved to the other side of Jen, opened the back door, and grabbed two rifles, but when he looked up through the window, Beard had broken into a run and was almost to the car.

Marc dropped one of the rifles while he got out and shut the back door.

As he was doing this, Jen's laser fire from her mouth shot straight up and magically bent, twisting back down. Marc turned to Alex and saw him staring up at it, his eyes completely focused.

The hot, thin line of fire hit the ground on the other side of the sedan as if probing for a target, small tendrils of white smoke caressing it near the dirt. But then the entire fiery laser bent just above the sedan, shooting straight out, hitting Beard in the eye when he was three yards from the car. The thin laser line stopped just as his feet came out from under him, and his body hit the gravel, skidding to the car.

Shades and Older-guy looked at each other and retreated to their armored jeep. For the first twenty yards, the two paramilitaries sprayed bullets as they swiftly walked backward, the bullets thudding dully into the armored sedan. It was only when they were twenty yards from the jeep that Shades and Older-guy turned their backs and ran.

Older-guy got two bullets in the back and went down hard.

This isn't happening! a part of Marc shouted. Days ago he was a normal kid, and now he was fighting for his life? Sweat above his brow, Marc pushed away the fear as best he could by exhaling hard twice. Gripping the military standard-issue rifle, Marc spun and fired, hearing himself shout as he did, since he'd never before shot at a person, even one trying to kill him. Though he peppered the armored jeep's windshield with white stars, a bullet didn't land at the base of Shades's skull until Alex took the rifle from Marc and aimed better.

Shades fell as he got to the Jeep's driver's side door.

Marc was dazed and weak with jitters. As he sank to the ground behind the armored sedan, his shoes sounding like a velcro rip against the dirt road, Marc noticed Jen sitting there with her phone out.

"You're texting?" Marc shouted.

"I'm still trying to reach Marah—I wanted to bend all their minds to stop this attack before it started, but it brought the fight to us instead!"

"Why can't you use your mind powers now?" yelled Marc.

"I tried! It's not working!" she said. In response to his look, she said, "I've never done it before while I was being shot at, okay? We haven't been able to help the Sorceron," she said. "They have no idea—"

The deafening sound of an explosion from the direction of the Dragonlair took the rest of her words, knocking her into Marc.

Her head snapped back in the blast's direction. "I'm going to Dragonlair," Jen said, her hand against the sedan to stand. "Make sure they're down. See you there. Meet you at Jasper's if we get separated." Jen seemed to intuit Marc and Alex's collective nod in agreement, because she never looked back to see it. She ran full speed through the trees.

Marc and Alex quickly but tentatively approached the armored jeep. As Marc dragged his still-shaking body forward, keeping up with Alex, he felt like he'd just been through the most intense video game ever invented. He knew he and his friends could have died. Marc's heart still raced, and his breathing had only slowed a little.

When they neared the jeep and saw that the bodies hadn't moved, they relaxed. "We can use these weapons against them," said Alex. "Let's—"

A shot went off.

Alex dropped to his knees hard, his eyes bewildered, dark pools, and Marc dove to the other side of the jeep just as another round screamed past his ear.

By the time Marc hit the ground, he had put it together; Older-guy, the one with two bullets in his back, must have been wearing bulletproof Kevlar and had played dead. He had slowly rolled over and shot Alex through his chest, and tried to get Marc too.

Alex lay on the ground, the nine millimeter still in his left hand, and Marc's dawning knowledge that he left the rifle at the car turned his blood to ice. Sure, he could heal from a couple of bullets eventually, but he wasn't so sure about a lot of bullets or a shot to the head.

"You little freaks!" Older-guy grunted with a pinched brow and nervous breath. Marc could tell he was slowly standing to come around the jeep and finish him off.

Thoughts raced. Marc had no idea what he could possibly do, crouched there, unarmed on the supposedly safe side of an armored jeep. He could use his powers, but what if they didn't work? What if he screwed up?

He had had it clear in his mind how this was supposed to work out. They would come up here and they would warn the Sorceron who were training for a war against 'the humans' that the war would be arriving at their doorstep a lot sooner than they realized. But now, all of those plans were shattered like bits of glass on a dirt road. Instead of warning or saving the Sorceron in a blaze of glory, that task was left to Jen alone. Alex was shot, and here Marc was, cowering behind a jeep, hoping to stay alive.

His confidence wavered as the doubts flooded his mind. Marc heard Older-guy's first ragged footstep on the dirt road, a scuffing sound, louder than usual in his stressed-out state of mind.

Suddenly, in a moment of clarity, Marc knew he had to access the Vibe. Things Steve had said made him doubt it even existed, but he felt it inside, simmering beneath all other emotions like a pilot light. He thought of the lessons Jen had said earlier: contain your fear, stay in the moment, don't think of the end result, let go, be relaxed yet focused. Be confident, yes, trust in your training, yes, but one thought—as unexciting as it was—reigned over them all.

Focus on your breathing.

FORTY

GETTING HELP

Marc focused on his breathing.

His eyes were shut, beads of sweat impersonating tears in microscopic pools on the skin surrounding his eyes.

Suddenly, something Jen said to him during his training jumped into his mind like a hurricane's eye, interrupting the swirling self-doubt that plagued him, "No one accomplished anything great while they were afraid of doing it."

Marc closed his eyes, focused, and breathed, and as he lifted his arm, the jeep flew straight at Older-guy with the strength of a free-falling horizontal elevator, pinning Older-guy against the tree behind him with a metallic groan, crushing the life out of him, leaving only an empty half-smile on his face. Involuntary spasms in Older-guy's left arm squeezed off two more rounds from the nine-millimeter auto he still held, dirt and bark on the ground jumping; a small chip of dark wood bounced off Older guy's dying, vacant face.

Marc winced when he heard the shots. Deep in his heart, he knew it was dumb luck that Older-guy had been close to that tree. He also knew that had the jeep needed to move more than a few feet, he wouldn't have been able to do it. He'd be dead right now.

There wasn't time to dwell on it.

Marc half carried, half dragged a semi-conscious Alex to his car.

Briefly ignoring the jitters that teemed through him, and the luck with which he had just escaped death, Marc felt pumped—fresh confidence from being able to move the jeep to stop Older-guy—feeling like he could do anything. How hard can driving Alex's Camaro be? But when Marc took the wheel of Alex's Camaro, the confidence quickly evaporated. His driving was like a herky-jerky dance between the gas pedal, the clutch, and his inexperience. He tried his best to push through the self-doubt that once again tore through his thoughts, berating him for how bad he was at everything. As Alex's body jolted and shook with each lurch of the car trying to get into gear, Marc wondered how much Alex's own blood was healing him. He looked up and saw the smoke billowing from behind the Lair's main building as distant gunfire sounded.

"Alex. Alex! Are you healing? Tell me you're healing! If you are, I need to help the others . . ."

"Go," is all Alex said with effort, his eyes slits of pain.

After parking on the side of Miner's Drive, Marc got out and, crossing the street, saw the overturned armored trucks, one of which had barreled sideways into the entrance of the Dragonlair's main building, and he immediately knew it was Jen's handiwork. He coughed from the smoke still wafting out of the building's wound.

Marc's vision jerked and jolted as a huge blast wave rattled his knees, sending him to the ground.

Another huge explosion, from the far side of the meadow behind the main building. He looked up with fearful eyes scanning the building as his palms held the cool, pine-needle-strewn earth.

"Jen," the words escaped his mouth as a worried sigh.

When Marc got inside the main building, climbing over the big, armored truck that Jen had sent through the front entrance, he saw the Dragonlair battle's aftermath. Gagging at the sight and stench of blood that seeped from the bottom of the truck, Marc's eyes squinted against the smoke from the small fires on the floor. He got closer and realized that two of them were the bodies of fallen paramilitary toughies—friends of Beard,

Shades and Older-guy—their heads completely engulfed in flames. The vaulted ceiling of the main building loomed above him, and he took one of the two symmetrical staircases that led to the second-story landing overlooking the main entrance.

Two Sorceron from the seventy-sixth generation tended to the wounds of a Dragonkyn lying on his back on a stretcher on the floor. It wasn't clear who the wounded boy was, until Marc got closer.

Victor.

It took a moment to register, but when Victor's eyes showed recognition, there was a hint of surprise, followed by a look of indifferent bitterness.

"You . . ." he said quietly, and the Sorceron who attended to him now stopped to see the boy Victor spoke to, ". . . brought them here?" Victor said this with a seething hatred simmering beneath the words.

Marc's eyes looked confused, even angry. "No. No, I tried to stop them." He wanted to say more, that he returned despite Victor's orders to have him killed, that he did it for the other Sorceron, but Victor's face twisted in pain from his wounds. He turned away from Marc with a painful groan, and Marc knew this was the end of their conversation. A long, hard talk about why Victor had tried to have him killed would have to wait. The older Sorceron resumed their conversation about Victor's comfort, the wounds he sustained, and how easily he could be transported. Full recovery was expected.

Running down the hall, searching for Jen and Marah, Marc tried to see through the smoke of the fires still burning throughout the main building.

The back hallways were littered with the glass from the shattered windows that faced the meadow. *What could have exploded like that?*

It was then he heard the approaching sirens.

Marc hated the thought of abandoning his search for Jen and Marah, but didn't want anyone to take him into custody for questioning when Alex was still hurt in his car, and thought it best to meet up with Jen later, praying she was okay and that she'd at least be able to find Marah. Marc dashed out of the building and ran for the entrance of the property. The sirens were clear at first, a single song, but soon mixed with the wails, beeps, and electronic grunts of many other emergency vehicles.

The first responding vehicle was a fire engine, a big red block with chrome accessories that lumbered into the entrance as Marc reached it, coming the opposite way. The fireman at the wheel ignored Marc, or hadn't seen him.

He ran down the side of the road and crossed, walking to the car, trying not to call attention to himself. He coughed from the smoke still in the air. The bright afternoon sun made everything glow, and its heat condensed in Alex's dark Camaro. When Marc got in, he was met with the heat of a hundred blow dryers, and the black leather seat felt just as warm as the burner at his home when he first realized that the human experience of pain from burning no longer applied to him.

"Need...doctor . . . still . . . bleeding . . ." Alex said weakly, and with determined eyes, Marc drove carefully to Fairplay. He felt frustrated and swore a few times at the Camaro's stick-shift when the car lurched and pitched. A passing driver gave him a look of half-fear-half-anger. By the time Marc got onto the paved road, he felt a little better about driving, though he still wasn't sure about some of the road signs, or the difference between fourth and fifth gear.

His entire body tensed every time a cop car passed him, lights and sirens shrieking all the way to the Dragonlair in the opposite direction. Marc was sure any of them would pull him over at any moment, but they didn't. He didn't know how many laws he was currently breaking, but he knew that getting caught driving without a license, carrying a seventeen-year-old kid with a gunshot wound wouldn't be in his favor. His eyes were focused on two things, obeying the speed limit and driving as every other car drove, which wasn't easy. He winced when the rumble strips groaned at him loudly for driving too close to the edge of the road.

When Marc got back to Fairplay, he took Alex to a veterinarian—the first doctor's office he passed—explaining that he and his cousin were playing around with his dad's gun and it went off accidentally.He didn't want to go to a normal hospital because he knew they had to report stuff like that to the police. At six feet both ways, the veterinarian was a large man. His monotone voice asked Marc where his cousin was shot.

"In the chest, but I think it's more his shoulder."

"I think I need to call someone, kid," said the doctor.

"Uh, okay, but just look him over first, okay?" said Marc nervously, hoping to heaven Alex's blood was healing him as he and the doctor spoke.

The doctor gave him a quizzical look.

"Please!" Marc begged, and finally, the vet checked the wound.

The bullet had passed right through Alex, and as the doctor stitched him up, he explained what a miracle it was that Alex wasn't in more critical condition, given the location of Alex's bullet and exit wounds on his torso and back. The big, balding doctor sat on an older, complaining stool, breathing heavily as he stitched up Alex, and Marc noted, after his panic subsided, that it was the first time he'd seen a man breathing as heavily while sitting as anyone else would be while running.

"I can't believe I'm just treating this as a flesh wound. It must have just grazed his lungs, though I can't imagine how," the doctor said with labored breath.

Marc feigned an innocent expression, full of wonder about the 'miracle' that saved his 'cousin.'

Forty-One

Meanwhile, Back at the Lair . . .

When Jen reached the Dragonlair compound, the battle was already underway. She realized immediately that the enemy—wherever they'd come from—had no doubt correctly guessed that if these dragonkids were fireproof, grenades could blow them apart, killing them. She crossed the space between the entrance at Miner's Drive and the front of the Dragonlair's main building in twenty seconds and stopped when she saw two of the black-garbed goons standing just inside the front doors, spraying bullets into the main building. Screams erupted from those inside. Despite Jen's attempts to warn them, the attack had taken them completely by surprise. Men in black tactical gear, with special fireproof helmets that made them look like some sort of space cops, were fanning out, spraying the place with intermittent gunfire and grenade launchers.

With all of her telekinetic strength, her eyes focused with purpose, Jen lifted the nearby armored truck that brought these demons to their doorstep. It was heavy enough that it fell twice on the way, but after a few seconds, she was able to throw it through the front of the building with enough force that the high glass and dark wood of the entryway splintered and shattered like a little house of toothpicks stomped by a heavy boot. The impact instantly crushed the two men clad in black.

Until they watched their own military-grade vehicle go through the front of the building, Stone's men seemed confident in their task, but not now. After watching Taymor rip a helmet off one of their comrades and turn his head and body into a six-foot, limp torch, three of Stone's space-cop men fled with panicked shouts into the forest, their minds crumpling under the weight of an enemy whose existence challenged all that they understood about the world.

The advantage had decidedly changed in favor of the Sorceron Dragonkyn, and this realization began to percolate in Stone's eyes, cracking his poker face, when he barked orders into the small, black, two-way radio attached to his shoulder, yelling for the men at the perimeter to come up quick and flank the enemy.

He only got static in response.

Stone's eyes were empty, the unmistakable look of genuine fear hanging onto his face like a dirty smudge.

This was when Stone brought out what he called the big gun, a flash-bomb weapon he always kept close as a last resort. Given the unlikely event that he and his team would ever end up on the losing side of a firefight, Stone always brought this along to take out as many of the enemy as possible before his own death, a final, defiant retaliation to anyone able to kill him and his team. He took it from his satchel, amidst the chaos, and quietly slid beneath the last armored jeep he and his men possessed that had not yet been turned against them in some way.

—

Marah may have been quiet in peacetime, but not in battle. With her powers of strategy, it was no surprise that Marah was the one to find Stone cowering beneath the armored jeep holding nothing but a phone and a small metallic contraption the size of an American football. Stone had been writing a text when she popped her head down, surprising him. "Ah, you must be maggot number one. Their fearless leader," Marah said.

He dropped his phone and grabbed his metallic prize, his last resort. Stone's face was maniacal yet detached. With his oh-yeah-take-this determination pushing its way through the stark fear in his eyes, Stone's face seemed a cracked version of itself, like a crazed robot finally springing a faulty wire.

A cacophony of chaos and panic filled the air, and the death struggle of both human and Dragonkyn alike began in earnest.

For a split second, Marah's eyes registered panic when she realized what Stone held in his hands and what it would do, but then, like the nearby trees standing in solemn witness to the carnage, she stood straight, lifted her closed, peaceful eyes to the sky, and exhaled.

In a flash of light, the bomb detonated. People from all over the area would describe a small earthquake. The blast ripped apart the jeep and Stone, of course, but also the last two of his men still firing their weapons nearby. It also claimed Marah, the gentle but brave 'adopted sister' of Marc who had made him feel like he wasn't such a newbie. The blast also killed Felipe, the Sorceron loyal to Victor whose leg was wrapped from the previous night when Jen made his own sword go through his leg. Felipe had been hand-to-hand combatting one of Stone's men twelve feet from the jeep.

The jeep shrapnel from the blast was the culprit to blame for Felipe's death. It inflicted deep scratches and wounds to many others, as well as a chunk out of Jaden's side. He screamed in pain until long after the paramedics reached him.

The blast wave knocked Jen back fifteen feet into the trees just as she was trying to telekinetically lift one of the space cops still firing at them, whom the blast ultimately killed with another piece of shrapnel.

When Jen regained consciousness, her breath was labored and she shook all over. "What the—" she groaned as she lifted herself to her elbows, the lights from the emergency vehicles in the open field behind the main building lighting the side of her face.

Jen began to move when a loud, sharp cry sprang from her throat. It was only then that she saw the piece of metal in her thigh. She managed a painful grin as she looked around, her mind still hot with the knowledge she was still in a battle. She thought of how tough she always fashioned herself and tried to be as her eyes stared at her first real wound. Her thigh was bleeding, but probably not as much as it should have been. The searing metal must have partially cauterized the wound, a salutation gift for its new sheath. Jen ripped part of her shirt off, swallowed the sharp pain and then, with trembling hands, took the metal out of her leg, using part of her shirt as a tourniquet. Her slipping consciousness grasped at her eyelids to pull them down, but she caught her breath and blinked to stay awake. Her back hurt from hitting two small branches when she was thrown into the trees. *Could have been a lot worse*, she thought. Already feeling queasy, Jen neared the tree line that bordered the meadow and saw the slaughter. Many bodies lay where hours before they had been laughing and training.

That's when she saw what was left of her friends.

After turning and vomiting behind her, Jen composed herself, then limped her way through the smoke to the only remaining white van on the other side of the property, southwest of the main building, as the pops of intermittent gunfire still sounded. Keys were under the driver's side mat, as always.

When Jen arrived in Fairplay, she abandoned the van in a quiet alley off a quiet street a few blocks from Jasper's. She stopped the engine and a moment later, a gasp escaped her, followed by short sobbing that released all she was feeling. It only lasted four seconds before she recovered, stuffing back all the pain, regaining composure, something at which she'd become an expert. Leaving the keys, she wiped her eyes and walked away from the van's empty form, away from the guilt that she remained alive while so many of her friends did not.

Back at Jasper's in Fairplay, Alex, Jen, and Marc sat quietly at their table. Alex was hopped up on plenty of painkillers, and though they knew he would be good as new within twenty-four hours, many of the friends they knew at Dragonlair wouldn't.

Felipe, Marah, and twelve other Sorceron were gone. Jen's face looked ashen.

Marc seemed to take the news hardest of all.

Marah. The few memories Marc had of her wouldn't leave his mind.

Marah, the girl who taught Marc about Erifice, the first Dragonkyn Marc had bonded with, was gone.

The loud sound of two waiters colliding, plates crashing to the floor somewhere in the restaurant with hushed, hurried laughter was the background music to their pain.

Life went on for others, which seemed to magnify the agony they felt.

A spent firecracker, frayed and hollow.

Useless.

That's how Marc felt. He couldn't explain why the news of Marah's death affected him so deeply.

The aching depression, vast and empty at once, grew within him like an inner ocean, until Marc could feel it tearing at the seams of his emotional sanity.

Marc excused himself to the restroom as thick tears came unsolicited from his eyes. A gasp of frustration burst from him when it took longer than he wanted to get out of the booth they sat at.

He entered the restroom sobbing, not caring at all that his open sobs made an uncomfortable, peeing stranger leave quickly, the spring door of the plastic trash can slamming loudly as he did.

Marc's entire purpose for returning to the Dragonlair was to protect the innocent Sorceron from an enemy that he was responsible for somehow. Where was Marah?

Can I speak Erifice to her thoughts now, beyond the grave? he cried in his mind.

Please? he prayed.

Yes, he knew about heaven and hell and all that. He knew she was in a 'better place,' though he hated it when people said that, because she wasn't. The best place for her was here, with them. Alive.

What exactly was she doing now? Who could she see? Relatives? Friends? St. Peter at the pearly gates? Marc agonized over his responsibility for her death, and gagged when his sobbing and breathing conflicted. He coughed, breathing heavily, wiping his eyes.

Right at the moment he felt the most hopeless, the most depressed, he felt it.

The Vibe.

The invisible fire, the energy that connected all matter to all Dragonkyn, teeming beneath all his anger, fear, grief, and depression. There it was, like a friend softly saying words of empathy, *I know. I know.*

After about fifteen minutes, Marc was able to compose himself and returned to Alex and Jen, who sat quietly at the table. They had known Marah and Felipe. They had laughed with them, argued with them.

The Sorceron were scattered. All three quietly agreed that Victor would regroup, that he and the survivor from generation seventy-five and seventy-six would build the Sorceron back stronger than what it had been, but that was a short discussion, a worry for another time. Now, they mourned their friends.

Jen had a deep scratch on the side of her head, and the blood from it had gathered atop and down her ear. Jen's brown eyes gave a scrutinizing glance to the people in the booth next to them, who smiled politely, trying to hide their scrunched up faces, reacting to the trio's stench of blood, sweat and smoke.

As the three spoke over the meals they were too wound up and beaten down to eat, a connection between them settled into their pores, one reserved for those who face an enemy together in battle.

Outside, by the car, with the wind playing with their hair, they stood together, not saying much. Jen's freckled nose sniffed. She passed a sleeve under it.

"We have to get Marc home," Alex said.

"We have to tell Marc's mom that he's a Dragonkyn," added Jen over the whoosh of cars passing by on the nearby road.

"Yeah," Alex said, nodding slowly with tired eyes.

"Where will you go after you drop me off?" asked Marc.

"Not sure," Alex said. He had already thanked Marc profusely for getting him to that veterinarian. Marc's arm muscles still complained at him for the herculean task of half-dragging, half-carrying a seventeen-year-old kid fifty feet to his Camaro.

"We'll probably stay with a friend of mine for a few days until we can tell your mom, together," added Jen. Marc offered that they could stay with him and his mom, but Alex and Jen declined, saying they wouldn't be far away.

They talked details, planning exactly when they would tell his mom as two loud honks from passing cars shouted over Jen's words. Jen suggested they wait a few days after Marc got back into a normal routine. "Why get her son back and freak her out about who he is on the same day?" she reasoned, while other details and thoughts of *what now?* were left for another day.

They drove back to Marc's hometown mostly in quiet contemplation, and for the first time in many years, Marc felt like he had more than his mom and Luke who cared about him.

FORTY-TWO

Stone Sorrow

Drakesel knew Stone and his men were dead. He had no exact evidence besides the text he received, but something in his gut, something he had grown to trust, knew without a shadow of a doubt.

His day started out more jovial than most; things were looking up according to the reports from the presidents of all of his company's subsidiaries and divisions. For the last couple hours, his sister's dog had whined and fussed for no reason, perhaps foreshadowing the news that came. Sunlight from the glass wall on the west side of his large office lighted half his face when he got the text from Stone.

Difficult to kill. Guns not ef mmmake sure they ar

The text immediately drained the self-satisfied grin Drakesel had worn since reading the day's reports, and the unlit cigarette in his mouth was now forgotten, hanging limply from his bottom lip.

Having not received another text from Stone despite several he had written in response, Drakesel had a sneaking suspicion that he wouldn't be hearing from Stone ever again.

"What's the matter, sir?" said Jonathan as he entered the office, seconds after being summoned. When Jonathan heard the news, he went straight to work, shredding all paper and melting to oblivion all electronic documents related to the special ops mission that the company had legally called R&D expenditures.

Drakesel was troubled, but not about having the fiasco leaked nor brought back to haunt him. Everything had been covered. Nothing in the armored vehicles could be connected back to him or his company: not the men Stone recruited, not anything they wore. Even the VIN numbers of the vehicles themselves and embossed IDs were obliterated.

One would think that sending fourteen men to their deaths would be the source of Drakesel's troubled mind, but no. Drakesel was troubled because he now knew the threat was real. He knew these dragon people his family had always warned him about actually existed, and if the huge sums of money he'd spent on this first failed offensive had only gained him this one piece of confirmed knowledge, it was worth every penny. Losing any amount of money stung, but he could make more. Now, Drakesel had a choice: he could fall back into the shadows and keep his eye on those Stone had identified, or with the intel Stone had gathered, he could try another tactic to finish the job himself.

After so many generations of rumor and conjecture, he could be the hero his family had long sought against this menace they feared would return. With his money and connections, James Leopold Drakesel could finish this once and for all.

Forty-Three

Pantsing the Policeman and a Surprise

It felt strange being back in Rifle again, the town feeling like clothes he'd outgrown.

After they'd gone to Marc's house to clean up a bit and put on new clothes they'd bought, they went to the Big Creek Diner. After Marc had introduced his new friends to his mom, and after she had fiercely hugged Jen and Alex for bringing back her boy safe and sound, they fell quiet as she got back to work, casting them occasional smiles as she held her tray and pot of coffee. Everyone noticed the spring in her step just having her son back under her care, and it made all the customers and her co-workers smile. Alex, Jen and Marc ate a meal she refused to let them pay for.

Marc wistfully looked around. It was the same ol' diner, but it seemed smaller than before.

They sat at a booth near the window from which they saw, getting out of his cruiser with all the confidence and bravado of a Roman senator, Deputy Brandwhite, wearing his hat again like it was glued on.

"That's him?" asked Jen.

"Yep," said Marc.

They walked outside the diner and when Brandwhite saw the three teenagers with eyes so confident, all he could do was chuckle nervously.

"Hey, boy," Brandwhite said. "Haven't you done something wrong I should know about? Why aren't you runnin'?"

"I dunno," Marc said, looking him square in the eye. "Why aren't *you* runnin'?"

Brandwhite laughed like it was the funniest thing he'd heard in ten years. "Whoa, now, that's a hoot. Who, uh, who are your, your friends here?"

"We're from out of town," said Alex.

"Well, welcome to these parts. Be careful the company you keep," Brandwhite said with a dismissive chuckle. The deputy then tipped his hat and turned away.

After a moment or two, when they were twenty feet away, Jen turned, shot her laser fire at the back of Brandwhite's belt holster, and a second later he jumped with a sharp pain, but then he shouted to the Lord, his pride falling as fast as his pants around his ankles. He stumbled stupidly toward his car, the moment made even funnier the more he yanked at his trousers, desperate to pretend it wasn't happening.

Marc's mom asked him to pick up some milk on the way home, so Jen and Alex dropped off Marc at the older convenience store a couple blocks from his house.

"When should we tell his mom?" Alex asked as the car gently sounded the alarm that Marc had unbuckled his seat belt.

"Tomorrow. We'll stop by early," said Jen.

"Sound good. Thanks, guys." Marc got out of the car and could still hear the beautiful sounds of the Camaro's engine driving away as he walked into the store.

The clerk at the store was Mr. Khaledi, an immigrant from Iran who spoke with a thick accent and drove an older, pristinely-preserved Porsche. He was known around town as "the Persian with the Porsche," a nickname he treasured. He was wary of kids in the neighborhood, always afraid they would shoplift, and when Marc entered, Mr. Khaledi gave him a guarded glance.

As Marc opened the door of the cooler, he saw a boy from school down the aisle near a stack of boxes wearing gloves. They both exchanged a nod for a greeting. Jeffrey Davis was the stock boy working minimum wage, a light-brown haired kid Marc knew from his Science class. Though Jeff didn't talk much, and they didn't know each other very well, Marc liked him because he wasn't the richest kid and was sort of a loner. Marc, as much as anyone, could appreciate that.

"Whuh?" escaped Marc's lips with astonishment.

As he approached the counter with the jug of milk, several things on the counter floated in the air.

Why was this happening? You've gotta be kidding me!

Marc had no idea why his powers were suddenly freaking out, lifting things off the counter with Mr. Khaledi's back turned. Marc quickly put the milk down and grabbed at a tiny box of *100% Energy* bottles floating in the air, trying to force it back onto the counter.

Just as Mr. Khaledi turned around to face Marc, the other boxes and cardboard advertisements lowered themselves. By the time Khaledi looked at him, everything seemed back to normal.

"Yes, hello. I'll be right with you, okay?" said Mr. Khaledi holding a clipboard.

Marc's eyes were panicked. Right when Khaledi turned away from him again, Marc looked around to see several more boxes of things for sale—from candy to hair products—lift into the air, hovering a foot above where they usually sat. Marc couldn't breathe. Quickly putting the money on the counter, Marc grabbed the milk and hurried out of the store.

"Money's on the counter. Keep the change!" he cried over his shoulder as he left, a gust of fresh air hitting his face as he did.

There, outside the store, was Jeffrey Davis with his hands on his knees, elbows locked. Was he okay? Marc thought he was crying about something.

"Hey. You okay?" That was when Marc noticed that Jeff was shaking with laughter. "What? Wait. What?" Marc said, and when Jeff looked up and saw Marc's shocked face, he laughed even harder.

"The look on your face was priceless!"said Jeff.

"You mean, you're—"

"I'm a Dragonkyn, too," Jeff said between gasps of breath. "Oh, that was great."

"You scared the crap out of me! I thought I was doing that!"

Jeff continued to shake with laughter. "I wanted to pull that prank way before now, but I haven't seen you in here for a while."

Finally, Marc wore a smile, the first since the attack on the Sorceron, but all the while, a certain guilt poked at him for enjoying himself. He also wondered why the Vibe hadn't told him another Dragonkyn was nearby. He knew he somehow had to work on that.

"I think you and my sister and me are the only three in town," said Jeff. Did Marc know he had a younger sister? He wasn't sure. "I've been watching you. The acne you had—I had it too. You were all self-conscious at school. Believe me. I've been there. It all hit me at the end of last year."

It was only at this moment that Marc became aware of the stupid grin on his face. "Wow! There's more of us! Right here in Rifle! Wait. So, when did you find out you were Dragonkyn?"

"Beginning of May, I think, but they just barely showed up to recruit me," said Jeff, still smiling.

"The Sorceron recruited you too?"

Jeff balked a chuckle. "What—Victor? Heh, no way. That guy's crazy. Naw, you're with the Iberian-American clan. I'm talking about the Welsh-American clan. They say there are more of us than any other type in the U.S."

"Is that true?"

"That's the rumor, but it makes sense. Wales is the birthplace of all dragons after all."

"So—wait, really?"

"Of course. Thousands of years ago, but, yeah."

"That's right. Your dragon ancestors are from Wales."

"Along with my human ancestors. Yeah. Are you telekinetic?

"Yeah. I can move a few different things."

"Wow. Different kinds of things? You must have a lot of power."

"Not really," said Marc. "I'm sort of horrible."

After a pause, Jeff said, "Okay," as if to say, *if that's what you think*.

Marc was struck by how matter-of-fact he said it. "So, uh, what's your lesser power?" he asked.

"I can smell precious gems and metals."

"That is great. And, uh, what—you move paper as your greater power?"

"Yeah," Jeff said. Marc felt a bit dizzy with how vast it all was as Jeff continued. "Kind of a dumb telekinesis if you ask me. Maybe my ancestors loved trees. Who knows how we have the powers we have. The guy who recruited me can move anything petroleum-based. It's pretty cool."

Marc was still smiling at the thought that not only did he know another Dragonkyn in his home town, but that he might also have a new friend. "Jen's like that for us. Can your guy move a car?"

"A car? Who can move a *car*?" Jeff asked, intrigued, but right then Mr. Khaledi poked his head outside.

"Jeff. Where have you been? Get in here. Break's over."

"Gotta go," said Jeff.

"See you around."

"See ya."

FORTY-FOUR

MOM CAN'T COPE

The next day, Marc's mom sat perched on the edge of an old recliner, her face as vacant as the half-burned-down house Marc had seen before he went to Denver.

"You're a . . . a what?" she asked, still tired from her double shift the day before.

Marc, Jen, and Alex sat across from her on the couch. Jen had a spoon she had stolen from Jasper's. She lifted it to her mouth and breathed on it, orange venules in her throat appearing before she did; after a few breaths, the spoon turned red hot. Jen took the molten spoon with her bare hands and pinched it, molding it to look like a small, metal taco. Marc's mom started with surprise, but held a blank expression. She lightly smiled, as if her boy had brought home magicians he had met during his travels. She stood and immediately started straightening up pillows on the couch. As she did, she noticed the drapes and wanted to close them.

With everything on her mind, she didn't want to hear this, and as exhaustion tugged at her eyes, she politely smiled at her guests. Then, her smile faded abruptly and she excused herself to her room. Marc followed.

There, alone together in her room, Marc continued to prove it to her, moving things with his telekinesis, keeping a flame under his hand for a minute, but when Marc finally got her to realize what was going on, his mom just stared at him.

"Yes, I understand, Marc . . . but at the same time . . ." she shook her head slowly with a tired expression. "I just need to sleep a bit more." Jenny's denial had turned into a paralyzing, emotional shock. She was a worrier by nature, trying to do her best for her and her son, and when part of her realized the news her son and his friends were giving would change their world forever, she naturally froze.

"Mom, I'm still me, okay? Hey," he said, and she finally looked up at him. "Mom," he continued, "remember when you told me to just 'be me' when it came to dealing with people who looked down on us?"

She nodded again, but didn't want to hear this pep talk.

Blinking, she finally said, "Perhaps a part of me always knew," but quickly interjected, "I just . . . It'll be okay," she said with no emotion, robotic. "I'm excited for you, I am. I just, just need to . . . sleep . . ." Wrapping the blanket she had around herself, Jenny lay on the bed.

Marc's eyes were in a daze when he left her room to join Jen and Alex.

"I can't believe it," he said.

"Just let her process it. It's not like you told her something that other kids tell their parents," said Jen.

"It's weird," Marc said softly. "She's acting like the lady at our church acted when her daughter told her she was gay."

"That's what happens when any mother finds out that her child is really different from herself," said Jen. "Believe me. I know."

Marc quietly noted how wise the statement was. Jen was a lot more mature than any other sixteen-year-old he knew.

"Let's leave her alone," said Alex. "We'll come back tomorrow and talk to her. Maybe it's just the shock of it. A lot's on her mind."

"Yeah," Marc said. "Thanks, guys."

After Jen and Alex left, Marc returned to the room where his mom lay inertly on the bed, still wrapped in the red gingham blanket, her feet in short socks protruding from the edge. He wanted to cry, wanted to comfort her somehow. He knew his mom. Never in a million years did he ever think his mom would treat this news as weird, or retreat like this. He had so much welling up inside him. Marc felt scared too, about himself, about others, about all of this. He thought of Marah and Felipe. He needed his mom now; he needed to share the weight of all of this with her, but she wasn't there. He couldn't remember a time when she had ever acted this way toward him. Left to carry the weight of all this alone, Marc's pained eyes turned watery.

As he neared her, Marc rubbed his eyes as he stared out the empty window with a lost expression, and sat heavily on the bed.

The feeling built up inside him, and when he realized he hadn't breathed, he closed his eyes and let out a quiet but heavy sigh.When he opened them, Erifice danced on the carpet of his mother's room. He smiled, as if seeing a dear friend unexpectedly, and with renewed hope, breathed Erifice more directly onto his mom and the bed and the floor surrounding her. Soon the entire room was awash in purple and blue-green flames. Slowly at first, his mom moved from the cocoon of her blanket.

"Honey! There's . . ." she started with panic, but swallowed the rest of the sentence with a quiet gasp. She lifted herself up, her back to him, head covered by the corner of the blanket she decided to crochet Christmases ago.

Would Erifice work with non-dragon folk? He knew no other power at his disposal to help make it better. He needed her. That's all it was. He needed his mom.

She turned to face him.

Understanding collected in her eyes and her lips parted. That's when Marc breathed again, when he knew that the Erifice had conveyed his feelings. Soon her eyes were the concerned eyes of the mother he knew, and they collapsed into each other for a hug.

They held each other for several minutes. He couldn't remember a time when his mom had held him so tight. They were still holding each other when his mom told him how much she loved him and apologized for not thinking about how he was taking all of this. She was amazed at Erifice, telling him she could see and feel all that he felt, and that was when the tears came.

They talked a while more; and he told her about his adventures, but spared her the stuff that would have made her worry.

FORTY-FIVE

WAKE UP. TIME TO DRIVE!

It was early the next morning when Marc heard hushed voices outside his bedroom window.

It was still dark, the tiniest hint of dawn giving a furtive glance behind the east mountain above the river. As Marc tried to work out in his head if he had been dreaming, the hushed voices he heard outside his window and the exploding sound of his front door collapsing bellowed into his ears like a cannon.

Bewildered, Marc soon found himself on the floor of his room, face down into a pile of his own dirty underwear—*I should have cleaned my room more often*—the crouching knee of a thick-forearmed officer pressed into his back.

He heard his mom shouting at them, and could tell by her voice that they were handcuffing her too.

The tan polyester cop-uniform pants made no sound as their occupants carried him and his mom to the four waiting patrol cars, the lightbars on top of which shouted like nervous holiday lights.

The cop that held the car door open for them was thinner, smaller, and seemed more levelheaded. His lips were a straight line, pity pouring from his eyes.

"You guys can't hold us without a reason!" his mom shrieked as she struggled against their grip on her. "You have to have a warrant or some kind of writ or something! Is this about the bill collector? Did he—I already told him . . ."

Marc stayed quiet. They were rough with him, and he heard himself loudly complain when they put the cuffs on, but otherwise he tried to stay quiet and calm, even though his mind screamed with what-the-funk-is-going-on-someone-please - help-us fear. Deep down, Marc felt the Vibration, and he knew as clear as a window that the best chance he and his mom had of getting through this was to gather details. So with anxiety weakening his muscles and his heart racing, his eyes gathered all they could: the looks on the men's faces, the fact that the men weren't local cops at all—just County Sheriff deputies; black guns in thick leather holsters; the mid-30s guy with the chestnut hair and blue windbreaker jacket standing on their front lawn. Was he forensics? Who was that guy? The man's face looked forgettable, but it was his eyes that Marc noticed as they marched him toward the vehicles. They weren't settled or resigned eyes, like any other normal cop might have, just a guy doing his job. This guy's eyes darted around, masking nervousness. Something was seriously wrong with this, but Marc didn't let out all the panic and worry that filled his heart. His mom was freaking out well enough for the two of them.

The flashlights the cops used and the light bars on the police cruisers left bruises in Marc's field of vision. They drove for two hours, and as those spots went from deep purple to blue to a greenish yellow against the slowly brightening sky, the shock and fear Marc felt had turned to anger. All he really wanted was to be a normal kid and make some money in life, to have stuff he'd never had someday. He had no idea who was behind all this, but he also knew that guy did not want to meet Marc right now.

He tried using his telekinesis as they drove, but all he was able to do was send the car they were in screeching across the road. And though it was fun to watch the driver freak out about the lack of control he had with the police cruiser, he didn't want to endanger his mom anymore, so he gave that up.

Many thoughts raced like changing TV channels. Yes, he had Jen's cell number written on a paper in his pocket, but Marc felt stupid—he should have known bad guys might find him since they'd been to his house before. Attacking the Sorceron lair didn't work, so why hadn't he thought ahead? Why hadn't he assumed they'd attack again the last place they'd been: his own house? Why couldn't he have been stronger? Smarter? Now he couldn't even protect his own mom when it was his fault she was in this mess with him.

She turned to him with a corner of her mouth tugging into a worried smile, and he knew he had to think and act like a man if he was going to get them out of this.

As the morning light stretched and yawned behind the mountains, the sedan they traveled in slowed, and Marc looked up. The building where the cops brought them didn't look like a police station of any kind. It looked more like the small, whitewash cinderblock office of a used-car salesman, tucked away among sagebrush and hills that could hide anything.

However improbably, it held an old block of three small jail cells along a parched green wall with bars and everything. He and his mom were in separate cells, each one slightly smaller than his own room.

Think, think! Marc screamed to himself as the echoes of the cell doors closed like quiet thunder. He had to get a hold of Jen somehow.

"Hey! We get a phone call!" he yelled to the I'm-bored-to-death-with-my-job guard, but the man walked away, ignoring him.

Great, he thought. *I'm stuck in a jail cell an hour or two from home and all the guards are either Deaf, or they're willfully ignoring my constitutional rights. Gee. Wonder which one it is.*

Then he remembered that Alex could see through someone else's eyes, though it left Alex exhausted. But could it work long distances? Wishing he'd had a longer conversation with Alex about his powers, Marc decided to find anything that could pinpoint their location, but sitting in a windowless cell, his hopes were fading. Fading, that is, until he noticed the map on the wall behind the guard's desk. Marc stood up bolt upright and neared the bars.

PARADOX, COLORADO, it said.

Paradox? Wasn't that southwest of his hometown? Marc stared at it for close to an hour, never looking away, hoping that by some chance Alex could see what he was seeing.

"Marc?" the voice came from a nearby cell.

"Mom?"

"How are you, honey?"

"I'm okay. Someone's really out to get us, huh?"

"I don't understand any of it," Jenny said with a solemn voice.

He knew his mom was in the next cell, so he blew Erifice all over the concrete wall that sat between them, and along the floor in front of her cell. He saw her hand reach out and touch some of it.

Don't worry, mom. It'll all work out, Marc lied in his mind, trying to soothe her. He didn't really understand any of it either, but he also felt a need to shovel out something positive. Staring at the bars of his cell, he thought he could perhaps get through them if he could make them a bit wider. Marc wasn't the absolute thinnest kid, but he was wiry, an advantage perhaps in this situation.

He practiced against the bars, burping up some fire, wishing he had a tenth of the fire-breathing ability Jen had. By this time, the Erifice had all but disappeared from his mom's cell, having run its course.

He had begun making the bars slightly creak with his telekinesis when the large door into the cellblock made a loud, metallic, echoed cry and swung open.

"A visitor," the guard said indifferently.

Marc's "For me?" went unanswered.

The guard unlocked his cell, and as Marc followed the guard, he heard his mom cry, "Hey! He's a minor, and I'm his mother! I need to be there with him! Hey!" she called.

"It's okay, Mom," Marc said over his shoulder, following the guard through the steel doorjamb.

Marc touched his pocket, feeling the bulge of Jen's flask of lix that he'd managed to slip in as he put his pants on, and for the first time that morning, he felt a little more comfortable about their chances.

FORTY-SIX

FALLING IN HATE

The guards brought him to a room in decay. Its walls sloughed white plaster, exposing old, open wounds of forlorn cinderblock. A large desk was in the middle where a well-dressed man sat, a guy so out of place he looked like a tuxedo in a chicken coop. The man's large, expressive eyes watched every move Marc made. Two silver, metallic-looking suitcases sat on the floor near the desk. *Do they plan on moving me and my mom to Fiji or something?* Marc wondered. Anything of real value in their house really could fit into two suitcases.

"Is this the warden's office?" Marc asked wryly, doing his best to wrap his fear in sarcasm, but the man ignored it.

"You must be Marc," the man said.

"No, I'm Daniel. Do you usually break into people's houses and drive them for miles without knowing who they are first?"

The biggest cop in the room, a Latino guy, the one who had brought him here from his cell, took out his nine-millimeter pistol and slammed it on the desk.

If his intention was to intimidate him, it worked. The cop had slammed down the gun with such ferocity and speed that it rattled Marc big time, but he absolutely refused to give them the satisfaction of thinking they had scared him.

Not.

One.

Bit.

Marc swallowed hard, looked at him, and said, "Wow. You must hate that desk."

The big cop sneered at Marc, and started toward him.

"No, it's okay," said the older man at the desk. The big cop stood down with eyes that didn't, and after a long pause, meant to deepen the feeling that they were undoubtedly in control of Marc, the man at the desk finally spoke. "I'm Captain Drake, and uh, you're in a lot of trouble, son. We found heroin and thousands of dollars in your house. Care to explain that?"

Marc's eyes glanced at the other four cops in the room, all of them wearing sunglasses and practicing their best tough guy sneers. It was almost comical. They acted like guys who had seen cop dramas of the 1970s as research for their roles.

"You're full of it," Marc said.

"Doesn't matter," Captain Drake spoke each of the following words like a finger poking in Marc's chest. "You're in trouble and you need my help."

"You're not a real cop," Marc said. "None of these guys are."

Captain Drake chuckled miserably. "What makes you say that?"

"Because if the sheriff's deputies were really planning on kidnapping my mom and me, they would have been from Garfield County, and none of your guys are wearing anything with the words *Garfield County* on it. That's why you brought us here outside the county. We're in Montrose County, right? And if so, where are the Montrose County deputies?"

"Nice theory, kid. Actually, I should have been clearer. I'm with the FBI, and these men are from a unified multi-county police force helping us today since we're short staffed in the area. You and your mom are looking at years behind bars. Is that clearer for you?

Marc's eyes seemed unsure. How could this be true? Might there be some other person who wanted to frame him and his mom—some other unforeseeable enemy besides the men at the Lair? No, he decided. It was all a lie. This guy or someone higher up had sent those goons to kill his friends at the Lair, and went back to the only place they had as a lead, Marc's own house.

Marc stared ahead but said nothing.

Then, Captain Drake did something peculiar. He looked around, nodded at one of the other cops, and faced Marc.

"Look, Marc, we brought you here because—"

The gun the cop had slammed on the desk lifted all by itself, pointing toward Drake. Without flinching, without a speck of fear in his eyes, Drake took the gun from the air and laid it back on the desk.

"Let's stop playing around here, Marc," said Drake. Marc was astonished that he didn't seem worried at all about a floating gun in the air.

You know about my powers, Marc thought.

"I'm here to offer you something."

Drake took one of the suitcases, placed it on the desk, and Marc heard the metal clasps snap open.

Drake turned the suitcase to face Marc.

"Open it," he said.

"It's a trick," Marc said.

"Okay, I'll open it," Drake said, and when he did, Marc saw that the suitcase was filled with cash. Marc had never seen so many hundred-dollar bills. There were also stacks of fifties and twenties.

He wasn't sure exactly how long he just stared at it. It made the money from the robbery look like a kid's allowance.

"Uh, what's that for?" Marc asked, suddenly defenseless.

"You," said Drake.

"Me? For what?"

"I need your cooperation, Marc," Drake said, leaving his chair, nearing him.

Marc was still stunned.

"Let's start over. I'm Special Agent Drake, and we have a problem. We know about all of you. The government's been tracking your kind for months now, all over. So we decided to bring you here to make you an offer, and it's a simple one. Keep me informed of the whereabouts and plans of anyone who is, well, like you, and the money is yours."

When Marc's mouth was finally able to say something, he choked out a feeble, "Does the government really pay people off like this?"

"You're kidding, right?" asked Drake with a smile. "Of course they do."

A pause.

"So, you guys didn't attack the Lair?" Marc asked.

Drake played dumb. "Uh, okay, see? This is the kind of stuff we need to know," Drake said, sitting on the end of the desk, close to Marc, with all the empathy of a school counselor. "Now, what's this *Lair* you're talking about? You say someone attacked it?"

"Yes," said Marc, his anger subsiding at the thought that these guys weren't responsible for killing Marah and the others. The money still sat on the desk.

"Get this down," Drake said, snapping at one of the guards, who looked like an actor now forced to improvise, searching for paper and pen. "What did they look like?" asked Drake, his eyes intently meeting Marc's with feigned concern.

"They looked like some kind of space cops or something. They were heavily armed." Marc gave the best description he could of the men, now believing, hoping, that Drake really was who he said he was.

Marc felt the Vibe within him.

Another weight on his chest, clutching his heart like a vise. If his experience at the Lair was any indication, the feeling told him they weren't cops, or FBI, but deep down he was also scared, wanted so badly to trust someone, anyone, to share this burden.

Still, how could Marc have believed Drake—if that was really his name? What convinced Marc? In the end, it was the thing that makes many men rationalize away the truth and believe a lie; it was something Marc never had before in his life, and it filled a nearby suitcase to the brim.

"The only way we can help you," said Drake, "is if you feed us information about your kind. Be our informant, and your government will be there to stop those who oppress you."

Marc still stared at the money with eyes transfixed. He slightly nodded.

"But, uh, Agent Drake, why all this? Why bring us to this place?" Marc asked, briefly shaking himself from the spell the money cast over his mind.

"We needed a cover. We needed it to look like you were in trouble, in case others were watching," Drake said, the lies coming so easily.

It made sense to Marc. Drake gave him a card.

"I'll be at this address until Sunday, and you can reach me on this cell whenever. Go talk to your mom. We'll have someone take you home in thirty minutes."

"Thank you," Marc said, looking up at the man responsible for killing his friends.

Drake's eyes seemed disarmed by the boy's sincerity. He mumbled, "It's no problem, kid. It's, uh, it's our job. Eh, thank *you* for helping us help you."

After Marc went back to his cell, the taller henchman approached.

"I thought your name was Drakesel," the taller one asked.

Drakesel rolled his eyes.

"What about the other kids?" asked the other one.

"I said they're on their way," Drakesel spat with impatience.

"Want my opinion?"

"Sure," said Drakesel, his eyes looking at the building they were in with disdain. "I love the yammering of lesser lifeforms." He turned and put the other suitcase on the table, checking the contents, letting his sarcasm hang in the air, and the cop paused, not knowing if that was a yes or no.

"Well, uh, sir, look. This kid is dangerous. Who knows what he could do to this place, and second, that's a lot of money you just gave away for nothing."

Drakesel exhaled loudly, as if to express the depths of contempt he had for idiots. “First, it’s only a hundred grand. Smaller bills are at the bottom.” He paused and looked in the direction of Marc’s cell. “And if that kid can bring the others to where I can finish them all, the dividends far outweigh the modest investment.”

Forty-Seven

Shaquan, Meet Shaquan

The guard in charge of driving Marc and his mom back to their house was a local bouncer-for-hire named Shaquan, very different from the extreme, hard-core type of guy Stone had hired for his crew. Built like a tank on legs, Shaquan didn't want to make this trip, but they hired him to do it, so he agreed, especially when the main boss gave him an extra couple hundred as a tip. After stalling as long as he could, he sighed and grabbed the keys off the desk with his dark-skinned hand. Checking his iPhone, he saw all the text messages his family were sending to each other, and wished he were with them.

Then he got a call.

"Yo," he said, answering.

"Shaquan, where you at?" The voice asked.

"Workin'."

"Working? Geez. Again?" But when Shaquan didn't answer, the voice said, "Did I lose ya? Hey! You there, Quan?"

Shaquan would have loved to answer, but he had never been so speechless in his life.

There, blocking the door to the cell where the kid and his mom were held, was a slightly smaller version of himself in a red t-shirt. It was like he was looking into a mirror.

Shaquan didn't notice when he dropped his phone.

Back in his cell with the suitcase full of money, Marc quietly sobbed to himself, wishing he could wrap himself in the earth and disappear from shame.

"Honey, what's wrong?" his mom asked.

"Nothing," he said. "It's okay, mom. We're going home soon."

Doubt collected in her eyes. "Honey, please," she said, but he didn't respond. Tears welled in his eyes because of his weakness. He should have refused the money at the slightest possibility that those guys were responsible for attacking the Lair.

But he didn't, and his self doubts were waiting to pounce.

You're nothing. You're just a little turd, the voice in his mind—his father's voice—said, and for a moment he was the little boy in his house before his father left.

Stop. Please, he responded. *Daddy—*

No, came the icy reply. *You know I'm right. You're weak. You've always been weak.*

His very soul crumpling within itself, his own doubts piled on. Y*ou call yourself a Dragonkyn? Your firespew is nonexistent. Nothing more pathetic.* Tears came unbidden.

At the height of the anguish within himself, there, in his mind, he saw Jen, waving, and he immediately knew she wasn't too far away.

A new voice he heard. As faint as it was, it was definitely not his own, nor was it his own thoughts:

Why so sad, buttercup?

Marc's eyes blinked, amazed, then looked up, squinting in confusion. *Jen?* He thought.

The one and only, the voice said.

How is this possible? Wait. Where are you, and why is your voice so low?

I sound like a man now? asked Jen.

No! Low in volume! Marc thought, shaking with a quiet laugh. *Serious! What's going on?* Marc thought as loud as he could with a smile on his face.

He waited for a second, and it was as if they had a bad Wi-Fi connection between their minds.

I thought you couldn't access my mind! Marc thought.

I can't with my powers, and, yeah, for every other Dragonkyn, Erifice is mostly pictures and feelings. But with you and me, as long as I'm using Erifice, I guess I can use words!

But—

I've been Eriflowing the outside of your cell's wall.

You're kidding!

Nope. Brought a few friends, too.

You did?

A few seconds later, the door to the cellblock opened, and Demitrius in a red t-shirt walked in like he owned the place.

They both laughed.

For twenty full seconds, all that came out of both of them was a sneaky, knowing, simmering laughter, part of which was the joy of knowing each other was still alive, that turned cackling as Demitrius opened the small cells that held Marc and his mom. Demitrius must have left the Sorceron, too.

"I got the guard tied up. I think he's just a guy—not involved with anyone who did this. Bad guys must've left, and I say we still make him drive you home."

They were all outside the small jail house: Jen, Alex, Demitrius, Luke, Marc, his mom, and of course, Shaquan the guard, hands bound with his own handcuffs, sitting in the passenger seat of the 'police cruiser' nearby.

"Hello, again!" Marc's mom called to Jen, and embraced her. They chatted as if Jenny Mondragon were being picked up from the mall—talking about life, the fun similarity of their names, and Marc's mom getting dragged into all this craziness. As Marc watched them, he was happy to see Jen with his mom. She needed a new 'mom' person in her life, Marc reasoned, and he couldn't think of a better lady for that job.

When Marc saw Luke, they hugged like they hadn't seen each other in years.

"How did you find us?" asked Marc.

"It was Erifice. The eriflowing you did when you were driving here and with your mom in the jail cell helped us track you.

"So, Erifice is also a kind of GPS with all Dragonkyn?"

She nodded proudly.

"So, it wasn't me staring at the map of Paradox, Colorado?" asked Marc.

"No," smiled Alex. "I can't be that far away from someone and be able to see what they see, but I appreciate your confidence in what I can do."

"Well, at least they let you pack a suitcase," Jen said.

"Honey, where did you get that?" Marc's mom asked, and that's when Marc told them they had a new ally in the FBI.

Fast-forward a few minutes, Jen had put it all together, and she was furious.

"You're completely full of it!" she yelled.

"How?" Marc volleyed, protecting his own shame of screwing up as much as his desire to keep the money. "The government pays people all the time!" Marc said.

"Why would they have to pay you to *protect* you and the rest of us?"

This stumped Marc, but he defended it anyway. "Oh, so now you're an expert on how the FBI handles things?"

Jen looked at Alex, but he just smiled at the ridiculousness of Marc's argument and walked away toward Shaquan, who Demitrius was watching.

Jen neared Marc. "So, these guys abducted you and your mom from your house, drove you two hours away, and put you in a cell so they could, uh, pay you a lot of money to be an informant?"

Marc looked at her and said nothing.

Luke jumped to his friend's defense. "Well, *yeah*. It sounds dumb when you say it like *that*."

Jen smirked at Marc with a lifted eyebrow. Marc looked to his mom, but she gave him the same look, and that's when he sat down and fought tears. "I'm sorry, okay? I saw the money, and . . ."

"Where is this guy now?"

"I don't know. He gave me a card."

Jen called Alex back over, and without consulting her, he approached Marc, put a hand over his eyes and closed his own. After a few moments, he said, "Got it."

"Got it?" Marc asked. "Got, uh, what, exactly?"

"I know what the guy looks like."

"Oh yeah? What does he look like?"

"The older guy? Big eyes, greying hair on the sides. Nice suit."

"Whoa!" Marc said. "You can read my thoughts just by doing that?"

"No, no," Alex countered. "I can't read minds. I can only see what you've seen in the last twenty-four hours."

It was almost noon when Drakesel and his men had everything situated at the standard-issue cabin he had rented with the long, sagebrush-lined driveway.

"They're finished digging? How does it look?" Drakesel asked the foreman he hired, a short man whose cap-in-hand, shy personality seemed permanently fixed to his demeanor.

"Yes, sir. Eh, looks very good."

"If I see even a hint of bulldozer or earthmover tracks out there, there's nowhere you'll be able to hide, do you understand?"

A phone rang.

"Just say FBI," Drakesel commanded from across the room.

"Say FBI, and then w—" started the bodyguard nearest the phone.

"That's it. Just FBI."

The bodyguard picked up the phone tentatively. "Uh, hello, FBI," he said, and Drakesel's eyes were daggers. The man wilted and handed the phone to him, expecting to get slapped.

Drake forced a smile. "This is Agent Drake. Yes, hello, Marc. I'm glad you called."

FORTY-EIGHT

THE FIRST METAMORPHOSIS

Marc's mom Jenny had a habit of biting her nails when she was nervous and right now she was almost turning them into a full course meal.

"Mom, don't worry."

"I'm not worrying," she said, but he knew her too well.

"Yes, you are, but you don't have to. We have to go after this guy. He killed our friends."

"I know, I just..." Jenny Mondragon let the words hang there, a sentence and a fear without completion.

He gave her a hug, and the worry in her eyes only lessened a bit after Jen and Alex promised they would all protect each other, and she even smiled a bit after Marc stuck Luke's pocketknife into his arm—this time no blood—to show her how much he'd changed since puncturing his arm at her work with a fork. In the end, though with tears, she gave her consent.

Luke wasn't happy about going home with Marc's mom, not one bit, even though he knew it was for his safety, so he hid his discontent with humor.

"I've given you the best years of my life!" he said with over-the-top drama.

"C'mon, bro. You can come the next time, I promise." Marc said.

"No! Your tongue speaketh lies! Lies!" Luke said with a Shakespearean flourish, and then stuck his face close to Marc's, breaking character, his volume dropping. "But serious? I can come the next time? Okay. Deal," he said with a mischievous-but-warm smile.

Shaquan the guard, Marc's mom, and Luke had driven home in Alex's Camaro. They gave Shaquan a bit more money to take a bus to wherever he needed to go from there.

Marc sat in the backseat of the sedan Drakesel tried to pass as an unmarked police car, driving toward the place they would confront the man who took the lives of his friends. A part of Marc wondered if they had enough evidence that this Drake guy was the one they wanted. He wondered if they should simply confront him, not attack.

No. This guy killed their friends. It was him, and the Vibe confirmed it.

Until now, they had all been quiet—Alex driving, Jen in deep thought in the front seat with her foot on the dashboard, Marc in the back. Jen shifted, turning back to Marc, her left elbow on the back of her seat. "Marc, this guy thinks you're coming to negotiate or give him information, so our attack should take him by surprise," Jen said.

Marc looked at her. "I know, Jen."

"Yes, well, I know you know, but I also know you value life. And that's good, but remember. If we have to fight, we have to fight, okay?"

Marc said nothing. He only stared at her with a searing, leaden gaze, then looked away.

Jen returned to looking at the road that moved fast beneath them. "Uh, okay, good. Yeah. You're ready," she reassured herself, trying to erase what she said. "I think if we stick with our plan, we'll be in good shape."

Alex moved one of his hands on the steering wheel to hers, his eyes not leaving the road.

Quiet took over as they drove, a calm before the storm, but Marc felt ready. Using their powers together, they would take this guy by surprise. Marc's mind filled with the things they planned for Drake's demise.

Marc's face was serene confidence, but then, like an alarm sounding in his mind, it wasn't.

One second he felt the Vibe and the confidence that comes with it, and the next he felt attacked by the same self doubt that always showed up at the worst times, like Zoosh at school, who teased and bullied people just because he could.

You can't do any of this and you know it, the self doubt told him, pressing his insides into the back seat, through feelings more than actual words. Marc's eyes suddenly looked lost, confused, staring at the chasm of darkness that opened up within him, mocking his feeble powers.

He wanted to burst into tears, scream, jump out of the car. Marc couldn't let Alex or Jen know how he was feeling. They always seemed so sure of their place as Dragonkyn, about what they had to do, about their abilities, and now he hated them for it. He stared forward, silently begging God, the universe, whoever was up there, that Jen not turn around again. He'd break if she did, if she looked at him even once, he knew he would.

What was he *doing?* Why was he here?

YOU'RE AVENGING MARAH'S DEATH, a part of him argued in response.

Yes. Of course he wanted revenge for his friends who died as much or more than any of them, but chasing this guy, going off on some hunting expedition that could easily end up as a suicide mission isn't what he signed up for. What good would it do for all of them to die right now? If this guy Drake had the money to pay him off *and* hire an army to attack them, what could three dragonkyn do against that?

It was only when Marc itched his eyes that he realized how much his hands were shaking.

The old, one-lane highway stretched before them, and there they were, three children of fire, racing down a fuse of highway, burning down toward whatever impending explosion awaited. It was the feeling of the car rushing to carry them to so many unknowns that scared him most. As they turned onto a long, dirt driveway that led to a distant cabin, he felt his heart drumming fast. He knew, if not consciously, that it was his old friend self-doubt that fed the fears that ate his insides, sickening him enough he wanted to puke.

Shut up! He tried yelling at these thoughts that had swallowed him like a tsunami, but no empty, positive affirmation he tried worked, and the panic rose in his gut like water in a sinking ship.

A groan of absolute dread escaped him, and as Jen turned around to ask what he said, Marc leaned forward, pretending to tie his shoe.

What happened next happened fast.

Brakes locked up, and then the car fell.

The road literally gave way, disappearing from beneath them. With the impact, a loud hum rang in Marc's ears.

There was dust everywhere, and it was slightly darker, as if they'd gone into a weird tunnel.

Marc blinked, his mind trying to work through what had just happened, and for a moment, he stared forward in a stupor.

'Captain Drake' must have created an illusion, turning the stretch of driveway that led up to the cabin into a ditch at least fifteen feet deep and as wide as the driveway itself.

"Jen! Jen!" Marc heard Alex yell, but Jen was unconscious.

Marc blinked. Dust was everywhere. *Of course,* he thought. *This guy was waiting for us the entire time.* If fight or flight instinct hadn't taken over, Marc would have been too paralyzed by the doubts that held him. Somehow, he climbed out the open window of the back door, squeezing between the car and the side of the ditch, dirt rushing into the car window as he did. He heard Alex shout through the dust and confusion, "Marc, can you get out?" Alex turned his worried dark eyes to Jen, who, except for the gash on her forehead, looked asleep.

Now on top of the car, Marc looked up at the fifteen foot climb that separated him from surface ground.

Using his telekinetic powers, he lifted himself awkwardly to the top of the ditch, quickly diving into a nearby bush in case someone were targeting him the moment he got to the surface.

Marc heard a muffled scream coming from the ditch. "I can't fit through the window!" Alex shouted in panic.

Alex kicked at the back window, trying to break the glass.

"Hold on!" Marc said, about to use his own telekinesis to lift the car out of the pit, but then he peered above the bush to see a jeep fast approaching from the cabin, a cloud of dirt trailing behind it. He took the flask of lix from his pocket. Knowing he didn't have much time, he unscrewed the top, and suddenly, time seemed to slow and his mind went quiet.

A memory of something Marah had told him came into his mind as clearly as if she had appeared, whispering into his ear:

"If you seek the Vibe and nothing else, *it'll awaken powers you never knew you had."*

The words "and nothing else" stood out with such force in his mind that the memory of her words felt as real as the ground he stood on. Marc looked at the flask of lix, this strange beverage that everyone said enhanced Dragonkyn powers. Now, in a flash of thought, he realized he never needed it, that in fact, this stuff may have *stifled* his powers the entire time. Exactly how, he wasn't sure. All he knew was that he needed to trust these words.

He only needed one thing.

The Vibe.

Two hundred feet away, the jeep stopped on the banks of the ditch, a rent-a-thug behind the wheel.

Decision time.

Marc tossed the flask into another bush as he stared forward, his eyes peering at those who would take his life. He gulped, trying to remember everything Jen had taught him about using the Vibe.

Somewhere, in the slow motion quiet of that moment, searching in the darkness of the center of himself, Marc found it, vague but getting clearer, a source of power that seemed covered up until now.

Drakesel emerged from the jeep with two thugs holding semi-auto machine guns, dressed in dark clothing, plus two boys about Marc's age, who wore tattered clothes—the smaller of the two in sweats and the bigger in a faded green t-shirt.

Marc stared at them from just above the bush. He knew if the men walked twenty feet in either direction, they'd clearly see him.

He had never faced anything close to this before. The overwhelming fear continued to lash at him, clashing against the Vibe, the feeling screaming in his mind, *I'm not ready for this! I'm just not ready for this!*

Marc focused on his breathing. It was all that was left.

Turning his attention back to the war that waged within him, he searched for what to do next, and like words to an unknown language, suddenly becoming clear to him, he knew that this was his time, his moment, and he somehow relaxed and stayed focused.

A wellspring of the Vibe, the invisible fire within him, awakened, more powerful than ever.

Marc could hear the boys saying something to Drake as they got out of the car. He couldn't hear exactly what was said, but he could tell that they had some kind of accent. *Australian?* He couldn't tell.

Marc looked at the other thugs. Drake came to the edge of the deep pit he had dug for their welcome and called down to the entombed vehicle.

"Hello, Marc! I see you brought some friends. Here to give me some needed information for the government? Was the money not enough?" he said sarcastically.

Drake walked along the edge of the pit, pride dripping with every stride. "Let me introduce myself. My name is Drakesel," he said, but then his voice spoke through clenched teeth, a deep grudge dipped in vengeance. "I want my family name to be the last thing you hear."

Bright fire erupted from the boys' mouths, and soon the deep ditch and the top of the sedan leapt with big, orange flames.

Marc's eyes were wide with worry. No, his friends in the pit couldn't be burned, but fire can do more than burn. It can steal the air they need to breathe.

"I'd like to introduce you to my new friends from the other side of the pond. Just my way of fighting fire with fire," Drakesel said with a confident laugh in his voice as he checked the ammo clip of his .45 automatic pistol.

Marc immediately knew some things. First, these boys were like him, but seemed different from any he had met before. Could they be the Rogues Marah had told him about? Second, Drakesel's confidence about his upper hand must be big enough to show his cards like that—having the kids spew fire—announcing their powers so brazenly.

And third, they didn't know that Marc was already out of the ditch.

Marc knew he only had one shot at this.

He steadied his breathing, and when he raised a hand toward them, the big jeep flipped on its side, crushing one of the thugs and the smaller of the two Rogue Dragonkyn who stood near it. The thug driver—now upside down—shouted panicked curse words, trying to free himself from his safety belt.

It happened so fast that Drakesel started away from the rolling vehicle, letting out a high-pitched gasp of worry as he did.

The worry turned to anger. "Where are you!?" Drakesel bellowed, firing seven or eight rounds from his automatic pistol into the car on fire at the bottom of the ditch.

The only thug standing near Drakesel brandished his gun with panicked jerks in different directions, and the Rogue in the green t-shirt, who didn't seem the least bit sad about his friend who died, began sniffing the air like a dog.

Marc threw his hand out toward them, but instead of telekinetically moving them, he felt a powerful, opposing telekinetic force block it and send him back ten feet.

Pain tore through Marc's lower back as he landed, a thick branch puncturing him an inch deep, just barely missing his spine.

The same force then lifted him off the branch, ten feet into the air, and slammed him back to earth hard. Stars exploded in his field of vision, and Marc, crying out with a whimper, felt himself lifted in the air again. Now helpless, Marc flew steadily toward the Rogue who stood with his arm pointed toward him. From out of Marc's shocked-but-tired eyes, he could see

Drakesel and his thugs cheering like fishing buddies who had caught one. Marc's energy and confidence waned, and though he searched for the Vibe within him, he couldn't feel it. As he landed in front of the green-t-shirted kid, panic set in.

"Wait, wait," Marc said, but as soon as he landed, the telekinetic force shoved Marc back against the overturned jeep. More stars exploded into his vision upon impact, and Marc briefly blacked out before he fell to the ground.

Lying there in the cakey ground near the jeep, blood from his back gurgling into the dirt, Marc vaguely regained consciousness when the Rogue jumped on top of him, raining down blows. Marc weakly blocked a few with his arms, but most landed. The kid used no special powers, no fire, just fists. Green-t-shirt boy, more proficient in the art of fighting, was toying with him.

With every hit, Marc felt overwhelmed, weak, his confidence gone, feeling that he couldn't defend himself, especially with a kid decidedly larger than him.

Just before resigning himself to his fate, Marc felt a sudden clarity in his mind as the blows landed, as if Marah were there, quietly whispering, *You are more than you have believed yourself to be.*

The beatific moment evaporated when Marc saw the steel of the blade the kid brandished to end him. Eyes wide, Marc grabbed the fist that held the knife with both hands.

As they struggled, an indescribable yet calm focus centered Marc's mind. The anger inside him was no longer rash, nor was it impulsive, and every ounce of self-doubt, the voices in his mind that sounded like his father's, left him like a scared shadow frantically hiding from sunlight.

The exhaustion he felt lifted, leaving a feeling of absolute authority, born of feelings and pictures flashing through him:

His father who left.

The mean things he used to say.

Drakesel's lies.

His mother's struggles.

The Sorceron who died.

Marah.

The regal dragon from his dreams, staring at him with a sober, expectant gaze.

The Vibe flooded his body again, and his chest expanded—a low, baritone hum seeping from his voice box as he heard himself snarling, hissing.

When Marc looked up, the bigger boy's eyes carried fear for the first time, and Marc firescreamed an angry beam of inch-thick laser fire from his mouth, spearing the boy through the eye.

It stole every command the Rogue in the green t-shirt had over his body, and he dropped into the dirt, still and lifeless.

Marc could almost hear his dream dragon command him.

Now stand.

As Marc stood, he witnessed for himself the extent of his incredible transformation. He felt that he'd become larger, taller, his legs and arms pure strength, his shirt tight across his skin that was now a darker shade of an ancient shield. Only when he turned the nearby jeep's side-view mirror toward him did he see that his head and neck had transformed into that of a magnificent dragon, with almond-shaped eyes the color of fiery lava. An incredulous gasp escaped him when he saw himself. He wanted to stare longer, so many questions in his mind, but a preternatural calm overtook him. The Vibe seemed to tell him he had work to do. Marc felt an amount of power flow through him he had never before imagined. It was as if anything were possible. He closed his eyes, and breathed for a moment, a sense of relief and gratitude growing as much as his confidence.

Marc then looked around for Drakesel, but all he could see was a big, thirty-something guy in dark clothing on the ground with his hands up in 'I surrender' mode, his semiautomatic rifle already thrown out of reach.

Big, mechanical whooshing sounds filled the air. He turned to see a helicopter lifting off from behind the cabin and Marc felt a few things all at once:

Anger in his snake eyes.

A tremor at the top of his back.

His shirt tearing away from his body.

Marc lifted into the air even before he saw the talon-adorned wings that had sprung from his scapulas. He blinked in disbelief and couldn't breathe. Wobbling at first, his immense wings sending him into the jeep's tires that pointed to the sky, Marc grunted, trying to work the new appendages with his mind. His large, muscular human legs twisted, a foot on a tire. Once he got his bearings, he exhaled sharply, flying straight for the undercarriage skids of the dark-blue helicopter.

He shot upward into the blinding cloud-scattered sky with clenched teeth, determined.

As he climbed, his breath out of reach from the exhilaration of flight as much as the effort to fly, he saw that the helicopter was still a few hundred feet away, but he was gaining on it. Part of the reason for his breathlessness was due to how fast he could fly, how much air his wings could push with a single thunderous flap. He'd never been on a plane before, and now he didn't need one. A part of him chuckled at the irony as he climbed farther up, low clouds meeting him like a long lost friend. Out of the corner of his watering eye, Marc saw distant birds parallel to him.

Just as he reached the helicopter, Marc shot a bolt of thick laser fire from his mouth, hitting its blue side. When it wobbled, Marc darted away, but as he came back, the helicopter banked hard right, and Marc's eyes went wide as its rotors sliced through one of his wings.

"No!" Marc roared with a full exhale as he fell, half from the pain that tore through him, half from the knowledge that he failed, tumbling to earth like a dragon Icarus. Flapping wildly, his hot, angry eyes were only able to glimpse Drakesel's helicopter escaping over the mountains, trailing smoke from its only injury.

His immense wings thrashed at the air, and though the pain was excruciating, he flapped hard just before he landed on the hard earth, causing only a tweak in his ankle.

Marc limped toward his friends.

There were lots of reasons why Drakesel got away, first and foremost being his lack of experience with his newfound powers of flight.

By the time Marc made his way over to Jen and Alex, his wings had melted back into his scapulas, and his torn shirt hung limply over his shoulders. He was vaguely aware that his head was still different, though he didn't know in what way exactly. He figured his face completely returned to normal.

Jen had regained consciousness, had lifted the sedan out of the ditch, and both she and Alex sat on the dusty hood, Alex tending to the gash on Jen's forehead.

"Hey," Marc said matter-of-factly as he approached. "You two okay?"

They didn't answer. They just stared at him.

"Marc?" Jen asked, her eyes squinting.

"Yeah?"

"Was that you in the sky?" She asked.

"Uh, yeah," Marc said, not stopping to consider how cool his accomplishment was, too wrapped up in failing to get Drakesel. "He cut my wing with the rotor blade. I think it'll heal, but maybe the cut is still—" he said, craning his neck behind him and twisting his right shoulder to look at it.

Again, Jen and Alex just stared. Marc's head looked human again, but a sharpness to his features remained, dark scales lining the snake eyes that peered from beneath his brows.

"You uh, you look different," Alex said matter-of-factly.

"Oh. Uh, yeah," said Marc, still not knowing how to process it all.

"Marc, you did it," Jen said with amazement.

"No, I didn't. That Drakesel guy got away."

"No, not him. You. You made it to the next level in the Dragon Order."

"I did?" Marc asked. "You mean, I'm a Dragon Lord?"

"Uh, no, not that high, but you're not a Wyrmling anymore!"

"Really?"

"No! See, many of the other generations before us had what they called dream councils, when many leaders had the same dream, and they've predicted for a long time that when a Dragonkyn, a 77th, could manifest any part of his physical form into that of a dragon, they'll have reached Draignor, the middle level of the Dragon Order," she said with quick, breathless words. "You're a Draignor! No one's come close to reaching it before you. I always thought we'd all get there in our twenties or thirties—ow," she said, wincing as Alex finished putting the bandage on her forehead.

"Who are you, ya freak of nature?" she said with a grin.

"No one," Marc said with a smile. "I'm, I'm just me."

"Serious. How did you do that?" Alex asked.

"I don't know," Marc said, his body wanting to collapse from exhaustion. There was no celebration this time, no fist pumped in the air. If anything, these new abilities sobered him.

"I think I discovered something that may help our powers," Marc said, and they were paying attention. "We gotta get rid of the lix. Believe me. We don't need to drink any of it."

"Good tip. Here's to hoping we're all sprouting wings soon by giving up that stuff," Jen said, smiling. When no one said anything for a few seconds, she jumped down from the sedan, adding, "Well, forgive all the crap I thought or said about you. You're the real deal."

"Thanks." Marc smiled sadly, missing her backhanded compliment, still bothered that Drakesel got away.

She picked up the suitcase with two bullet holes in it. "Seems like he really didn't want it. We'll give some of it to the poor kids in the next town. They'll love it."

Alex took a few steps toward some dark clouds forming over the distant mountains and paused. "Does anyone have fix-a-smashed-radiator powers? 'Cause if not, it looks like we're walkin'."

And for the first time in what seemed like forever, they all laughed.

FORTY-NINE

SEEMING DIFFERENT

The sun rose again, and a semi-normalcy returned to Marc's life, with some exceptions. Some of the money Drakesel left was used to help Jenny Mondragon buy her own house a few streets away to prevent any more surprise attacks from Drakesel or anyone he might hire. It was smaller than their white, rented house, but with a bigger backyard and a place to call their own, they weren't complaining at all.

After the hellos and 'welcome back' gestures from a couple of neighbors, it was just him and his mom again.

"How's my hero?" she asked in the kitchen, bathed in morning light.

"Half asleep," Marc said with a tired smile, grabbing a box of cereal from the cupboard.

As Marc's mom smiled, gathering up the things on the table, forever cleaning up, the moment slowed a bit. Marc watched her, realizing in an instant that his mom was, in fact, a person. He always knew this on a surface level that yes, she was a person, just like him. He wasn't sure why he thought of it right then. She had always been there for him, and he knew he would always be there for her.

School was school, but it felt good to be back, to stand in those hallways again, to smell the musty scent of the older building, and to listen to the drama that some kids invented to fill up their days.

Lunch was a bit lonely. To most, Marc was still the kid from the poor side of town—out of sight, out of mind—but Marc didn't care.

"Move it, dork," one of Zoosh's friends said, holding his tray of food.

Marc quietly scooted in his chair so the bigger kid could get past, and the bigger kid threw him a disgusted, 'you're a loser' stare, seeming to resent that Marc didn't say anything or retaliate in any way.

Marc exhaled a quiet half chuckle, shaking his head at the kid's desperate need to prove he was tough. Perhaps now, for the first time, Marc could appreciate how different he was from the masses. It was his secret to keep. He knew what he could do, and felt no need to show it off to anyone just to gain the approval of those he really didn't like anyway. He was a Dragonkyn, and though he sensed this journey was just beginning, he felt excited about its future.

Between fourth and fifth period, he saw Zoosh walking around, stiff as a robot in his torso cast, most of his cranberry-colored shirt hanging off him, along for the ride. Having had to rely on others for the last couple weeks, he seemed more humbled, and when he saw Marc, he gave him a quick lift-of-the-head greeting—perhaps the most genuine nod of hello Marc had ever received from the guy.

When he saw Katie after lunch, the feeling was a mixture of excitement and the deepest caring and warmth. It was as if his eyes were a person, slipping into a luxurious hot tub. He also felt grounded inside himself enough that he only grinned, instead of excitedly running up to her like he wanted to.

That was when she did something so unexpected it shocked both Marc and Luke. Wordlessly, Katie approached him and hugged him. It was more than just a quick 'buddy' hug. Electric shocks bolted through him when she touched him, and something rushed inside. He felt dizzy as he tried to calm his racing heartbeat with steady breathing, and simply enjoy the moment. She held him for two full minutes, her face against his chest, a girl simply wanting to feel safe in her boyfriend's arms.

Yes. They were now officially boyfriend-girlfriend, because Katie O'Hannon simply never hugged *any* boy like that, and she had told many friends that if she were ever that affectionate with someone, he'd be the one.

Marc was the one.

As Marc's arms enveloped her, Luke did silent jumping jacks of excited gestures behind her, his eyes two ping pong balls, freaking out that the girl everyone wanted was now officially Marc's girlfriend. It almost made Marc laugh, but he only exhaled with a small smile, enjoying the feeling of holding her. Katie had no idea about any of what had happened to Marc recently, but did she sense it somehow? He liked her warm breath against his shirt.

"Welcome back," she said when she broke the embrace. "See ya later," she added, and walked away with a flirty smile.

As Marc and Luke rode their bikes back to Marc's neighborhood from school on that unusually hot day, they decided to take the long way home. Though Luke begged Marc to tell him all about what happened while he was away, Marc didn't feel a need to share most of it, not yet, and that surprised him. Luke settled for talking about the school gossip Marc missed out on.

They walked their bikes, in no hurry to reach home, and when their conversation dropped into silence, Luke looked at Marc, studying him.

"You seem different," Luke finally said.

"Different?" asked Marc.

"Well, different good, I guess," said Luke. "I mean, Katie did just give you the hug of the century out of nowhere. I dunno, just—just, different. Uh, more sturdy?"

"Sturdy?" Marc asked with a quiet chuckle. "How's that?"

"I dunno, never mind. Just, more chill—older, maybe? I dunno. Do you notice anything different?"

Marc thought for a moment, and he looked around at his small town, so far from anything 'important' happening in the world, and an overwhelming sense of gratitude filled him. He had missed his hometown, the million different textures of the mountains above the Colorado River, the trees at the very top and the barren strip just below them—some sections looking like stone knuckles atop mud-caked fingers that gripped the hills below, like silent, wise grandfathers who never die. He looked to the hills east of town, at the deep green trees and light green meadows resting against the deep azure above.

"Other places are cool, I guess, but it's just nice to be home," Marc said.

Luke said nothing; he just gave him a warm smile, and they walked on.

For the first time it seemed, Marc felt like an important part of the small town where he lived, a permanent fixture, grounded. He felt like he belonged.

He thought of the people he knew that weren't Dragonkyn, and a small amount of pity seeped into his heart. They knew of only one kind of fire, but Marc knew there were three: Firespew, Erifice, and the Vibe.

FIFTY

THREE DREAMS IN ONE

That night, Marc dreamed again, and it was like three dreams in one.

The first and second were wordless. In the first, he was in a white room, so white that he couldn't tell where the walls met the floor or the ceiling. He was alone in this space. All that was there was a jeweled locket attached to a leather strap. The majestic dragon from earlier dreams was not there, and Marc was puzzled, feelings of abandonment tugging at him, like when his dad died.

The second dream was another warning dream.

It was difficult for Marc to see this growing, supernatural threat—something his dreams had vaguely warned him about in the past, an enemy that had haunted Dragonkind's existence in the early days.

The silhouette that Marc saw in his dream was humanlike, sort of. It was big and powerful. Most of what Marc saw were furrowed, angry brows above wide-set eyes, its pupils horizontal, like a goat or a horse, the opposite of the vertical irises of a dragon.

In his dream, Marc felt tired. *Why can't I ever see a bright future? Is this a real warning from my dragon ancestors, or a dream inventing some kind of danger?*

It was then, in the last part of his dream, that he saw her.

Marah.

She looked like royalty, wearing an ornate silver hairpiece that flowed down, bracing her long neck. A wise, loving smile radiated down to him like Erifice.

"Always seek the Vibe. It will never fail you."

"Will I see you again, even in dreams?" Marc asked, his eyes welling with tears.

"Of course. I will be near you. I promise," she said. "But you must never repeat in your mind the lies you tell yourself about yourself, for your self-destructive thoughts are whispers from demons who know all the good you will do if you accept yourself."

"I promise," Marc said, but soon his smile faded a bit. She wasn't real, and it saddened him that his subconscious mind would give him such false hope.

When he looked, her eyes seemed offended, as if she'd read his mind.

"Dreams and the people in them are as real as you are," she said. "This is how we help. We accomplish much in dreams on behalf of the living, though they often stay unaware."

"You do?" he asked, mystified and curious about the pursed smile on her lips like she was hiding something.

"Yes. Here's one example," Marah said, and suddenly Marc knew the reason for her secret-hiding smile, because there, in that moment, he heard a voice.

It was a familiar voice, a man's voice, fading in and out, desperate to be heard, its tone one of absolute love and sincerity.

My son, the voice said, and Marc couldn't breathe for a moment.

His father's voice continued to press through dimensions to be heard.

Please forgive me...all the horrible things I said to you.

Please. I—

That was all the voice was able to say, and it was gone. For the rest of the dream, Marc felt the destructive names his dad called him, all the words burned into his mind, lifting, one by one, unlocking the control they'd had on his mind.

When Marc opened his eyes, his pillow and face wet with tears, his three dreams were all a jumble in his mind.

Marc couldn't remember much about his three dreams, or why he'd been crying, but he didn't feel sad for some reason. They seemed so vivid as he slept. Perhaps they'd return.

He sighed, humbled by all that he had yet to know about this new world and his place in it.

Thinking of the Colorado River a few blocks away, he thought of a new simile. He no longer felt like dead cells on the side of the artery river. He felt that the town was like a misunderstood person, and the consistent river was its beloved, eternal clock, slowly continuing forever and ever.

For the first time in a while, Marc was content to ride that current, unafraid of where it might lead.

ABOUT THE AUTHOR

Nathan Smith Jones has been a public school English teacher for many years. He believes equally in the power of stories and in the power of the Vibe—the feeling that connects all dragons. He lives in Utah with his wife and five children.

www.dragonkyn.com